The Seventy-Four

M.C. MUIR

Other books by M.C. Muir

Under Admiralty Orders-The Oliver Quintrell Series:

Book 1 – Floating Gold
Book 2 – The Tainted Prize
Book 3 – Admiralty Orders
Book 4 – The Unfortunate Isles
The Oliver Quintrell Trilogy *(Books 1-3 Box set)*

Books by Margaret Muir

Sea Dust
Through Glass Eyes
The Black Thread
The Condor's Feather
Yorkshire Grit (Box set)

Words on a Crumpled page (Poetry)
Uncanny (Short stories)
Goats (non-fiction)
King Richard and the Mountain Goat (Young adult)

Acknowledgements

I wish to extend thanks to my editor, Matthew Keeler for his professional services. Thanks also to Roger Marsh, maritime writer and journalist who has an encyclopaedic knowledge of ships of the Napoleonic era.

As always, I appreciate the valuable feedback offered by Jan Everett, L.C. Collison, Malcolm Mendey, Rose Frankcombe and Nerissa Warner-O'Neill.

And, last but not least, to my son for setting up my web page.

The Seventy-Four

Under Admiralty Orders -The Oliver Quintrell Series
Book 5

M.C. MUIR

Copyright © M.C. Muir
November 2016

ISBN-13: 978-1536840087

ISBN-10: 1536840084

All rights reserved. No part of this publication may be reproduced or transmitted in any form or by any means without permission in writing from the copyright owner.

Chapter 1

Rio de Janeiro - Guanabara Bay
February 1805

Oliver Quintrell perused his Admiralty orders for the fifth or sixth time. A rap on the door of the great cabin interrupted his concentration.

'Is there anything you require?' It was obvious from William Liversedge's tone that he was concerned about the amount of time his fellow captain was taking.

'A moment,' Oliver replied, folding the paper and returning it to the envelope bearing his name. He was conscious he was merely visiting His Majesty's ship *Stalwart* and was presently occupying the captain's private domain. After offering an apology, he begged Captain Liversedge to join him.

'A glass of wine?' William said, seating himself at the table.

Oliver nodded and glanced out of the windows spanning the full width of the 74's stern. Beams of sunlight streaming in enhanced the richly upholstered furnishings, yet despite the windows being open, there was not the slightest breath of breeze and the humid tropical air of Guanabara Bay was far from refreshing.

Oliver sat back as the cork was pulled from the bottle, listened to the familiar *glug-glug-glug* of the rich amber liquid as it was poured and watched as it swirled around the glass. Accepting the drink, he took a moment to savour the aroma before swallowing deeply.

Captain Liversedge looked at his friend, cocked his head to one side and waited.

'Forgive me, William,' Oliver said, touching the envelope on the table. It was addressed to: His Majesty's frigate *Perpetual*, Captain Quintrell. The word SECRET, printed in large red letters, glared back at him. 'Are you aware of the contents of this despatch?'

The commander of the 74 sat down. 'Not entirely,' Captain Liversedge replied. 'I was provided with only limited information by the Lords Commissioners, when they ordered me to intercept you here in Rio. At the time, rumours were floating about the corridors of the Admiralty but I have learned from experience that rumours monger only misinformation and mischief. In answer to your question, the full extent of my knowledge is that I was to meet you here and deliver this envelope to you. However, from what you have told me, I understand you are carrying some items of value.'

Oliver nodded and withheld a cynical smirk. He was bemused that the Sea Lords and Navy Board showed little regard for the unexpected contingencies that constantly befall ships at sea. 'What if my journey from Gibraltar had not been delayed for several weeks?' he said. 'What if I had charted a course south, watered in Recife and decided to bypass Rio de Janeiro, or alternatively chosen to sail down the Slave Coast of Africa?' Frustration was evident in his voice. 'What if my ship had been taken – as it was for a time – and I had been unable to regain it? What if I had followed my original orders and sailed directly to the Antipodes? Tell me, William, what damned fool clerk in Whitehall decided to send you halfway across the globe to intercept me here? No one, not even I, could guarantee that *Perpetual* would make port in Rio de Janeiro.'

Leaning back in the chair, Oliver Quintrell inhaled deeply. He was not asking for or expecting answers. 'Forgive me. I have endured an exhausting voyage since we left Gibraltar. But, tell me honestly: if I had not arrived in this harbour yesterday, how long would you have waited for me?'

'I cannot say. Like you, I follow the orders I am given.'

'My apologies, William. For many months, I have been tossed from one duty to another, met one catastrophe after another, including the loss of my ship and the struggle to take it back. I feel as though I have been navigating a cross sea.'

Captain Liversedge leaned forward, his elbows on the table, his fingers touching as if in prayer. 'My instructions were to wait here for news of your pending arrival – or of your fate. When word was passed from the Portuguese frigate recently arrived in the Bay informing me that you had left the Western Isles on a course for Brazil, it was news I greeted with great relief. On hearing that, I had no doubt you would make landfall in Rio soon after. However, as the days passed and you failed to arrive, I found myself biding time, wondering what had become of you.

'I have been in Rio almost a month,' he continued, 'and, in that time, have lost several seamen who, on becoming impatient, deserted. I also suffered unrest from the crew for denying them the opportunity to go ashore. I am certain you are familiar with the problems that occur if sailors, deprived of their pleasures, are not allowed some freedom in a port such as this.' He relaxed back into his chair. 'Apart from that, with a complement of five hundred to feed, the ship's supplies are dwindling. The crew are becoming impatient. They are anxious to return to the Channel which offers the possibility of action and prize money – something this harbour does not afford. I admit I am also eager to head home.'

Oliver admitted his officers and men were not relishing the prospect of a long voyage deep into the Southern Ocean. And, while he had not yet fully digested the ramifications of the revised orders he had just received, his main concern was their present situation. 'Have there been any sightings of enemy ships off the coast hereabouts?'

'I heard of two Spanish convoys – one out of Callao and the other from Buenos Aires. They both headed north since I dropped anchor here. Well-laden ships, I understand, packed with cases of gold and silver intended to replenish Spain's coffers.'

'And pay her dues to Napoleon,' Oliver added cynically.

'Yet I encountered not a single foreign ship when I sailed from England. In all honesty,' Captain Liversedge said, 'I admit to finding the inactivity rather tedious. The heat and humidity of this late summer air make for a very sultry atmosphere. It not only drains one's strength but saps one's mental energy. I look forward to returning to Europe.'

'What is the latest news from England?' Oliver asked.

'When I left, there was talk in Whitehall of a major sea battle looming. The Spanish have been supplying their ships at Cadiz and Ferrol and the French are recalling their convoys from North America. Our spies inform us that the combined fleets are planning to mount a decisive attack to crush the British Navy.'

'That possibility has been mooted since before the Spanish first swore allegiance to Napoleon,' Oliver said.

'Indeed, but mark my words, this year it will come to pass.'

'Then, like you, I would prefer to be patrolling the Channel or the Mediterranean rather than the waters of the South Atlantic.'

Oliver rose from the table and walked over to the windows. The vast expanse of Guanabara Bay stretched many miles to the north and west. In his opinion, few harbours in the world offered such a safe and sheltered inlet. The soaring granite outcrops and steep mountains surrounding the bay provided strategic locations for watchtowers and gun batteries. No ship could enter the harbour without being seen.'

Captain Liversedge poured another glass of wine for his visitor and invited him to join him. 'Are you at liberty to share the contents of your new orders with me?' he enquired.

Returning to the table, Oliver removed the paper from the envelope, smoothed the creases from the single sheet and placed it on the table at his friend's right hand. 'Read it for yourself, William. I am instructed to transfer the special items I am carrying to you, and return in company with *Stalwart* to Portsmouth. There is nothing more.'

It took Captain Liversedge only a minute to absorb the details of the secret despatch he had conveyed from England. He was perplexed. 'I do not understand,' he said. 'What is the dire significance that necessitates you aborting your prior orders and turning about? What or who are you transporting aboard *Perpetual* that is so important that you must sail in company with a 74-gun ship of the line?'

Oliver shook his head. These new orders countermanded his previous sailing instructions and the news had taken him aback. He had no option but to accept the change and share the relevant details with Captain Liversedge. As such, he explained about the four cases of Spanish treasure hidden aboard his ship, how he had come by them and been entrusted with them. He advised his friend that the chests contained minted silver and, to the best of his knowledge, there was no gold or precious stones in the consignment. He added that his original orders, received in Gibraltar, had instructed him to convey the coins to Van Diemen's Land in the Southern Ocean, due to the desperate need for currency in establishing a new British settlement there. But, according to his new orders, the treasure was to be returned to England aboard HMS *Stalwart* – the 74-gun man-of-war.

Until now, the presence of the silver and its location within His Majesty's frigate *Perpetual* had been known only to himself and a handful of his men and, for months, he had striven to maintain that secret. However, with the physical transfer of the treasure chests to the third rate, very soon, hundreds of men, namely the officers and crews of both British ships, would be aware of their existence and nothing would stop word leaking to the wharfs and docks of Rio de Janeiro and beyond.

'So,' Oliver said, 'the Admiralty, in its wisdom, has decided. We sail for England. That news will be well received by my men. Making the transfer, however, will be a tedious task. If you will permit me to arrange the details, I will advise, in due course, how and when it will take place. In the meantime, I must beg you to delay your departure for at least another week. I am in dire need of canvas and cordage, and must arrange with the victualling store for essential supplies.' Oliver drained his glass and refused a refill. 'There are several other pressing matters I must attend to, but I will not bore you with those. There is much to do and the sooner everything is attended to the better.'

As the captain's boat approached the British frigate, the pipes shrilled from the gangway. In answer to the call, sailors poured up from below and shuffled into untidy lines on the forward deck. Under the watchful eye of the bosun the sailors stood in silence, the sun beating down on them.

Stepping onto the deck, Captain Quintrell automatically glanced forward and aft – an observation few would have noticed. Though his face showed no change in expression, his attention was immediately attracted to a handful of men who had not responded as smartly as others to the call. They appeared reluctant to follow orders and present themselves in line. To Oliver, it was quite apparent the conversation these men had been engaged in was of a more pressing nature than the demand of the pipes marking the return of the ship's captain.

For the present, his observation would keep. He would deal with it later.

Oliver lifted his hat, acknowledging his command, an action that was second nature to him. His respect for the service and for his vessel, *Perpetual*, went without question, though he exhibited no outward emotion. His face remained expressionless as he inspected the ship's officers, never glancing at any of them directly.

'Welcome back, Captain,' the first lieutenant said. Like every man aboard, he was eager to hear the outcome of his captain's visit to the British 74-gun third rate anchored half a cable's length away, but he refrained from putting the question.

'Dismiss the men, Mr Parry, and join me in my cabin, if you please.'

'Aye aye, Captain.'

The calls of the junior officers and the scuffing of leather soles along teak deck timbers muffled the sound of Oliver's shoes as he stepped down the companion stairs to his cabin.

Casson, his steward, was waiting below for him. 'Can I get you anything, Capt'n?'

'A glass of lemonade, thank you.'

Having removed his coat, Oliver dribbled a small amount of water from the pitcher into the china bowl on the wash stand. After loosening his stock, he dampened a cloth and wiped his brow and neck before opening it and sinking his face into it.

'Am I disturbing you?' Mr Parry called from the doorway.

Oliver turned, dabbing his face on a fresh folded towel. 'Come in and sit, Simon,' he said. 'Damnably hot out there in the sun.'

Without commenting, the first lieutenant did as indicated and paused for a moment until the captain had completed his toilet and relaxed into the wingback chair. 'I trust your meeting aboard the 74 was satisfactory.'

'Indeed it was,' Oliver replied. 'It was good to renew my acquaintance with an old friend. You will remember the last time we parted company his ship had been under heavy bombardment and was heading to port for repair along with a prize-of-war we had taken.'

His first officer nodded. 'I can presume, therefore, that he reached Kingston in one piece.'

'As did Lieutenant Hazzlewood and Mr Smith aboard the prize vessel. They are sailing with Captain Liversedge, so I look forward to speaking with them both in due course.'

'Indeed,' Simon Parry said with an inquisitive expression on his face.

'You are expecting news,' Oliver stated with a hint of cynicism.

'I think I am not alone. I believe every man aboard is hoping for word of when we are likely to sail.'

'Interesting,' Oliver said. 'My impression of the mood on stepping aboard was one of disenchantment and disappointment rather than hope. Have you sensed it?'

The lieutenant's answer had to wait while Casson delivered the refreshments. 'There's some nice green cheese, if you fancy a bit. The one you like.'

The captain thanked his steward and both men remained silent until he had quitted the cabin and the door was shut.

'I admit there is a degree of discontent amongst the men,' the lieutenant observed. 'Probably brought on by uncertainty.'

Oliver was quick to reply. 'A sailor without a grievance is like a baby without a teat. Is that not so?'

'It is true. But I believe the men have some justification to their claims. They have put up with much since departing Portsmouth over six months ago.'

The captain asked him to explain.

'Having been virtually imprisoned on the ship in Gibraltar—'

'*Imprisoned*?' Oliver snapped. 'Careful, Simon, those are strong words.'

'Beg pardon, sir. I was merely repeating the murmurings I have heard. I should have said – *confined*. In Gibraltar Bay the men were confined to the ship for many weeks.'

Oliver could feel his dander rising. 'For their own good, I might add, due to the malignant fever that was raging in the colony at the time. Continue.'

'And when we sailed, we encountered trouble off the Western Isles where both officers and crew were subjected to evil threats and some to actual imprisonment by that piratical privateer.'

Oliver's frown mellowed to a look of satisfaction. 'I believe we delivered Captain van Zetten his due deserts.'

Mr Parry agreed. 'But now, with the exotic sights, smells and temptations of the bars and bordellos of Rio de Janeiro located only a few hundred yards away, the crew are again confined to the ship knowing that very soon they will be sailing to the Antipodes far across the Southern Ocean – a voyage of six to nine months without once touching land. With a seaman's natural appetites satisfied only by shore leave, I believe the current feeling of discontent could be mollified if the crew were permitted to go ashore for a brief spell or alternatively if you would allow some females to visit the ship.'

Oliver shook his head. 'You surprise me, Simon.'

The lieutenant was unperturbed. On board the frigate, the welfare of the crew was the responsibility of the first lieutenant and the facts he had related to the captain were well-founded. He had witnessed unrest on other ships beset by similar circumstances and knew that in extreme conditions discontent could lead to serious unrest, even mutiny.

Captain Quintrell was not blind to such eventualities. 'I heed your comments. As you know, one reason I did not allow females to visit the ship in Gibraltar Bay was because of the fear of them transmitting the malignant fever that was decimating the population there.'

'But there is no fever here.'

'Humph. Perhaps I should seek the surgeon's views regarding transmission of the Spanish Pox if females from the local bordellos are allowed aboard to entertain the men.'

The lieutenant shrugged his shoulders. 'My observations were merely in response to your comment about the mood that greeted you when you came aboard. I will say no more and, if you will permit me, I will take my leave.'

'Simon, please remain and say no more on that score.'

The lieutenant resumed his seat.

'I have been withholding the information I have just received. I am in receipt of new orders from the Admiralty. We will be heading north. We are to return to England. I believe that news will raise a few spirits.'

Simon Parry was delighted and, for a moment, was lost for words. 'Am I permitted to pass word to the men?' he said.

'Not until I have spoken with the other officers.'

'Of course,' the lieutenant replied hiding his disappointment.

'I think that calls for another drink,' Oliver said. 'And a toast. To England.'

The officer was happy to echo the captain's words.

The pair drank and enjoyed a few minutes of comfortable silence while privately contemplating the homeward voyage.

'I take heed of what you say,' Oliver said, returning to the conversation as though there had been no break. 'As you know, I value your opinion above any other. You are my eyes and ears on deck. However, I have a feeling my concerns may run deeper than mere seamen's gripes and grievances.'

The smile left the first lieutenant's lips and his brow creased. 'I do not entirely understand. To what are you referring?'

'Tell me what you know of the group of men who attracted my attention on deck when I came aboard. If I am not mistaken, that is the same cabal I have seen engaged in conversation on several occasions in the last few weeks. Would that be so?'

'Quite probably,' Simon Parry replied. 'I assume you are referring to the landsmen who signed in Ponta Delgada. There were half a dozen of them joined the ship at that time.'

Oliver nodded. 'I know the ones. What have you learned about them since they came aboard?'

'Their physical details are recorded in the muster book – but as to their character and behaviour, I know little more than you gleaned from the authorities in the Azores. I can confirm that not one of those men is a sailor. The only time they ever spent at sea was aboard the ship they took passage on from Liverpool.'

'The ship that sank, taking with it all their possessions and money,' the captain added.

'Do you believe their story?' Simon Parry asked.

Oliver nodded. 'I do. Mr Read, the British Consul, is an astute man who would not easily have been duped. He told me of their misfortune and their intention to head for America where they were originally bound. Have you spoken with them?' the captain added.

'Not personally, but I was told they wanted to leave the ship as soon as we touched Rio. Their plan was to sign on any vessel that was heading north. But, with your change of orders, that would not be necessary.'

Oliver agreed. 'Have you had any problems with them?'

'There have been no charges brought against any of them. They were allocated to various stations and were not kept together. However, when off duty, five of the original group are invariably seen together, as you noted earlier. Since we dropped anchor, I am aware these men have been the most outspoken about being confined. They demand to be paid off.'

'Do they, indeed? For such a short time with the ship and with slops issued to them when they first signed, they will be lucky to have accrued any wages.'

Oliver glanced from the window to the granite dome that dominated the entrance to Guanabara Bay. In the distance, beyond that, the angular mountain peaks rose even higher. In the bright cerulean sky, black frigate birds circled the ship on wings spanning more than six feet. Captain Quintrell shook his head in an attempt to dispel the memory of his last visit to this harbour. The birds stirred images he preferred to forget and the accompanying feeling of foreboding was not easy to shrug off. From the expression on his first officer's face, he wondered if he was having similar feelings.

'What troubles you, Simon?'

'There is something about one of those men that unsettles me.'

'Any particular reason?'

'No, it's just an uneasy feeling. It appears he has the ability to gather a crowd around him and they listen to what he says. He attracts attention like a dead whale attracts sharks. At night, also, I have noted small groups murmuring in muted tones. Mr Nightingale has witnessed it also. It irks me but it's not irregular enough to reprimand the men for.'

'If you recollect, Simon, I never wanted to take those men aboard in the first place, but I was obliged to do so. Personally, I have had no quarrel with them. In fact, Michael O'Connor, who is currently acting as my scribe, is proving to be a useful asset and I would not want to lose his services. The other five, I cannot pass judgement on. All I can say is that for the present, no one leaves the ship without my permission.'

'So be it,' Mr Parry said. 'However, might I remind you of the Portuguese sailors we plucked from the sea?'

'How can I forget them?' Oliver sighed. 'I intend to speak with the port authorities tomorrow and arrange for their transfer as soon as possible. Is there anything else?'

'What of the two women – Mrs Crosby and Mrs Pilkington, and the boy, Charles Goodridge, who has been annoying some of the men with his antics. Will you permit them to stay aboard?'

'My views are that it is neither practical nor proper for the women to occupy precious space in the carpenter's workshop. Since visiting the 74, I am considering having them transferred across. I will advise you of my decision later.'

'But what of the doctor's views?'

'What do you mean – "What of the doctor's views"? This will be my decision and will have no bearing on the doctor's views.'

'But—'

'What are you trying to say, Simon? I know that Mrs Pilkington has been assisting the doctor in the cockpit.'

'Not only that,' Simon said cautiously.

'Are you suggesting there is more to that relationship than that of a surgeon and a pair of willing hands?'

Oliver's gaze questioned his lieutenant. 'Jonathon Whipple is a professional medical man.'

'But he is man not without feelings.'

'Are you saying he is attracted to this young woman?'

'I cannot speak for the doctor. I merely observe the way he looks at her and the manner in which she responds to him. I believe they share a certain mutual attraction and perhaps fondness.'

'Then all the more reason the two women should go. I trust I shall hear no more of this matter.'

'It was just a feeling.'

'Another one of your feelings, Simon?'

'Do you never follow your intuition, Oliver?' the lieutenant asked.

'I cannot afford to. I follow Admiralty orders to the best of my ability.'

Despite a slight awkwardness, Simon Parry had another matter to address. 'There was one more thing.'

'Go ahead,' Oliver said.

'During your absence, charges were laid against one of the fo'c'sle hands. I've had him placed in the hold under guard.'

'What man, what rating and whose division is he in?'

'Franz Gorman. Able seaman. He's in Mr Hanson's division.'

'The offence?'

'Fighting on deck.'

'A minor scuffle?' the captain asked.

'A little more than that. I did not witness it myself but, from what I heard from Mr Hanson, he tried to strangle one of his mates. He accused him of mutinous talk and had the loose end of the starboard mainbrace wound several times around his neck. Apparently, he was trying to push the sailor over the side either to hang him or drown him.'

Oliver frowned. 'Was it just talk or did the other man provoke the attack?'

'No. The sailor claimed he was merely sharing a joke when Gorman jumped on him.'

The news was not what the captain wanted to hear. 'Why does this sort of thing occur when I am off the ship?'

The first officer shrugged. 'Coincidence, Captain. What punishment will he receive?'

'Let it be two dozen at the grating, though he deserves more.'

Mr Parry hesitated as if intending to question the captain's decision but it was only for a fleeting moment. 'Two dozen it will be, sir.'

'Call all hands to witness punishment, if you please, and pass word to the bosun to come to my cabin.'

'Right now? Would it not be more appropriate tomorrow after the morning call?'

'Right now, Simon. I have much to attend to in the morning. Let us get this over and done with as quickly as possible.'

Chapter 2

The Cat

Grasping the stout handle, Oliver slid the hempen cat from its red canvas bag. Allowing the nine tails to drop to the floor, he shook them apart as vigorously as a dog shakes its coat after emerging from a duck pond. Then, resting his hands beneath the knotted thongs, he draped the implement along the length of the table and carefully separated its tails. Not having been cleaned, the lash was thick with congealed blood and, towards the ends, the knots were flecked with tiny pale fragments. He studied them for a moment, before closing his hand around one of the tails, grasping it tightly and purposely pulling the knotted rope through his closed fist. Twice he winced silently to the passage of the hard knots over his skin.

On reaching the end he released his grip and examined his hand. As expected, his palm was blackened with old blood, but it was also punctuated by spots of fresh red blood.

'O'Connor!' he called to the ginger-headed man sitting at a side table. 'Put down your pen. I would borrow your magnifying lens and require a small dish and a pair of tweezers. Immediately, if you please.'

The items were delivered to the table within seconds.

'Anything else you'll be wanting, Capt'n?' the writer asked.

'I need your attention for a moment. Tell me what you see here.'

Michael O'Connor studied the cat of nine tails extended across the table. 'You mean those?' he said, pointing to the tiny specks adhering to the knots.

'Yes, those flakes.'

'Salt?' the man suggested.

'Please take a closer look.'

The Irishman curled his nose. 'Is this the lash that was used on the sailor from the fo'c'sle?'

'Yes. The man had committed a crime. I believe you have been on board one of His Majesty's ships long enough to be familiar with the Articles of War and the punishments laid down by the Admiralty.'

'Yes, Capt'n, that I have.'

Leaving the table, Oliver poured an inch of water into the basin on his wash stand, dipped his soiled hand into it then dried it gently and re-examined his palm. It struck him how different his palms were to the leather-hard, tar-stained hands of the sailors in the tops. His were soft and spongy – and now scratched.

Holding the magnifying lens to his eye, he leaned over the knotted rope and examined it more closely.

'See that,' he said, touching one knot with the tips of the tweezers.

O'Connor leaned forward. 'Skin?' the Irishman questioned vaguely.

Oliver thought not. After worrying a particle that was lodged in the spun hemp, he pulled it free with the tweezers and held it in the ray of light streaming from the window. After dipping it in water, he studied it again through the magnifying lens and passed it to his scribe.

'A fragment of glass?' O'Connor enquired nervously.

'You have heard of such things.'

'I have, indeed. The practice is not new,' he sighed dolefully. 'It is cruel enough to flense the skin off a man's back with rope or leather, but to score it with broken glass is the Devil's own work.'

From the expression on the man's face, Oliver was convinced his concern was genuine and not contrived. 'It is not glass,' Oliver said. 'I believe this is a fragment of rusted iron and I imagine it was scraped from the round shot on the gundeck.' Not committing himself further, the captain looked again at his own hand. 'The skin on a man's back is no thicker or harder than that of a gentleman's palm,' he said. 'The cat is cruel enough when swung with venom but a cat seeded with glass or rusted metal can be lethal. It can strip a man's back of skin and muscle and lay bare the bone.' He turned his face to his clerk. 'Kindly ask Dr Whipple to attend me here and then return to your other duties.'

The ginger head inclined towards the captain in the manner of a polite social gesture. Michael O'Connor was unaccustomed to a sailor's salute. He still had much to learn.

Oliver Quintrell studied the fine scratches across the palm of his hand yet again. The bleeding had stopped. Then he focused his lens on the cat's other tails splayed across the polished surface.

By the time the ship's surgeon joined him, he had several tiny pieces of rusted iron sitting in a glass dish that he had concealed beneath a handkerchief.

'I understand you examined the man who was punished last evening?' the captain stated.

'I did,' the doctor replied. 'His back was terribly shredded. He will live, although—'

'Although what—?' Oliver questioned.

'I believe the punishment was excessive.'

'He was sentenced to two dozen at the grating – and that is what he received. You witnessed it yourself.'

'Unfortunately, I did.'

'Believe me, Jonathon, it is not something I enjoy ordering nor do I enjoy witnessing punishment but that number of lashes was lenient considering what the man had done and would not be regarded as excessive on most ships.'

'I have witnessed the same amount of punishment elsewhere, and more, but this time—' the surgeon shook his head. 'By the time the man was taken down, his back resembled a plate of minced liver.'

Oliver ignored the remark. 'No doubt you cleaned the wound.'

'As best I could for his pain was exquisite. In my estimation, he will not be fit for duty for more than a week.'

Removing the cloth covering the small dish, Oliver slid it along the table for the doctor to examine. 'Did you find any fragments, like these, in his wounds?'

The doctor studied the fine particles. 'If such foreign material was present, it would have been washed out on deck when his back was dowsed with sea water or, perhaps later, when he was brought down to the cockpit and I cleaned it myself.'

'What if it was not?' the captain asked.

'Then the fragments, of whatever they are, will be absorbed by the scar tissue as the wound heals. Like splinters of wood that enter the skin during battle, if left alone, they eventually fester and work their own way out.' The surgeon looked up at the captain. 'Are you saying that someone deliberately pierced the knots of the lash with these needle sharp claws?'

'It would appear so.'

'That is diabolical. How could anyone do that? Does the cat usually remain in your cabin?' he asked.

'Not until recently. A new cat is made after every punishment and the bosun and his mates are the only ones who have access to it.'

'You think it was one of those men.'

'No,' Oliver said bluntly.

'Did anyone have a grudge against the man who received the punishment?'

'Perhaps the man he tried to harm. I will endeavour to find out.' With that, the captain gathered up the implement, wound the thongs around the handle but did not return it to the red bag. 'Casson,' he called. His steward responded immediately. 'Do me a favour. Drop this over the side.'

The steward raised his eyebrows. 'Right now, Captain?'

'Right this instant.'

'Aye aye, Capt'n.'

Oliver turned to the ship's surgeon. 'The bosun is not short of old rope. If he has not already done so, I will instruct him to make a new one forthwith.'

As the steward could be heard running up the steps to the deck, Oliver removed the other items from the table, washed his hands and thanked the surgeon for offering his opinion.

'Join me for dinner this evening and pass word to Mr Nightingale and the officers on deck. I have some news to share.'

'Thank you,' Jonathon Whipple replied. 'I shall look forward to it.'

The table had been almost cleared, apart from a large platter of strange exotic fruits, many of which the young midshipmen had never seen before and took delight in making jokes about. Sitting at the head, Oliver tapped the crystal decanter with a spoon. 'Your attention, gentlemen,' he called.

The banter came to an immediately halt.

'I trust you all enjoyed your supper.' The captain's words were applauded around the table. 'Might I suggest you take special note of the tenderness of the beef? Cook went to great lengths, at risk to life and limb, by going ashore this morning to purchase it directly from the slaughterhouse. Be advised, it will be the last you will eat until we reach our destination. The pork, however, is unaware of its fate and is happily eating its fill in the manger.'

The company laughed, raised their glasses and proceeded to drink to the health of the pigs.

Sitting on the captain's right, Mr Parry remained silent. As if infected by the disconsolate mood of the men, his spirits were somewhat deflated. He was anxious to hear the captain share his news with the other officers in order that the necessary arrangements for their forthcoming voyage could be put in place.

With the attention of everyone around the table, the captain remained seated to address the assembled company. After taking a sup from his glass, he spoke. 'Brandy, gentleman. Enjoy, for this is the last bottle from Napoleon's vineyards that I have in my pantry. I considered this a suitable occasion to have Casson bring it to the table and when you hear the news, I am sure you will all agree. In the meantime, I propose we win this war against the Frogs so we no longer have to rely on English smugglers to replenish our stocks.'

Oliver held out his hand to quieten the mirth. 'Let me thank you for dining with me and inform you we have things to celebrate. Mr Hanson,' he called. 'Stand up – no don't stand up, you will knock your head. Remain seated. Gentlemen, let me advise you Midshipman Hanson has today achieved the grand age of seventeen years. I offer you my congratulations, young man. At almost twice your age, I only wish I could turn back the clock.' Oliver winked at Mr Mundy, his sailing master. 'But on second thoughts, perhaps not.'

Knuckles rapped on the table in agreement.

'However, you were not invited to join me to hear that news. As you all know, yesterday I called on Captain William Liversedge aboard HMS *Stalwart*. The captain and I have been friends since we were young lieutenants serving aboard a first rate. For your information, he is a fine officer held in high esteem by the Admiralty. During the course of my visit, he handed me an envelope containing new orders which he had carried with him from the Admiralty in London. Gentlemen, you will be pleased to learn we sail within the week.'

The response was spontaneous and enthusiastic. The captain's words were repeated by almost everyone.

'And,' he held his audience in suspense, 'we will not be sailing alone, but in the company of the third rate.'

'Excellent news,' the sailing master said.

'And that is not all.'

Wine glasses stopped betwixt table and lip. Mouths remained opened. Eyes widened. Ears flapped. Only the sound of footsteps creaking across the planks of the deck above disturbed the silence.

'We are not heading south as was originally ordered. We are returning to England.'

'Heaven be praised!' the sailing master said.

'By all the saints, this is good news!' the doctor added.

Clapping his hands in joy, the rose-tinted flush of embarrassment that had coloured young Mr Hanson's cheeks immediately drained and his pursed lips broadened into a smile stretching from ear to ear.

Across the table Mr Nightingale and Mr Tully shook hands. 'I told you so,' Mr Tully said.

Oliver leaned back from the table slightly surprised at the overwhelming response. 'It appears the new orders meet with everyone's approval.'

'Indeed, they do.' Simon Parry said. 'It will come as a tonic to the men. Am I now permitted to pass the word?'

Oliver leaned towards his first lieutenant and whispered in his ear. 'With my steward and two of the ship's boys hovering outside the door, I would not be surprised to learn that word is flying up the companionway steps at this very instant.'

Righting himself, the captain continued. 'Let us be serious for a moment, gentlemen. There are several important matters that must be attended to before we can depart this harbour. Orders for fresh supplies and stores must be placed and the goods received on board in the next few days. I call on you all to ensure they are handled safely and stowed efficiently. I want no unruly behaviour as occurred yesterday. Lashing a man to within an inch of his life does not solve problems – it only succeeds in making an undisciplined man worse. On a more positive note, I trust this news, which you are at liberty to share with your divisions, will lift the crew's flagging spirits and bring a renewed sense of optimism. To add to that, two bags of correspondence, carried from home aboard the 74, will be delivered tomorrow and can be distributed to the men.'

As the last word any of the crew had received from loved ones was in Gibraltar, there was a sense of eager anticipation.

'The most pressing matter to attend, however, relates to the Portuguese sailors we rescued and are accommodating below deck. Arrangements must be made for them to be put ashore or transferred to another ship. I trust those men will not soon forget the service *Perpetual* afforded them.'

'All credit to you, Captain,' the sailing master said.

'Nay,' Oliver replied. 'Aboard ship, no one serves alone. For the present, however, enjoy the wine and eat up the fruit for what is not consumed this evening will be feeding the fishes of Guanabara Bay in the morning. In the meantime, let us raise our glasses as, in a few days, God willing, we will be raising our yards, jibs and staysails and delivering life back into our indolent canvas. Gentlemen, I give you a toast – heading home.'

'Heading home.'

With laughter and excited voices buzzing around and across the table, Oliver took the opportunity to speak in confidence with the doctor, seated on his left.

'From your response to my new sailing orders, I take it you are pleased.'

'I could not be more delighted,' Dr Whipple said.

'You surprise me, Jonathon. I thought you were quite at ease with us heading south in accordance with my original orders.'

'Initially, I was happy to go wherever the cruise took me. But on being given the choice, I would dearly love to step on English soil again. There are matters I should attend to before spending another year or two away from home.'

'And where is home?'

'London, for the present.'

'Not Dublin?'

'I left Ireland in my youth to study at the University in Edinburgh. When I joined the ship, I told you of the death of my father and the loss of the family's estate. Because of that, I have no reason to return to Ireland and, indeed, no desire to do so. If I did return, I would not find the country the way I left it in the mid-nineties. Much happened at the time of the uprising and in the years preceding the rebellion. Ireland is no longer the home I grew up in.'

'I understand.'

The doctor quickly turned the subject of conversation from himself. 'From the mumblings of the officers, I think most of them welcome your news.'

Oliver sighed. 'I believe I am in the minority in this occasion.'

'What makes you say that?'

'I am probably the only one who regards the passage back to England as a retrograde step and one fraught with danger.'

'How so? I know danger lurks beyond the next wave on the high seas – you have reminded me of that many times. But, from what you have told us, we will be sailing in the company of a 74-gun third rate man-of-war. Surely that will provide us with a safe escort.'

'Permit me to correct you there, Doctor. *Perpetual*, being a frigate, is a fifth rate ship, and is, therefore, seen to be escorting the 74 and not being escorted by it. In times of war, however, a 74-gun ship is a vulnerable target – a prize worth pursuing by both French and Spanish squadrons. As our new course will carry us across the routes sailed by both those countries' navies, I can only hope we do not encounter any of them.'

After glancing about to make sure his conversation was drawing no attention, Oliver lowered his voice to a whisper and continued.

'Tell me about the use of the cat of nine tails, Jonathon.'

The doctor was taken aback by the sudden change in the captain's subject matter. 'Hardly a suitable topic for the dinner table,' he suggested.

'It is important I know your views,' Oliver said. 'Interestingly, the Irishman who is acting as my scribe did not seem unduly shocked at the use of a seeded lash.'

The doctor smiled sympathetically. 'Any Irish-born man would have heard of such a lethal weapon. Those who felt it on their flesh often did not survive.'

Oliver waited for him to continue.

'The Irish know much of man's inhumanity to man – most often from personal experience or events related to members of their families. I've heard tales of the treatment of prisoners and of convicts shipped across the seas and of the cruelty inflicted on them by their British overlords. Terrible stories.'

'You speak with the verve and tone of a United Irishman.'

The surgeon sighed. 'You live your life within the wooden walls of a small floating community set apart from the rest of the world.'

'I have lived beyond these walls,' the captain replied defensively. 'I have witnessed wretches on the docks of many a port in Britain and abroad.'

'But you have not witnessed abject poverty until you have lived in Ireland. Poverty brought about by British rule.'

'You were not born of that peasant class,' Oliver reminded.

'No, but I am of Celtic blood and, though I lived most of my life in England I have heard the stories first-hand and I understand the feelings shared by Irishmen, both Catholic and Protestant alike, and their bitter hatred of British authority.'

'But the rebellion of '98 was quashed, was it not?'

'The uprising was put down, but the spirit behind it was not and never will be. The flame was lit almost two hundred years ago when Irish slaves, many of them children, were first sent to America. That flame will not be extinguished until Ireland has gained its independence.'

'I trust you are not suggesting that all the Irishmen serving aboard British ships feel this way?'

The doctor raised his eyebrows.

'Tosh!' Oliver exclaimed. 'There are thousands of Irish sailors serving in the Royal Navy. Our ships are filled with them and there are many qualified and skilled men like yourself serving in senior capacities. Over the years, many officers have risen to the rank of Admiral.'

'I am fully aware of that fact and am reminded of it whenever I hear Gaelic verses sung or hummed on the deck. I know the accents of the Irish hands, I know the county and sometimes the very town those men hailed from. But despite their differences, they are all of one resolve. They will not tolerate traitors and, on the other hand, they will always support one of their own kind.'

When the captain's steward reached over the table to fill their empty glasses, the conversation came to an abrupt stop. After that, nothing more of significance was shared or said and the company departed when the wine was exhausted.

The following morning, the first lieutenant was on deck. As the watches had not been stood down, all hands were engaged in the morning chores. The decks were holystoned and swabbed, the brasses polished and glass windows cleaned. When that was finished the men brought up their hammocks and stuffed them into the netting atop the bulwarks. After washing their clothes, various items were hung about the deck to dry. While the sun brought a mid-morning temperature of over eighty degrees, the humidity held the dampness in the garments.

The degree of pleasure the sailors took in bathing was measured by the crude jokes, laughter and fun they shared. With a pump and hose rigged in the bow, one man soaped himself while another directed a powerful jet of cooling seawater over him. Those who preferred to bathe themselves in a bucket of brine drawn from the sea occupied the area around the heads and cursed when the hose was inadvertently or deliberately directed at them.

When the suds, sand and flecks of seaweed had been washed into the scuppers, the noise subsided and the men took advantage of free time to relax. While some stood silently by the rail gazing blankly at the broad bay, others smoked or chewed on a piece of tobacco, or played games. A few occupied their time splicing old rope or teasing it apart to make oakum-stuffing for a pillow.

Aloft, the bosun was busy in the rigging while the sailmaker and his mates sat in the shade of the waist with folds of canvas spread across their legs. With needle and palm they occupied their time repairing a torn topgallant sail.

There was no wind and had been none for several days. While presently, no one complained, such conditions, if they persisted, would prevent the ships from proceeding from the harbour in two or three days' time.

Wandering aft, Oliver stood at the taff rail and looked across the still water to the third rate man-of-war anchored less than a cable's length away. She was indeed a fine looking ship. Her sails were neatly furled for the harbour, her brightwork gleamed and the sun reflected from her east-facing stern windows.

Command of such a vessel was envied by many aspiring post captains. Boasting two gun decks, *Stalwart* carried 28-guns on the lower deck, mainly 24- and 36-pounders, and the same number of 18- to 24-pounders on the upper gundeck. There were also nine and 12-pounders on the quarter deck and substantial bow and stern chasers plus swivel guns mounted on her rails and in the tops. Her weight of metal was enormous and the firepower she could bring to bear in battle made her a formidable force. It was not surprising that Britain chose to build more 74s than any other rate of fighting ship.

Though her crew numbered around five hundred men, the captain could see very few sailors either on deck or in the 74's rigging.

'That group of men over by the heads, they are of your division, are they not?' the first lieutenant asked.

The midshipman looked to the group of a dozen men standing around the pin rail beneath the foremast. He nodded. 'Most of them are, but not all.'

'And what do you think is so engrossing that they are hovering around that spot like ants on a dead cockroach?'

'Beats me,' the midshipman said, shrugging his shoulders.

'Well, I think it is time you made it your concern. The matter men are discussing when they congregate in such a manner, speaking as they are doing in hushed tones, should be a concern.'

'I'll go and enquire.'

'Hold fast!' Mr Parry ordered. 'Observe a while.'

The midshipman dithered for a moment before stepping back and doing as he was instructed.

'It appears the taller of the men is doing all of the talking and has everyone's ear. Who is that sailor?' the senior officer asked.

'He's not a sailor. He's just a lubber. A landsman signed at the last port.'

'One of the six men who came aboard in the Azores?'

'Yes, sir,' the midshipman added with a slight grin. 'I hear he's a bit of a joker and tells yarns. That's what gets the men's attention. He and his mates call themselves the Wexford lads.'

Mr Parry was not amused. He had been troubled by this man's antics previously and was conscious he had even attracted the captain's attention.

While the pair continued to observe, a whisper ran through the group and all eyes shot aft towards the quarterdeck. Within seconds, and without prompting, sailors peeled from the group in a nonchalant fashion and wandered to other parts of the forecastle or threw a leg over the forward hatch coaming and descended to the deck below.

On witnessing their behaviour, Mr Hanson, with the lieutenant's prompting, strode over to the handful of men remaining there. One old salt laughed inappropriately but said nothing. Another sneered through toothless gums – a quid of tobacco stuffed in his cheek, the black juice seeping from the corners of his lips. Another quickly stuffed the stem of his pipe into his mouth and drew deeply on the cold empty clay.

'What goes on here?' Mr Hanson asked.

The man, who had taken centre place in the group, pulled a feather from the band of his hat and poked a piece of pork sinew from between his back teeth. After looking at it, he placed it on his tongue and made a show of eating it.

The midshipman gave a disparaging look.

'Not a thing goes on,' the man said. 'Just tittle tattling. There's no law against that, is there?'

'Tell me, what was it that was of such interest?'

'Oh, nothing really,' he claimed, fanning out his fingers of one hand and running the end of the sharpened quill under his grubby nails. 'Just planning a small celebration for when we sail. Saying farewell to the port. A bit of music and a jig on the deck, if the officer-of-the-watch will allow it.'

'Look at me when you are talking to me,' the midshipman said. 'And put that disgusting thing away.'

'Whatever you say, Mr Hanson, sir.' The lilting Irish accent was unmistakable.

The middie took a deep breath. 'Since when have the men celebrated leaving port?'

The Irishman waggled his head from side-to-side, in the manner of an Indian sailor. 'Can't rightly say but when I put the idea to the lads they took to it right away.'

'They did, did they? I thought you and your mates were anxious to leave the ship.'

'Aye, that we were, but it seems we aren't permitted to. So, if we can't get off, we'll have to make the best of a bad thing.'

'You think it's a bad thing to continue sailing with this frigate?' the young middie asked. 'Didn't this ship give you a berth in Ponta Delgada after you'd been pulled, near drowned, from the North Atlantic?'

'Aye, it did. At the request of the British Consul,' he added boldly.

'I don't think it is necessary to bring the British Consul into this discussion. From now on, I don't want to see any gatherings either on deck or in the mess, day or night made up of more than four men. Do I make myself clear?'

'Clear as Waterford crystal, Mr Hanson, and I guarantee that is the finest glass there is, believe you me.'

Exhausted of any other argument to level at the men, the midshipman returned to the quarterdeck and reported to Mr Parry.

'What was the fellow's excuse for the meeting?' the lieutenant enquired.

'He said the men just wanted an excuse to kick their heels up a bit and depart the bay as soon as possible.'

'Indeed,' Mr Parry said. 'Remind me, what is that man's name?'

'Murphy. Joseph Murphy.'

Chapter 3

A Confrontation

Having returned to his cabin to collect a package he had put together earlier, Captain Quintrell stepped up to the quarterdeck and stood for a moment observing the deck and listening to the familiar squeal of hemp straining through the blocks as his boat was lowered from the davits. Casting his gaze forward, his attention was drawn to a boy on the gangway, only twenty yards from him.

As if prompted by a sudden urge, the lad leapt up onto the rail, grabbed the shrouds and shinned up the rigging with the agility of a foremast Jack. His bare feet bounded from one ratline to another, never missing a step whilst his hands barely touched the ropes. When he reached the main yard, he leapt across to the starboard footrope as confidently as if striding across a puddle in an alley. With one arm lightly hooked over the spar, he glided gracefully along the rope. When he reached the end, he leaned from the yardarm and examined the large block through which the main brace ran. Appearing satisfied with what he saw, he slid back to the mast, jumped nimbly across to the larboard arm and repeated his inspection. From there, he headed up, climbed out around the futtock shrouds and continued aloft to the royal yard.

While he was exchanging a word with the masthead lookout, the bosun's voice boomed up from the deck. 'You boy! Get down here, quick smart. I ain't going to scrape your innards off the deck when they're splattered all over it.'

On hearing the order, the lad, not yet five feet tall, wound his leg round a stay and took the quickest way down. Landing lightly on the rail, he dropped to the deck and presented himself, a satisfied grin on his face.

'Didn't I tell you to see to the pitch pot?' the bosun yelled.

'I did. I stirred it for ages, then I stirred it some more. Then I thought I'd take a look at the yards?'

'You did, did you? And was the running rigging to your satisfaction?'

'Yes, it was,' the boy replied seriously.

Having stopped to observe, Oliver was tempted to smile but refrained.

'Well, from now on,' the bosun growled, 'you'll keep out of the rigging. That's my business and not yours. Away with you. I don't want to see your face on deck again.'

Like a seasoned salt, Charles Goodridge knuckled his forehead and scampered off to the forward hatch where he disappeared down it quicker than a rabbit escaping into a warren.

'Save your energy, boy,' the bosun yelled after him. 'You're going to need it when you're carrying powder.'

As his boat was not yet ready, Oliver headed along the gangway to speak with the petty officer. 'That is the boy who came aboard with the shipwrights in Gibraltar, is it not?'

'Aye, Captain.'

'What do you make of him?'

'He's more mischief than a Barbary ape. He'll leap onto anything that's fastened down, swing from one line to another, if he thinks no one's watching him, and climb without fear.'

'Is that so?'

'I have to nail his shoe to the deck if I want him to keep still for any length of time.'

A voice from the water below interrupted the conversation. 'Boat's alongside, Captain,' the coxswain called.

'Thank you, Wootton. I will come aboard.'

From the entry port, Captain Quintrell climbed down the ship's side and, after taking his seat in the stern sheets, placed the package between his feet. The coxswain already had his instructions – to steer for the Portuguese frigate sitting at anchor a mile away.

It was the same frigate that had left the main island of the Azores with its sister ship, *Pomba Branca* – the *White Dove*. Encountering that vessel on his way to Rio had left a lasting impression on Captain Quintrell and a sour taste in his mouth. Having agreed to rendezvous with *Perpetual* and *Pomba Branca* at the Fernando de Noronha archipelago off the coast of Brazil, the Portuguese captain had failed to meet that obligation. Having wasted valuable sailing time waiting for him, Oliver was anxious to hear his explanation and to learn why he had parted company with his sister ship and made sail for Rio de Janeiro alone.

Since that episode occurred several weeks ago, Oliver Quintrell had sworn that if the opportunity arose, he would confront the frigate's commander with the dire consequences of his failures that directly resulted in the tragic loss of *Pomba Branca* and the lives of many of its crew. He also intended to present him with the survivors of that disaster – the sailors he had rescued. These men urgently needed to be transferred to the port or to a Portuguese ship.

It was an unsavoury business and although Oliver felt little satisfaction would be gained from the confrontation, he intended to go through with it. With those thoughts foremost in his mind, he sat bolt upright in the stern of the boat and did not take his eyes from the Iberian ship as he was rowed up the bay.

After being formally welcomed on board by the vessels senior Portuguese naval officers, Captain Quintrell was ushered to the great cabin and offered refreshments. He declined. When the servant left and he was alone with the commanding officer, Oliver wasted no time in broaching those questions that had been vexing him for the past few weeks.

Bombarding the frigate's captain with the full extent of the tragedy his actions had caused, speaking in cold, clear English, Oliver described the fate of *Pomba Branca*. He explained that it had not only been sunk by a privateer, but described how it had been plundered of everything of value including sails, spars and guns, and informed him that those who had survived had been taken prisoner. Holding nothing back, he described how the Portuguese officers and some of the seamen had been executed before his very eyes – their heads split open, their throats cut and their bodies unceremoniously tossed into the sea.

Showing little apparent regard for the lives forfeited on that day and offering no logical reason or apology for failing to keep the prearranged rendezvous, the Portuguese captain's supercilious attitude offended Captain Quintrell. Though there were flickers of discomfort in the commander's eyes, the word *apology*, which Oliver was expecting, never slipped from his lips.

Whilst controlling his anger and allowing time for the extent of the tragedy to be absorbed by the officer, Oliver placed the package on the table. After removing the twine and paper, he revealed the contents and placed them side-by-side on the table. Included was the *Pomba Branca*'s log book plus bundles of letters and papers but nothing of monetary value. Each item had been salvaged from the great cabin but not before the keel had settled in the sand and the washed over the decks. Water damage had sealed the log's pages and, the ink on the other correspondence had run rendering the writing totally illegible. Gazing down at the pathetic remains, Oliver wished he had dragged the ship's figurehead from the ocean and delivered it to the recalcitrant captain. Perhaps the life-size effigy of the woman cradling a white dove in her hands would have served as a poignant reminder to the officer of his flagrant lack of concern.

However, having carefully documented all the events that had occurred before, during and after *Perpetual*'s encounter with the privateer at the archipelago, Oliver handed his report to the frigate's captain. He then showed him an envelope containing an exact copy, transcribed by his secretary and signed by himself. It was addressed to the Commanding Officer of the Portuguese Navy in Rio de Janeiro. He advised the captain it was to be hand-delivered that same day.

With those matters attended to, Oliver had fulfilled his obligation, as he saw it, yet it still galled him that *Pomba Branca* had been left at the mercy of an evil privateer by its sister ship. The memory of the ship's officers – their legs crumpling beneath them as sharpened steel sliced their throats and blood streamed across the deck – was not an image he would easily forget.

After the unsavoury business was concluded, Captain Quintrell was eager to leave and declined an offer to dine on the ship. In his mind, there was nothing to celebrate. The only positive outcome from the meeting was that the Portuguese captain agreed to take the survivors – the sailors *Perpetual* had rescued, cared for and carried safely to Guanabara Bay. Oliver was obliged to thank the captain for that but for nothing more. The sooner the sailors could be transferred the better.

Oliver's face showed no emotion as his boat pushed away and slid silently down the bay. The steady dip of the oars echoed the heaviness of his breathing.

'*Perpetual*,' the coxswain hailed, as they neared the British frigate, announcing the return of her captain.

With unfamiliar bumps and rumblings reverberating right along the frigate's hull to the bulwarks of his cabin, Oliver bounded up the steps to investigate the sounds. After acknowledging Mr Nightingale on the quarterdeck, he joined the ship's carpenter leaning against the bulwarks on the gangway. He was watching a consignment of supplies coming aboard.

'What are those goods?' the captain asked.

'Stores for the carpenter's shop and bosun's locker,' Mr Crosby said, checking the inventory he was holding. 'Twenty cases of cut nails, twenty of wrought nails and twenty cases of copper nails.'

'That is a considerable quantity of nails,' Oliver observed.

'We barely had a nail left in the ship after handing over much of our stock in Gibraltar and then doing repairs to various vessels since then,' Mr Crosby explained. 'Mighty heavy those containers are,' he added. 'I hope the tackle doesn't break.'

'What else?' Oliver enquired.

The carpenter referred to his list. 'Lengths of sawn timber, paint, varnish, borax, turpentine and beeswax. You approved the list yourself only two days ago.'

'Thank you, Mr Crosby.' Oliver watched for a while as another consignment consisting of more casks and boxes was placed in the mesh of netting, hoisted from the lighter's deck, swung inboard and lowered into the frigate's hold through the waist.

'Spare spars and cordage will arrive later this afternoon. Bolts of cloth for the sailmaker are promised for tomorrow morning.'

'Good,' Oliver said, as he mulled over the volume of stores his warrant officers had ordered and for which he had given his approval.

Casting his mind back to Gibraltar, he recollected how generous he had been with his ship's supplies. But when Captain John Gore, *Medusa*, had limped into the bay and requested assistance, he had done what any other captain would have done under the circumstances. One reason he had not thought twice about handing over spars, cordage, canvas and more was because he believed, at the time, he would be returning to Portsmouth within a matter of weeks. That, however, had not happened and the Admiralty orders he had received before leaving Gibraltar Bay had instructed him to head to the Southern Ocean. Then, having proceeded to sea with his supplies greatly depleted, *Perpetual* had crossed paths with the evil privateer, Fredrik van Zetten. After the bloody encounter necessitating repairs to his own ship and after supplying spars and cordage to repair the privateer's brig, the tradesmen's lockers, the lazarette and the hold had been emptied of essential items necessary to keep the frigate at sea. Now, the prospect of sailing across waters infested with French and Spanish ships, without adequate spares, did not rest easy with him. Meeting an adversary and suffering damage, before he cleared the tropics, could spell disaster.

Satisfied the quantity of supplies ordered was justified, the captain nodded to the carpenter. 'Anything else expected today?'

'More victuals, I am told, but I don't have that list,' Mr Crosby advised.

Oliver thanked him and headed down to the cockpit. He needed to talk with the doctor.

When the captain entered the cockpit, young Tommy Wainwright popped up from behind one of the swinging cots where he was busy swabbing the deck.

'Leave us,' Oliver said.

'Aye aye, Capt'n,' the lad replied, returning his mop to the wooden pail and hurrying away.

'Good morning, Jonathon,' Oliver called.

From the writing desk, where he was working, the doctor rose and returned a cordial greeting. On inviting the captain to take a seat, he was surprised when the invitation was accepted. 'How can I be of help?' the doctor asked.

After looking around, the captain hesitated. Several of the swinging cots were occupied and a pair of sailors was sitting on deck with their backs resting against the bulwarks. With eyes closed, they appeared to be sleeping.

Jonathon Whipple anticipated the captain's question. 'Portuguese sailors,' he said. 'Apart from a few basic words, they do not understand English so you are at liberty to speak freely.'

Despite the doctor's advice, the captain lowered his voice. 'I need the benefit of your valued opinion,' Oliver said. 'I need to know the state of the cooper's equilibrium.'

The doctor raised his eyebrows. 'Bungs?'

'The very same. How stable is he?'

'He suffered a severe head injury,' the doctor replied.

'I am fully aware of that. Kindly answer my question regarding his equilibrium.'

'Are you referring to the man's mental or physical balance?'

'It is not his physical stability which concerns me. It is his mental composure and behaviour. He was obviously quite disturbed for some weeks following that unfortunate event.'

The doctor nodded.

'It is important for me to know if his memory is fully returned and serving him well and if he is capable of following orders.'

The doctor collected his thoughts before replying. 'James Tinker or Bungs, as the men call him, is quite old in comparison with the rest of the crew. He has been in active service for many years. He informed me in great detail about his work in HMS *Victory*'s hold, way back in '82, when she was refitted and her bottom sheathed in copper. On hearing his story, I see no problem with his memory. However,' the doctor was conscious the captain was waiting for a direct answer, 'prior to his accident he was a strong healthy man. In fact, so much so, the injury he sustained, which resulted in the swelling of the brain, would have killed men half his age. Others might have survived but suffered apoplexy, bouts of memory loss, fits and impaired speech or vision. Bungs, however has made a remarkable recovery within a relatively short time. As a result, I have already given approval for him to return to work for a number of hours every day. Mr Tully has agreed to give an eye to his progress.'

Oliver frowned. 'Mr Tully is hardly qualified to make a medical assessment.'

The doctor ignored the cynicism. 'I merely advised the lieutenant to report to me if the cooper's actions, speech or behaviour showed any noticeable change or aberration.'

The captain continued his enquiry. 'Apart from being under observation, are there any other treatments you are administering to ensure this man's continued recovery.'

'The necessary healing and repair is taking place within the cooper's skull, so I am unable to monitor it. There is nothing more that can be done. Mr Tully will check on his performance at work and his messmates have agreed to observe him at other times. I am confident they will support him and make sure he gets into no strife. I believe they, too, are anxious to see their shipmate return to his normal self as quickly as possible.'

Oliver smiled. 'To the crusty, cantankerous, feisty old devil he was before the injury. But I jest,' the captain said. 'The cooper's lassitude following the accident has seen him adopt a manner far removed from that of his previous self. I, for one, welcome his return to a more lively spirit. But let me repeat my original question, Doctor. In his present capacity, is he capable of following orders? I must know because there is a specific job I need him to do for me.'

'I assume it will not overtax his physical strength.'

'You can be assured I intend to call on extra hands to assist him.'

'That is well,' the doctor said. 'I believe he currently has a man with him who had been helping with the cooperage since we left the islands.'

'So I was told. Do you know this man's name?' the captain asked.

'McNamara. I have spoken with him briefly. He was born in County Wexford, as was I, but he hailed from Liverpool. He told me he was planning to leave the ship once we reached Rio. If he does so, a replacement to assist Bungs will be required.'

Oliver was concerned. If the man had been working alongside the cooper whilst his mental capacity was less than normal, was it possible he had learned of the secret that Bungs held?

'Thank you, Jonathon, I appreciate your candour. Now, I understand you had been wishing to speak with me. What can I do for you?'

'There is a favour,' the doctor said. 'My medical supplies have run low as a result of the action we encountered. They are now at a critical level. I would not wish to embark on a long voyage without replenishing my stocks. I need to go ashore and will require use of one of the ship's boats. Can that be arranged?'

'Of course,' Oliver said.

'And, also—'

Oliver waited.

'Would you permit me to escort the carpenter's wife, Mrs Crosby, and Mrs Pilkington into the town? There are items they need to purchase to tide them over the coming weeks at sea.'

Oliver frowned. 'You are presuming that I intend to permit the pair to stay on board. I think you are aware of my thoughts about females on His Majesty's ships and—,' with no change in his expression, '—I would feel quite within my rights to put them both over the side.'

On reading the response etched in the lines across the doctor's brow, Oliver mellowed his tone. 'As you are aware, I made an exception with these two when we departed the Azores and, since that time, both females have abided by the restrictions I placed on them. Subsequently, they both proved their worth when we came under attack. Of course, Mrs Crosby has a claim to stay aboard being the wife of the ship's carpenter. As for Mrs Pilkington—'

'Mrs Pilkington also made herself useful and is well regarded by the ship's boys.'

'This is not a nursery school, sir, and the ship's boys have no need for a wet nurse.'

'I understand,' Jonathon said dejectedly. 'However, I beg you to allow both women to stay with the ship, particularly as we now know we are heading for England. Connie – Mrs Pilkington has no family, only the boy, Charles, whom she has taken under her wing. And she provides good company for the carpenter's wife.'

Oliver eyed the doctor and considered an ulterior motive to his remark. 'Do I see more to this female's role in the cockpit than as an assistant?'

The doctor reached for his cane leaning against the bulwark, grasped it in both hands and rolled it between his palms. 'Begging your pardon. I trust you are not suggesting anything improper in our relationship.'

'I merely put the question,' Oliver replied. 'She is a fine looking woman who is much obliged to you for saving her life. If I am not mistaken, you alone administered to all her needs after the brutal attack on her person.'

'I performed my duties as would any physician in those circumstances.'

'Say no more. It was indelicate of me to raise the issue. Needless to say, I agree, the women should stay together along with the boy. However, I have considered speaking with Captain Liversedge and having them transferred to HMS *Stalwart*.'

'Is that necessary?' the doctor asked.

'In my opinion, it will be for the best. Presently the pair is occupying a section of the carpenter's workshop. Although Mrs Crosby is entitled to berth with her husband, in only a matter of weeks, when we arrive in Portsmouth, she will be reunited with her husband. I am sure she can manage a short period of absence from him. In the meantime, if the women are removed, the carpenter and his mates will have nothing to distract them from the performance of their duties. As for the boy,' he added, 'in a ship the size of the 74, all three should be easily absorbed. The boy's name will be entered in the muster book and I am sure the women will be provided with some useful occupation. They have both proved to be good workers when called upon in emergency. But I have yet to discuss the matter with Captain Liversedge.'

The doctor remained silent.

'However, in answer to your question, I will not permit the women to go ashore with you or with anyone else. You witnessed, first hand, the misadventure that befell the pair when they were allowed abroad on the streets of Ponta Delgada. I cannot chance that happening again. In the meantime, I suggest you invite the women to prepare a list of their requirements for you to purchase, on their behalf, when you go into the town.'

Although Oliver doubted the doctor would understand his motives, he had good reason for not allowing either members of his crew or the women to leave the ship. The memory of his previous visit to Guanabara Bay was foremost in his mind.

'I cannot afford to lose you or your equipment, Doctor. Therefore, I will detail one of the middies and a small detachment of marines to accompany you. Mr Parry will also be going ashore. I suggest you join him in a boat.'

Dejected, but not unduly surprised at the captain's deliberation, the surgeon tapped his stick on the deck. The display of frustration did not go unobserved.

'Will tomorrow suit?' Oliver asked.

Resting both hands on the head of his cane, Dr Whipple acknowledged. 'That will be fine.'

'I trust you can still defend yourself with that,' Oliver said, glancing down to the wooden cane. 'You impressed me with your skills in Alicante.'

The surgeon nodded and his face brightened. 'There is little space in this cabin for stick fighting but, occasionally, when the cockpit is empty or the patients are induced to sleep, I practice against an invisible enemy, much to the entertainment of the boys. Both Charles Goodridge and young Tommy Wainwright have asked me to teach them some of my moves.'

'Have you agreed?'

'I said I would if time permitted.' Then his serious expression returned. 'I pray I do not have to use my skill to defend myself.'

As he departed the cockpit, Oliver mulled over what the doctor had told him and considered the other matters he had to address in the coming days. It was essential the

Portuguese sailors were returned to one of their country's naval vessels as soon as possible. He was also obliged to arrange transfer of the Spanish silver to the 74-gun warship but he intended to leave that until the ships were almost ready to depart Guanabara Bay.

The news he had received about the cooper's state of mind was reassuring. Bungs was one of only three or four people who had been present when the four chests containing Spanish treasure had been placed inside four large barrels and hidden in the hold. He thought it unlikely the cooper had marked the barrels indicating their unusual contents for fear of them being identified. For that reason, Oliver was concerned the cooper's memory of the exact location of the specific barrels might have been lost.

Ships' holds, whether in merchant or fighting ships, were dark, deep and dank regions housing hundreds of barrels stowed side-on, one row stacked on top of another, reaching from ballast base to deck beams. Throughout a cruise, barrels were constantly in demand, continually shifted, hoisted from the hold, emptied in the galley, or wherever they were required, and returned empty, to be disassembled or shipped home intact. Barrels varied in size, but with hundreds, sometimes thousands of each, locating one particular item could be extremely challenging.

Placing one foot on the first step of the ladder leading up to the gundeck, the captain was alerted by a hissing sound.

'Yer ear, Capt'n,' the voice called in a loud whisper.

Oliver recognised it. 'What is it Bungs? I have urgent matters to attend to.'

'Be wary of Michael O'Connor and the rest of his mob! Just saying, I am. Best thing would be to rid the ship of them that's Irish.'

It seemed more than coincidental to the captain that he had just been speaking with the doctor about the cooper, and now here he was accosting him on the companionway steps. He knew the wooden walls of ships were porous and revealed many secrets but he doubted the cooper had heard the conversation he had just been having. His interruption certainly captured the captain's attention.

'What makes you say that, Bungs? You must have good reason.'

The cooper scratched a fresh growth of hair bristling from a scar running across his head. 'Well, my brain might have been tossed like flotsam in a maelstrom, but I can assure you I ain't as daft as I look, or as some folk take me to be.'

Oliver ignored that remark. 'Continue.'

'It's just that I was resting my eyes in the hold – not sleeping mind – a day ago, when I hear this tapping sound. *Tap-tap* it went and then again *tap-tap, tap-tap*.'

'And—?'

'I knew it weren't no rat with clogs on. I know that particular tapping sound pretty well. I knock on them barrels regular as clockwork every day. That's how I know which is full and which is empty and what's rotten and what's in each of them. I can tell if it's wine or water or beef or pork just by tapping.'

'Did you investigate to discover who it was that was making the noise?'

'I didn't need to. It were that fellow who were sent to do my job after I were *hindisposed*. It were one of them *red-headed* Irish croppies.'

'Don't you think it possible the man was merely imitating your routine?'

'Pig's arse!' he blurted, before slapping his hand across his mouth. 'Sorry, Capt'n, I shouldn't have said that. I reckon he was looking for the barrels with the coins stowed inside them.'

'Shh!' Quintrell said, quickly glancing around to ensure that no one was within earshot. 'Are you sure about that? Perhaps it was in your imagination.'

'Begging your pardon, Capt'n,' Bungs remonstrated. 'It might have seemed like my brain was double reefed for a spell but, I assure you, I never lost my memory or my nous. Trust me, Captain – just ask my messmates. They'll tell you, I got this *hintuition*. I can smell right away when something ain't right.'

The captain chose to ignore his comments. 'The man you heard, did he know you were in the hold?'

'No, he didn't. I was tucked away out of sight between a couple of big leaguers, well away from the spill of the lantern light, where no one could find me.'

The captain raised his eyebrows.

'I waited for a while after the tapping had stopped and, when I couldn't hear no footsteps, I got up and looked about, but he'd gone.'

Oliver lowered his voice. 'Do you think the man knows which barrels the chests were hidden in?'

'Aye, as sure as a jack flies in a breeze.'

'What makes you say that?'

'*Hintuition*.'

'But you said you didn't see his face.'

'I didn't need to. I knew who it was.'

'Thank you, Bungs. Go about your business. However, I suggest you spend less time hiding behind the barrels.'

But the cooper hadn't done with the captain's attention yet. 'One more thing, Capt'n – about the boy who was sent down to help me. He can go too.'

The captain looked puzzled.

'Young Charlie Goodridge,' Bungs announced. 'Too clever for his own clogs, in my opinion.'

'What do you mean by that?'

The cooper shrugged. 'Little squeaker thinks he knows it all. How old is he? Ten or a dozen years yet talks like he's an old salt-pickled tar.'

'Is that a problem for you?'

The old man poked his index finger in his nose and scratched around inside. 'Not as such.'

'Is he impudent or impolite?'

'Not as I've noticed.'

'What then? Does he refuse to do what you ask or speak out of turn?'

'Ah! That's it. It's the speaking that's his problem. *Yap, yap, yap.* He thinks he knows something about everything and verses an opinion about all manner of things. Then, he tells you about it, whether you want to hear it or not. And he sticks his nose into all manner of stuff begging to know the whys and wherefores, how this works or why this doesn't work. I tell you, Captain, it drives me crazy just listening to him. I can't do with him harassing me when I'm trying to work.'

Oliver considered some of the boy's questionable attributes reflected those of Bungs himself. 'And where is the lad now?'

'Don't rightly know since I complained to Mr Tully and he dragged him off.'

The captain frowned. 'I have more important things to concern myself with than the behaviour of one of the ship's boys.

'Are you going to do anything about him, Capt'n?'

'I beg your pardon!'

'Not the boy,' Bungs said, 'him that was tapping.'

Despite the cooper's blatant impertinence, his continued bickering, his unkempt appearance and his pungent unwashed odour, Oliver had a liking for the old tradesman. He was a skilled craftsman, had been on and around navy ships for decades, had served with him aboard two frigates and, because his accident had occurred when he had been ordered to board a privateer's ship, Captain Quintrell felt partly responsible for his injury.

'For your information and for your ears only,' Oliver said, 'I have been ordered to transfer the cases of coins to HMS *Stalwart* – the 74-gun warship in the bay. When the time comes, I will need you to identify the barrels in question and show me exactly where they are. Will you be able to do that?'

'Course I will. I might sound a bit simple, but I can turn it on, if I want to.'

The captain refrained from allowing a grin to crease the corners of his lips. 'I suggest you don't mention that to the officer-of-the-watch but, for the moment, it will best suit the situation if you maintain your present guise. To say too much could put you in danger. I know only too well the lengths some sailors will go for a pipe of tobacco worth only a copper or two.'

It was obvious from the smug expression on the cooper's face he was enjoying the privilege of the captain's confidence, if only for a short while. 'Do you want me to remove them barrels ready to hoist 'em on deck?'

'Belay that,' Oliver asserted. 'For the moment, don't touch anything. I will inform you when the transfer is due to take place and how it will be done.'

'I'll need some help.'

'I realise that and I will seek some strong and trustworthy hands to assist you.'

The cooper was quick to respond. 'Ekundayo would be a good choice, begging your pardon, Capt'n, for suggesting.'

'Indeed, I agree. He's a messmate of yours, is he not?'

'Aye and William Ethridge. He helped hide them chests away in the first place.'

'Thank you,' the captain said.

The short conversation, while irregular, had proved opportune and answered some of the questions that had been confronting him. Oliver knew the transfer would not be easy and that the wooden walls of sailing ships had ears. But, until now, the treasure had been untouched. He had minded it according to the promise he had made to Captain Gore in Gibraltar and would not free himself from that responsibility until the cache of coins was delivered into the hands of the Admiralty in Portsmouth or London.

Turning towards the steps he lifted his foot to continue but the gravelly voice continued.

'Do you think that fellow who was tapping the barrels was trying to steal the silver?'

'If that were the case,' Oliver said, 'it would be an impossible task for one man to accomplish on his own. Therefore, I suggest you forget about him. Let us presume he was just investigating the rumour that we are carrying silver from a plate ship. I fear it is now an ill-kept secret.'

'Aye, Captain. You can trust me,' Bungs said.

'Then this conversation is at a close. Let me hear no more mention of coins or treasure or Spanish silver or Michael O'Connor or the Irish for that matter. Those are issues I will deal with myself. The sooner you go about your business the better. And, in future, I would prefer you request an appointment to speak with me in my cabin rather than accosting me in the companionway.'

'Aye aye, Capt'n, whatever you say.'

Chapter 4

The Wexford Lads

When the final grains of sand slid through its narrow neck, the hourglass was turned and the ship's bell struck. Striding silently along the grey deck in the pale light that preceded dawn, the sailor completed his rounds, extinguishing the ship's lanterns. The glim above the binnacle stand was the last to be snuffed.

In the east, the golden orb was emerging from the sea, casting its orange glow along the horizon and forcing the night back into the heavens. While, in the west, the rugged mountain peaks were slow to cast off their nocturnal hues. The waters of Guanabara Bay still slumbered, the vast inlet stretching its arms almost twenty miles in one direction and seventeen the other. When a breath of wind stroked its belly, the surface shivered and stirred before settling back again. Only when morning arrived would the broad expanse cast off its grey shroud and adopt the colour of the sky. Around its edges, the petticoat of white quartz beaches awaited the sun's rays to set them gleaming.

Oblivious to the day unfolding around them, a woebegotten mob crowded onto *Perpetual*'s forecastle and along the larboard gangway. Having emerged from the forward hatch, prompted by the ship's bell and the bosun's threats, they had shuffled towards the entry port where a pair of midshipmen was directing them over the side and into the first of the boats waiting to carry them up the bay.

The line of individuals no more resembled sailors than beggars brought in from London's backstreets by a desperate press gang struggling to fill its quota, or a stream of war-weary soldiers dragging themselves away from a European battlefield.

Not a single head bore a hat and few wore shoes, though some feet were bound in rags. Brown stained bandages wrapped around cracked crowns or weeping stumps that once bore healthy limbs. They followed after each other, one man's hand touching the back of the fellow in front of him and, when the line stopped, they rested their weary bodies against the ropes coiled to the pin rails. Some leaned on a mate's shoulder. A couple supported their weight on roughly hewn crutches.

Just a few, scattered amongst the group, appeared remarkably presentable showing barely a trace of dishevelment in themselves or their clothing. But for the majority, shirts were ripped or stained with old blood, pitch or powder. Some faces wore the indelible blue imprint of powder burns. Yet despite their pathetic condition, the murmur of conversations had a distinctly hopeful air about it. One sailor lifted his arm and pointed towards the houses on the nearby hillsides, while those next to him gazed bleary-eyed in that direction. Some thanked the Virgin when they turned to step down the ladder and traced the outline of the cross on their chests.

A haggard old salt, his face sculpted by deep dry wrinkles, was helped by two younger men. When he reached the rail and it was his turn to disembark, he looked to the quarterdeck and called out the word: *'Obrigado'*.

Captain Quintrell nodded in acknowledgement. He was pleased to see the seamen disembarking and relieved they had all arrived safely in a Portuguese port. For a few sailors, Rio de Janeiro was their home but for most it was a port where they would be welcomed, fed, clothed and offered the opportunity to return to duty on one of their country's ships bound for Lisbon.

Not all, however, were so lucky. By the starboard scuppers, three men lay on stretchers, each covered by a blanket. Four other men sat alongside – their legs encased in strips of wood tied with twine and old rope.

Jonathon Whipple moved between them, taking care not to step on anyone's hand or foot. He was satisfied he had done all he could for the men whilst they had been in his care and pleased he had not lost a single man. Now his patients would be placed into the hands of another surgeon.

Lifting his arm weakly from the stretcher, one of the wounded sailors grabbed the doctor's leg and clung to it. He couldn't speak English but the tears, glistening in his eyes, conveyed all he wanted to say.

From the side, Captain Quintrell watched the first boat as it was pushed off from the frigate's hull, the blades dripping as they dipped rhythmically into the salt water of the bay. Fully laden, the longboat sat low in the water and swam slowly. From the thwart facing the tiller, a young man, sitting between two of the rowers, rose to his feet and waved. He was promptly jerked back into his seat by the man sitting behind him but not before the captain had recognised the face. It belonged to a young sailor named José who he had encountered on the island where the tragic event had taken place. In response, the captain lifted his hat and silently wished him well.

In contrast to the orderly movement of the Portuguese seamen, where barely a word was spoken, the emergence of a handful of boisterous characters from the forward hatch created a noticeable disruption. In attempting to make the front of the queue and get down to the waiting boat, the newcomers pushed forward, elbows out, jabbing and jostling those waiting patiently in line. Several Portuguese sailors cried out, swore or levelled their fists at the intruders but it didn't deter them. Because of the disturbance plus the fact these new arrivals were dressed in Royal Navy slops and each carried a bundle either under his arm or slung across his back, the midshipman at the entry port was alerted to their ruse.

'You there! What's your hurry?' Mr Hanson called, pointing to the worst of the offenders. 'I know you,' he said. 'You're Murphy, aren't you?'

He got no reply.

'Stop right where you are and stand aside. No one is permitted to leave the ship without the captain's permission.'

The tall man sneered cockily. 'So what are these Portugee Jacks standing in line for? A ticket to Davey Jones' locker?' Taking no notice of the midshipman's order, he pushed past anyone blocking his way. When he reached the gunnel he quickly swung one leg over the side, planted his foot on the top step and started his descent to the waiting boat. His mate, following close behind him, cocked his leg over the side and had his foot suspended in the air, almost touching the top step, when the middie grabbed him by the collar and yanked him back.

'Belay that!' the young middie shouted.

'You'll not stop us,' the man cried. 'We were told we could leave when we reached Rio.'

'No one goes ashore,' Mr Hanson said, gripping hold of the shirt with both hands, while the sailor wriggled desperately to get out of it. 'Cast off, coxswain! Do it now!' the young man yelled as he clung on.

Aware of the tussle going on above his head, the coxswain released the painter to the water, swung the tiller hard across and ordered the men in the bow to push off. Two oars clapped down on *Perpetual*'s hull and the oarsmen heaved against it. The longboat's bow instantly swung out from the frigate's side leaving one Portuguese seaman hanging from the ladder with his feet dangling in the water.

'Mr Tully,' the captain called from the quarterdeck. 'Attend to that commotion! And give an eye to the number of men in each boat. I don't want to be pulling those men out of the ocean for a second time.'

'Aye aye, Capt'n.'

From vantage points in the frigate's rigging and from the ship's rails, *Perpetual*'s sailors hissed and booed in response to the ruckus. Not understanding what was happening, the Portuguese sailors, still standing in line, had no alternative but to remain where they were.

After dragging the man by his shirt collar back onto the deck, Mr Hanson ordered Murphy to climb back. With only water beneath him, the Irishman reluctantly clambered back and regained the deck. At the same time, three companions of the pair continued pushing forward to reach their mates.

'Go to the mess and stay there,' the midshipman yelled.

'The captain said we could go ashore!'

'You half-witted dawcocks,' Mr Tully bellowed from the ratlines, 'Are you blind as well as witless? Can't you see that boat ain't going to shore! It's headed for the ship over yonder. It'd serve you right if you were taken aboard and found yourself in irons on a slave ship.'

The pair at the entry port glanced across the bay and then looked at each other, while Mr Tully jumped down to the deck landing only a few feet from where they were standing. 'No one leaves,' Mr Tully repeated. 'Not without the captain's permission.'

Turning to face the officer, a flash of intense hatred fired in Murphy's eyes.

Mr Tully had seen it all before. 'You heard the middie. Now shift your stinking arses and be quick smart about it. If not, I'll see you clapped in irons in our hold and I'll toss the key out of the nearest bleeding gunport.'

While the wording of the order and its delivery were not quite befitting the gentlemanly manners expected of an officer in His Majesty's Navy, Ben Tully's forecastle oration had the desired effect. Observing from only a few yards away on the quarterdeck, Captain Quintrell was quite prepared to overlook the colourful language. Of more interest to him was the man who had raised his voice. He turned to Mr Parry who was standing beside him. 'That sailor who raised his voice is Murphy, is it not?'

'He's no sailor, sir,' Mr Parry reminded. 'He claims he's from Liverpool but his accent tells a different story.'

'Have those men removed from the deck immediately,' Oliver ordered.

'Aye aye, Captain.'

Once the troublemakers had been returned through the forward hatch from which they had appeared, the signal was given for the coxswain to return his boat. Running it up alongside, the crew quickly grabbed the feet of the sailor who had been left dangling and pulled him aboard.

'How many more will she take?' the middie called down from the entry port.

'Another dozen,' the coxswain answered.

With order and quiet returned to the deck, Mr Hanson counted the foreign sailors as they climbed down the ship's side and clambered into the longboat. When all the thwarts were filled, that boat was pushed off and the final craft slid alongside to receive the remaining passengers.

Mr Tully supervised the despatch of those invalids unable to walk. With block and tackle rigged to the yardarm, the infirm were placed in a canvas chair, while those on stretchers were swung out and lowered gently to rest of the thwarts. When the last sailor had been settled, word was given for the boat to proceed up the bay. Their destination was the Portuguese frigate Captain Quintrell had visited the previous day. Only when the deck had been vacated could *Perpetual*'s routine return to normal and the sailors of the starboard watch attend to their regular morning chores.

Satisfied to have completed another necessary task on his mental list, the captain turned to his first lieutenant. 'I have a letter for the Port Admiral and one final order for the victualling store. I need you to go ashore and attend to these matters for me. Kindly inform the clerk in charge of the store that my requirements are urgent. Tell him I would be grateful if he would attend to the order personally.'

'Do you intend to go into the town yourself?'

'Thank you, no,' Oliver replied.

Simon Parry was surprised and glanced about him. 'Many argue this is the most beautiful harbour in the world.'

'People say what they will. I form my own opinion and I have no desire to go ashore or to linger in this port any longer than necessary.'

The lieutenant was happy to oblige.

'One other matter,' Oliver added. 'The doctor needs to replenish his apothecary's chest and purchase some personal items for himself and for the women. Be so good as to transport him and kindly remain with him. I would not like anything untoward to happen to him. I recommend you take a handful of marines and a couple of strong hands with you.'

'Do you think that is necessary?'

'Would I have suggested it if I did not think so?'

'I will make arrangements with the doctor, immediately,' Simon said.

'One moment,' Oliver interrupted. 'Before you go, ask Mr Hanson to prepare a report about this morning's disturbance. I want names and details of the troublemakers. I fear there may be more to their misbehaviour that just mischief.'

An hour later, the captain was perusing a list the midshipman had presented to him. 'You have only five names listed here yet there were six men joined the ship in the Azores?'

Mr Hanson nodded. 'I didn't include Michael O'Connor as he was not involved in this morning's ruckus. He certainly came aboard with the others, but he claims he was thrown with them by chance.'

'Chance, coincidence or convenience?' That old vein of cynicism had crept back into the captain's tone.

'I questioned him and he assured me that prior to sailing from England, he knew nothing of the others and was merely travelling with them. Against his name in the book, it states he was a writer for the Honourable John Company in Dublin.'

'Hmm. He told me that also, but Dr Whipple tells me the East India Company has no such office in Dublin.'

The midshipman looked confused.

'Ignore O'Connor,' the captain said. 'I have no problem with him and he has expressed no desire to quit the ship. It is the other five that interest me.' Oliver turned his attention to the sheet of paper and read from it. 'Samuel and Matthew Leary. Brothers. Ginger hair. From Liverpool.'

Mr Hanson grinned. 'At five feet two inches tall and looking like a set of twins, they'd make a fine pair of bookends.'

The captain was in no mood for humour. 'Kindly stick to the facts, mister.' He continued reading. 'It states here that Matthew Leary has scars on his back.' He regarded the midshipman. 'Do we know the reason for his injuries? Were they the result of punishment?'

'When the doctor examined the man, he reported that the scars were consistent with wounds inflicted by a sharp instrument such as a knife, sword or pike.'

'Not the cat?'

'Not the cat, sir.'

'Joseph Murphy?' Oliver noted the name with interest.

'He's the most talkative and conniving and attracts all the attention. Measuring six feet, he's also the tallest in the group and, at thirty-five years old, he's the eldest. No tattoos or marks. He also claims to be from Liverpool.'

Hugh Doyle was next on the list. Five feet four inches tall. Brown hair. Grey eyes. No scars or marks. Approximately thirty years of age.

'McNamara – Andrew,' the captain read. 'He's the man who is assisting Bungs with the cooperage, if I am not mistaken.'

The midshipman nodded. 'Black hair. Bald crown. Age thirty-two. Bares a six-inch scar on his right forearm. Average height.' With that, the midshipman had exhausted his list of the men's physical attributes.

'Is that all?'

The midshipman appeared to have more.

'Speak out,' the captain prompted.

'Although all five claim they are from Liverpool, when I quizzed the doctor a few minutes ago he claimed the men spoke as though they had just stepped off the boat from Dublin.'

'Enough,' Oliver said, folding the list and placing it in his pocket. As he did so, he noticed the midshipman regarding the absence of three fingers on his own battle-mangled right hand. 'One thing we know for certain,' the captain added. 'These men did not receive their injuries serving at sea, nor did they acquire their scars toiling in the cotton mills in Lancashire or scratching up potatoes from the peat bogs of Ireland. I think it far more likely they fought in the Irish rebellion and fled to Liverpool for safety.'

'That's a long time ago, isn't it?' the midshipman reminded.

'Only seven years. 1798. The important question is: on which side did they fight?' His statement met with a blank expression from the young midshipman who, seven years ago would have been hiding behind his mother's skirt.

'Besides these lubbers, there are other hands who have requested to go ashore?' Mr Hanson said cautiously being aware of the captain's views.

Oliver remained adamant. 'Were I to allow men off the ship, word of the consignment we are carrying would spread round the bay quicker than St Elmo's fire jumps from one mast to another. Therefore, I suggest you inform those who have not already heard the news that we are no longer bound for the Southern Ocean and will be sailing from this port within days and heading home. That prospect might quieten a few disgruntled voices.'

'But the Portuguese sailors who left the ship, won't they talk about the treasure?'

'I doubt they are aware of it,' the captain replied. 'Few of them speak English and, since being plucked from the sea, they have kept their own company and seldom conversed with the regular crew.'

'But the Irishmen?' Mr Hanson persisted. 'They understand English. They will know about the silver.'

Oliver scowled. The question was impertinent but it prompted the captain to reach a decision.

'I do not trust those men. Arrange for all five to be removed from the ship before their unruly behaviour infects the rest of the crew. As to them collecting wages, I doubt the ship owes them anything. They came aboard with nothing; barely the clothes they were standing up in. If I am not wrong, the purser issued them with clothing from the slops chest and since we left Ponta Delgada, they have been well fed and provided for with a clean hammock. I very much doubt the pay due to these landsmen would satisfy their debt to His Majesty's Navy Board.' He sighed. 'The Board does not take kindly to men leaving the ship in a time of war but the decision is mine. Get them over the side as quickly as possible and let us pray they hold their tongues about what *Perpetual* is carrying long enough for us to depart this harbour.'

Having taken his usual turns back and forth on the quarterdeck, the captain stopped abruptly. His attention was captured by two local boats heading towards the third rate. With insufficient wind to carry them, they were being rowed and, as they were heavily laden with boxes and trays of multi-coloured local fruits and fresh vegetables, their progress was painstakingly slow.

A longboat, packed with marines, having just shoved off from the hull of the third rate, was heading directly towards them. The coxswain's view of the approaching boats was obstructed by two of the marines who insisted on standing up in the boat. When he was finally able to see the water ahead, the local boats were almost upon him. Despite swinging the rudder across to avoid a collision, he was too late and the boats' oars collided in mid-air with one of the local craft. While nothing was damaged or broken, curses rang out from the Brazilian traders while the marines found the accident highly amusing. As the boats parted company, the soldiers' shouts and jeers became louder. In Captain Quintrell's opinion, the company of marines were already drunk.

Gripping his seat till his knuckles were white, the ashen-faced young corporal perched in the bow was unable to exert any control over the men. The abuse screamed from the coxswain on the tiller also had no effect on the riotous behaviour. When one of the soldiers deliberately stood up and rocked the boat from one side to the other, dipping the gunnels perilously close to the water, peels of raucous laughter exploded. The pomegranate-colour of the marines' coats was not only reflected on the shimmering surface of the water but on the inebriated faces of the men.

Shaking his head in disgust, Oliver turned from the rail and was approached by Lieutenant Nightingale. 'I have five seamen waiting in the waist to go ashore. Do you wish to speak with them before they disembark?'

'I have nothing to say to them,' Oliver replied curtly. 'Put them over the side before anyone else asks to join them.'

'Should I offer them the opportunity to thank you for delivering them safely from the Western Isles?'

Oliver's eyes narrowed and he stared to the angry grey peaks in the distance.

'Mr Nightingale, when did you last hear of a common seaman seeking out the ship's captain, to thank him? Once a sailor's period of service is complete and he has received his pay, nothing will induce him to linger. The five Irishmen were lucky to be entered in the muster book and would not have been granted a berth were I not obliged to honour a debt. His Majesty's Navy owes them nothing and expects nothing from them. Get rid of them.'

The lieutenant acknowledged. 'I will attend to it right away.'

That evening, Mr Parry returned to *Perpetual* and provided the captain with a report of his activities in Rio de Janeiro. He had handed the letter to the office of the Port Admiral, spoken with the clerk at the victualling store and accompanied the doctor while he purchased his medical supplies and visited several shops in the town to buy items for his own needs and those requested by the two women.

With another item struck from his mental list, there was one matter Oliver wished to speak with his first lieutenant about. After sitting down together and relaxing in the great cabin, Oliver broached the subject of crew numbers.

'When we sailed from Portsmouth, a year ago, we had a compliment of around two hundred men. A conservative number for a frigate, would you not agree?'

'An adequate number,' Simon Parry asserted, defending his area of responsibility. 'And by the grace of God, we have lost but a handful of men since then – mainly as a result of sickness. But we gained some skilled shipwrights in Gibraltar plus a few others.'

'I trust you are not including the women and boy as additions to the crew?'

'Certainly not. But, in support of the present crew, I contend they are able-bodied and well-disciplined and, like all British salts, each one is the equal of three French sailors.'

'And today you parted with five men,' Oliver reminded.

'I do not regard those Irishmen as a loss. They were lubbers and not sailors. Certainly, if I had found seasoned sailors off merchant ships or Company vessels wandering the wharfs of Rio, I would willingly have accepted them, but I am reluctant to press men off the beach in this part of the globe. The dockside rabble, hereabouts, is made up of drunkards, beggars and vagrants, most of whom do not speak English. Perhaps there are some hands aboard the third rate that would care to serve on a frigate.'

'You will not seduce men away from *Stalwart*,' Oliver said. 'Captain Liversedge has already lost about thirty men since he arrived here and cannot afford to part with any more. He has barely enough to man a ship of that size.'

'Then I can assure you, Captain, we will manage with the numbers we have,' Mr Parry said confidently.

'I hope you are right,' Oliver replied. Though it irked him, there was little point in procrastinating over crew numbers at this time as it was too late to change the situation.

The lieutenant politely reminded his superior that in wartime, though many lives were lost and despite suffering severe damage in action, ships invariably managed to reach a home port with only a handful of men working them.

With nothing more to be said on the situation, Mr Parry was about to excuse himself.

'A moment. There is one other minor matter,' the captain said. 'Tell me more about the boy you mentioned – Charles Goodridge.'

Simon Parry raised his eyebrows. It was not the first time that day the name had been mentioned to him. 'Is there a problem?'

'From what I hear, he is leading some of the warrant officers a merry dance. The bosun has washed his hands of him, as has the cooper, and cook complains that he talks too much. I need to know what the problem is. Do the officers have no control over him? I remember he came aboard in Gibraltar with one of the women, but I gather he is not related to her.'

'Mrs Pilkington is no blood relative. She lost her husband and infant children when the malignant fever ravaged the colony. At the same time, the boy lost his parents and was taken in by the widow.'

Oliver winced. It was difficult to hide the personal loss he too had suffered as a result of the epidemic. 'So many succumbed to the sickness. So many loved ones taken,' he sighed. 'Let us hope, when we next touch on the Rock, Gibraltar is free of that terrible malignancy.'

Not wishing to rekindle memories of the time spent there, Mr Parry continued. 'When Mrs Pilkington took the boy into her care, I believe the need was mutual.'

For a moment the pair considered the conundrum. The boy was proving to be a major aggravation but, at times, a minor inspiration. An enigma. 'To which parts of the ship has the boy been sent?'

'When he came aboard, he should have been entered as a powder monkey and sent to join the other ship's boys in the magazine. However, from what I observed, he was too quick witted and inquisitive for that role and he would have gained nothing from being there.'

'Probably a wise decision,' Oliver said.

'I was told that from the time he spent in and around the naval dockyard observing his father and the other wrights, he learned quickly and came to know every inch of a fighting ship from mast head to keelson and counter to transom. Despite his tender age, he possibly understands the structure of a ship better than many young midshipmen serving in today's navy.'

'I understand he is only ten years of age.'

Mr Parry nodded. 'Is it not a fact, the names of sons from titled families are often entered on a ship's books at an even younger age?'

'Indeed, in order to register years of service yet those young gentlemen never actually step on the deck of a ship until several years later. It is a covert means of advancing a young man's naval career,' Oliver said cynically. Patronage and privilege were subjects that reignited the deep-seated grievances he had long held.

'For the present, I have more to concern myself with than the comings and goings of a ship's boy. What surprises me, however, is how one minor individual manages to have midshipmen, warrant officers and some senior officers running around in circles not knowing what to do with him? Surely it cannot be such a difficult task allocating him to some station. If he lacks discipline, a serve over the gun might teach him not to disobey orders?'

'But he doesn't disobey orders,' Simon said defensively, 'in fact, it is to the contrary. The problem with young Goodridge is his overabundance of enthusiasm and exuberance.'

Oliver recalled the boy's antics in the rigging he had witnessed earlier. 'If he is capable of carrying boiling pitch without splashing it across the deck, send him to work with the team of caulkers on the gun deck. Let them employ him as an oakum boy. Surely he cannot get too enthusiastic about that job.'

Mr Parry was non-committal.

The captain continued. 'If he has spent time with his father in the shipyard, he should be familiar with that occupation. There is also the manger. I am told there are pigs to be fattened,' he said cynically. 'Alternatively, my steward can make use of him.'

'I will attend to it personally.'

Oliver thought for a moment. 'Don't waste valuable time on the boy. I am considering sending him and the women over to the 74. That will solve the problem.'

Chapter 5

Charles Goodridge

Captain Quintrell jumped up from his desk and burst out of his cabin.

'Casson! In Heaven's name, what is all the shouting about?'

The answer came from a whippersnapper not much more than half the captain's height. 'It's me, Captain. Charlie Goodridge. You said I was to give Mr Casson a hand. Well, I was trying to show him a better way to stack the preserves in the pantry but he wouldn't hear me out.'

'Casson, where are you?' Oliver called.

'I'm here, Captain,' the steward replied, rising from his knees from within the open pantry and knocking his head in the process.

'I do not know what is going on here,' Oliver exclaimed, 'but for goodness sake there is no need for either of you to raise your voices.'

Before the captain's servant had time to open his mouth, the boy jumped in again. 'I was just telling Mr Casson that if he did it like I said, it would save him time and he wouldn't have to crawl on the floor to find things and he would know exactly where everything was.'

'Young man,' the captain said, 'you will speak when you are spoken to or, within a very short time, you will find yourself scraping rust from a basket full of round shot in the magazine. I am sure Mr Casson is quite aware of the position of all the items in the panty as he put them there in the first place. Mr Casson has been acting as my steward for many years and I have no reason to question the way he conducts his duties.'

'But my way would save time.'

'Silence!' Oliver cried.

The boy's mouth snapped closed and remained tight shut. Casson glared at him, while returning all the jars, bottles and containers to the shelves, deliberately banging each one down as he thrust it back into place. Fortunately nothing broke.

'You,' Oliver said, addressing the boy. 'Come with me.'

Young Goodridge did as he was bid and followed the captain into his cabin. When he reached the door he hung back until he was instructed to enter and stand upright with his hands at his sides.

'So,' Oliver pondered. 'What is going to become of you?'

'Beg pardon,' the boy mumbled.

Oliver seated himself at the table and examined the boy whose name was bouncing off the ship's bulwarks like an echo. 'You appear to be observant. Do you know what that means?'

'Yes, sir, of course I do. I keep my eyes and ears wide open and that way I don't miss anything. That's what my father taught me.'

'I imagine your father was a good worker.'

'Yes, sir. He was a shipwright in Gibraltar. He'd learned his trade at the Deptford yard.'

'Is it your wish to be a wright like your father?'

'No, sir,' he said defiantly.

Oliver raised his eyebrows. 'You surprise me. From what I hear, you appear to be preoccupied with fighting ships. What will you be then?'

'I want to be an officer like you, sir.'

Oliver laughed. 'Indeed. And how do you hope to achieve that? Certainly not by upsetting everyone around you as you are doing at the present.'

Dejected, the boy looked down and, for once, seemed lost for words.

'I'm listening,' Oliver said.

'I don't rightly know, sir. My father said I had a brain between my ears and that was the reason he sent me to the school in the colony. He said if I learnt well, I might make something of myself one day.'

'Can you read?' Oliver asked.

'Yes, of course,' Charles said. 'In Gibraltar most folk spoke English and Spanish. The boys at school spoke both but not all could read and write both.'

'Do you speak Spanish fluently?'

'Yes, sir,' he said proudly. 'My grandparents lived in Alicante. My mother was born Spain but lived most of her life in the colony. I speak Spanish like a local.'

'Do you have any other languages?'

'I can understand a bit of French but cannot write it.'

'What else did you learn?'

'History, arithmetic, geometry, grammar.'

'Your father worked in the dockyard. Did he enjoy his work?'

'Aye, he loved working with timber and I heard tell he was good at his job.'

'I hear you spent your spare time in the yard when permitted.'

'Aye, sir, I helped around the yard when I could – fetching and carrying, swinging off the end of a saw or bagging the shavings. I've been climbing around warships for as long as I can remember. My father used to say I was like a rat sniffing out every nook and cranny. I near drove him and his mates crazy forever asking questions, wanting to know what everything was for, where it belonged and how it was made. I learned a lot.'

'Enough,' the captain called. 'On my ship, you must first learn to curb your tongue or it will hang you one of these days.'

The boy was puzzled.

'Tell me, do you consider yourself a troublemaker?'

'Me, sir? No, sir. Definitely not, sir.'

'That is not what I am hearing from my officers. I have had reports from the bosun, the cooper and the ship's master that you are an annoyance and, now, I can add my steward's name to the list.'

A pair of large dark eyes looked up at the captain reminding him of a starving hound desperate for a lump of suet. 'After considerable thought, I have decided what to do with you. You will not remain on board *Perpetual*.'

'But Captain?' the lad pleaded.

'Listen to me, young man, for I will only say this once. I have decided to send you over to the 74 where, because of your age, you would be normally be entered as a ship's boy. However, I must speak with Captain Liversedge first and ask what likelihood there is of your name being entered as servant to one of the midshipmen. If that is possible, you will perform whatever duties are demanded of you.'

Like a fish out of water, the boy's mouth opened wide then abruptly closed again.

'You will learn how to wash stockings, iron handkerchiefs, sew buttons on shirts, polish shoe buckles and press uniforms. These are all useful skills. Every morning, you will collect the midshipmen's hammocks and take them on deck for airing. You will fetch and carry as required, deliver the young gentlemen their meals and clean up after them.'

Charles's young brow furrowed.

'Don't worry, you will not be alone. There will be other boys to learn from. But remember, life aboard one of His Majesty's vessels is not all fun and games, and you will not run willy-nilly about the ship as though it is your private nursery. If you disobey an order more than once you will find yourself kissing the gunner's daughter. I trust you know what that means?'

Charles Goodridge nodded.

'An early introduction, such as this, will give you an insight into what it is like serving in the Royal Navy. You will quickly discover that life in service is far removed from the unfettered freedom of scampering up ratlines and sliding down backstays on a fighting ship in dry dock. It is quite possible that by the time we reach England you will have had your fill of waiting on young gentlemen and will be content to act as an oakum boy aboard *Perpetual*. What say you?'

'How do I become an officer?' Charles replied.

Taken aback, Oliver shook his head. The boy was certainly persistent. 'With much hard work and perseverance. Plus,' he paused, 'and herein lies a problem – ideally you require a parent or sponsor who can afford to outfit you with, not one set of clothes but, six or eight, along with a sea chest to store them in. And funds to furnish you with a personal store of private provisions sufficient to last for a year at sea, and also to provide you with a pocketful of spending money. Then, of course, you will require books, writing materials and nautical instruments. In most cases, it is highly desirable that you procure an introduction to an influential captain or admiral who, if not a relative, will take a liking to you and offer you a berth on his ship.'

The boy expression was glum. 'My ma and pa are dead. Connie is my only friend and she doesn't have any money.'

'I understand that is the reason you are here.'

The lad nodded. 'Will Connie go with me to the 74?' he asked.

'I presume you are referring to Mrs Pilkington,' Oliver said, without answering the boy's question. 'How old are you?'

'Almost eleven.'

'Then if you truly wish to become an officer one day, now is the time to become independent and start behaving like a man.'

Charles Goodridge blinked and as quickly as his mood had sunk, it surfaced as his thoughts leapt ahead. 'If the two ships are sailing together to England, perhaps I can visit Mrs P when we are in port.'

'It is unlikely we will touch land until we make Portsmouth,' Captain Quintrell said. 'But, if we do, there will be no time for indulgences.'

The boy screwed his nose.

'No time for social visits,' Oliver explained. 'Do you understand? However, there is no reason to prevent you from writing to her. I will even have my clerk supply you with a pen, paper and ink, and when you have written your letter ask the purser or midshipman to have it conveyed to her.'

The boy thanked the captain.

'In the meantime, try not to annoy people with your excessive eagerness. Keep your nose clean and be ready to leave the frigate when the call comes. In the meantime, do not broadcast the details of our conversation. Do I make myself clear?'

'Yes, sir.'

Oliver looked the lad up and down. 'Do you have dunnage? A change of clothing? Shoes?'

'Some things but not much.'

'Then I suggest if and when you go aboard the 74, you present yourself in clean and neat attire. Do I make myself clear?'

'Yes, sir,' the boy said again, raising his right hand and knuckling his forehead in the manner of a seasoned foremast Jack.

'You may go,' the captain said and watched the boy trot out. Only then did he allow his lips to give way to the grin he had been withholding.

With a fresh breeze punching out its sails, the cutter completed the crossing between the two British ships in less than ten minutes. Though Oliver had many things to attend to on *Perpetual*, once on the water, albeit for a short time, he appreciated the wind on his face and the smell of brine. With the easy movement of the frigate's largest boat on the bay, he looked forward to heading to sea.

After being piped aboard the third rate, and exchanging a brief greeting with Lieutenant Hazzlewood, Captain Quintrell was welcomed by William Liversedge and invited to join him in the great cabin. Though it was only a few days since he had sat at the captain's table and opened his orders, the thoughts that flashed through Oliver's mind were quite different to those he had experienced on his previous visit.

First he reflected that this expansive area was often occupied by an Admiral. No doubt in this very location, over the past two decades, senior officers had met, not only to eat and converse but to study the charts, to consider battle strategies and make important tactical decisions.

Then, for an instant, when casting his eyes across the full breadth of the warship's stern, Oliver Quintrell considered how vulnerable this area was. Should an enemy sail under the ship's stern and fire a full broadside at the cabin, iron shot would cannon straight through, pulverising anything or anyone in its path, smashing through bulwarks and delivering death and devastation to the deck beyond.

Shaking the thoughts from his head, he returned to the usually pleasantries: the weather, the local conditions on Guanabara Bay, the provisioning of the ships and the deficiency in crew numbers. Oliver then took the opportunity to request an indulgence of his friend.

'I realise you are shorthanded, William, and I know it is able seamen you require – not dead wood. However, I wish to beg a favour.'

'I owe you for more than one favour considering what you have done for me in the past.'

'You know me, William, I prefer to leave the past in the past. Let us concentrate on the present.'

The conversation was interrupted momentarily by the distant sound of eight bells ringing out from the 74's belfry, then a series of peeps from the bosun's whistle and a rumble of feet thumping along the companionways in response. Despite the ship being at anchor, the watches were maintained and there were still many chores to be attended to on a line-of-battle ship.

'How can I be of help?' Captain Liversedge asked.

'Two matters,' Oliver Quintrell said. 'Against my better judgement, I allowed two females and a boy to embark the frigate in Gibraltar.'

'Are these individuals of any particular significance or standing – the wives of dignitaries or high ranking naval officers, for example?'

'Indeed, they are not. The younger of the females is the widow of a shipwright. The boy is an orphan and, though unrelated to her, has attached himself to her apron strings. The other woman is the wife of my carpenter.'

'Would it not be more appropriate for the carpenter's wife to remain with her husband?'

'Perhaps. However,' he paused, 'I have no other females aboard and, more importantly, I have no suitable accommodation to house the pair. Presently their hammocks are slung in the carpenter's workshop, which is totally unsuitable. What I ask is for them to be accommodated aboard *Stalwart* for the voyage to England. I can assure you they are both well-mannered and will cause no problems, and will perform whatever tasks are asked of them without objection or complaint. Let me add, when we were under attack from a privateer in the Atlantic, both women performed duties that surprised even me. If you can assist me in this matter, I will be most grateful.' Oliver looked to his friend and continued. 'Do you have women aboard?'

'Three of my senior warrant officers are accompanied by their wives. These females also pose no problems and the crew are respectful of them. And the boy you mentioned?' Captain Liversedge asked.

'A rather bright young lad of ten or eleven years of age. He is surprisingly knowledgeable regarding the workings and construction of a ship having grown up on the dockyard in Gibraltar. He has aspirations to be an officer in Royal Navy one day.'

Captain Liversedge grinned. 'A lofty ambition.'

Oliver's expression was unchanged. 'I believe he has the potential to follow his desires but not the wherewithal or background or connections.'

'You would sponsor him yourself?' Captain Liversedge queried.

'You read me well, William. However, you are probably aware of my views on patronage and privilege in the Royal Navy. I have spoken out against that very subject on several occasions. My opinions have not changed, although I appear to be mellowing as the years progress. The fact is, I have no heir and it would give me satisfaction to watch a young man climb the ladder in the service, if he proved himself capable of it.'

'So what are you asking of me? I think you would not want this young man to serve in the magazine as a powder monkey with the other ship's boys.'

Oliver was quick to respond. 'He lacks title, wealth and influence and would, therefore, have little chance of entering the service other than through the hawse hole. However, he is intelligent and possesses an ample degree of precocious confidence – a little too much at times – plus a remarkably intimate knowledge of the timber components of a ship and their workings. Presently these qualities are being wasted and, for the sake of his dead father, I would not like to see them extinguished. In my opinion, a spell as servant to one of your middies or young lieutenants would provide him with an insight into life aboard a ship of the line. That will give the lad quite a different picture of a fighting ship when compared to the bare decks and silent bulwarks of a ship in the dockyard.'

William Liversedge did not think twice about the request. 'Convey them across. I will speak with my first lieutenant and make the necessary arrangement to find berths for all three.'

'Thank you, William – and if there is anything I can do in return.'

'You can assist me to get *Stalwart* safely home. Our course takes us via Kingston, Jamaica before heading out across the Atlantic.

Oliver was surprised. 'That is quite a detour and into hostile waters.'

'I am aware of that and wish it were not necessary. However, I have my orders.'

Oliver regarded his fellow captain quizzically.

'I have a *passenger* to deliver to the authorities there.'

'*Passenger*?' Oliver repeated, raising his eyebrows.

'I do not refer to him by name but as my *supercargo*. He is a political prisoner being exiled from Britain to the colonies.'

'Is he dangerous?' Oliver asked.

'Although he is under guard, he is no threat,' William Liversedge explained. 'I spoke with him several times on the voyage from England and enjoyed our conversations. He is Irish,' he paused. 'A literary man, a poet and a scholar. A man of peace. He is a gentleman who loves his country and deplores what has happened to Ireland and its people. But he is not a revolutionary or even a fighter.'

'Then why is he being exiled from Britain?'

'Because he was associated with members of the United Irish Party and because he had connections with judges and lawyers who were executed for their part in the rebellion. As a result, he spent five years in Ulster Jail.'

'On what charge?'

Captain Liversedge shook his head. 'Like several of the leaders, he was held on suspicion of conspiracy but was never charged. Eventually the court decided to wipe their hands of him and exile him. America was the usual dumping ground for such men but that country is now loath to take any more of our troublemakers.'

'Five years is a long time to be held with no charge,' Oliver noted. 'Does he bear a grudge? Is he bitter?'

'Not at all. He is a philosopher. A thinker. Though he believes in Ireland's independence from Britain, he swears that despite his poetry and prose inspiring many songs and stories, he had no hand in inciting any of the unrest. However, he firmly contends that the dream of an independent Ireland will always remain. That desire, he says, is a flame that will never be snuffed out no matter how many battles have to be fought and how many lives forfeited. Rest assured,' William said, 'he is of no danger to the Crown or to my command.'

'Do you believe what he says?'

'I believe his conviction, although I believe that dream will always remain a dream because the British will never bend.'

'So,' Oliver said, after glancing to the clock on the mantelshelf over the fireplace. 'When your *supercargo* is delivered to Port Royal, your duty in the Caribbean is discharged?'

'Indeed. I have no intention of staying in Jamaica any longer than necessary.'

'Is there anything else I should be aware of?'

Captain Liversedge thought for a moment. 'Nothing. Needless to say, I am eager to sail from here as soon as possible. All that remains to attend to is the transfer of the special consignment you have for me.'

With his cabin windows open to catch the cat's-paws of fleeting breeze, the cry, announcing a boat approaching, drifted across the water. Glancing out, the captain's view was of the new government buildings and warehouses skirting the shoreline with the mountains rising up immediately behind them. With no boat in view, it was obvious the call was coming from the direction of the 74 on the bay. Lifting his coat from the hook, Oliver dressed and waited.

A few minutes later, the jubilant voice of his steward, outside the cabin door, informed him in advance of the identity of his visitor.

'Well if it ain't Mr H,' Casson said. 'Ain't you just a sight for sore eyes? Just wait till Captain Quintrell sees you. He'll be pleased as Punch.'

After politely thanking the steward for his greeting, *Stalwart*'s lieutenant was shown into the great cabin albeit a little overawed by the greeting.

'Thank you, Casson,' the captain said. 'I think a glass of wine would be appropriate, if my visitor will be good enough to share one with me.'

Appearing somewhat embarrassed, Lieutenant Hazzlewood agreed.

'I can only echo the sentiments of my steward,' Oliver said, 'and I welcome you aboard *Perpetual*. Congratulations on your step up to lieutenant. Fourth lieutenant on a third rate, no less. I applaud you.'

'Indeed. Thanks to you, Captain.'

'No thanks are due to me. You served long and honourably as a midshipman, you passed your examination, after much hard study, and no one is more deserving of the position you now hold. Please sit and let us share a glass together.'

The officer did as invited and relaxed, the nervousness he had felt earlier slowly disappearing. 'As you can guess, I am here on behalf of Captain Liversedge. He sent his apologies for not coming in person. He is presently making preparations to leave Rio and is anxious to sail as soon as you are resupplied.'

'I am aware of his impatience,' Oliver said. 'I, too, am anxious to leave this bay. Kindly inform Captain Liversedge that I received word less than an hour ago that the last of the stores are now aboard and are being secured at this very moment. As such, providing the captain is in agreement, I will deliver the special consignment I discussed with him, this evening. Once that is done, *Perpetual* will be ready to sail on the morning tide.'

The lieutenant was sure that his captain would welcome the news.

'Good,' Oliver said. 'I am glad that is settled. Now, tell me, have you been keeping well?'

'Yes, sir, thank you, sir.'

On that note, the captain proposed a toast to the success of the man who had held the dubious honour of being the oldest midshipman to have ever served under him. 'Sixteen years, was it not?'

Lieutenant Hazzlewood nodded, blushing slightly and laughing nervously.

'And what of that young titled gentleman you served alongside. Algernon Biggleswade Smythe. Went by the name of Mr Smith while aboard *Elusive*.' Oliver smiled. 'I remember the day I despatched the pair of you to sail to Kingston in command of a prize vessel. Despite its condition, the agent paid a reasonable price for it, as you will be aware.'

'It was quite a challenge at the time but proved very worthwhile.'

Oliver leaned back. 'If you will forgive me for saying, you were the most unusual pair of shipmates I have ever encountered. You, with your northern accent and humble ways and Mr Smith with his drawing room etiquette, gentlemanly manners and eloquent speech.'

The lieutenant shuffled in his chair.

'Permit me to compliment you on how smart you look now. I remember the day you first presented on the deck of *Elusive* in an ill-fitting second-hand uniform standing alongside young Mr Smith. I heard he had a chest full of new clothes, enough to fill the racks of the best naval outfitters in Saville Row. I distinctly remember his uniform always smelled strongly of lavender. Tell me, how is Mr Smith?'

'Algernon – Algy, as I know him, is well and asked me to pass on his regards should I speak with you. He's not yet been appointed to lieutenant because of his age, but it'll not be long now. We still remain close shipmates.'

'That is well,' Oliver said. 'Perhaps one day we will all sail together again.'

'I would like that, sir.'

'But tell me, Mr H, Captain Liversedge informed me he is heading into the Caribbean and must touch on Kingston before we can head across the Atlantic. What do you know about the special passenger he is conveying?'

'The gentleman was put aboard in Portsmouth under close military guard. I understand he is being exiled from

Britain. I know little more about him than the fact he is locked up at night but during the day is at liberty to exercise on the quarterdeck with strict instructions not to speak to the officers or crew. It seems a bit odd to me. Mr Smith agrees.'

'Thank you, Mr H. As the stop in Kingston will be brief, it may not be necessary for me to drop anchor there. That is well. My concern is that our route into the Caribbean fetches us close to some of the French and Spanish islands.'

'Captain Liversedge has also expressed that concern.'

'Then we must all be extra vigilant.

The lieutenant agreed, and after draining his glass rather hastily, replaced it on the silver tray. 'I was instructed to make this a brief visit,' he said apologetically. 'Algy – Mr Smith is ashore with the third lieutenant. We posted broadsheets around the town a week ago in an attempt to attract some experienced hands. The captain is hoping we will be able to fill a couple of boats with men from the docks before we sail tomorrow.'

'Good luck. It is not an enviable task.'

'Thank you. As to the transfer of goods you spoke of, I will be on deck at dusk to assist in receiving them.'

Oliver Quintrell shook hands with the officer and wished him well. 'Perhaps at a suitable time during the cruise, a dinner could be arranged aboard *Perpetual*. That would provide me with the opportunity to meet with you and Mr Smith again, and allow us time to reminisce.'

'I would like that and I know Algy would too.'

Chapter 6

The Barrels

Having passed word to the 74 that *Perpetual* would be ready to sail the following morning, there was a general hubbub of activity aboard the frigate. On deck, all loose items were securely lashed down after the final supplies had been stowed below and the hatch covers fastened. In accordance with Captain Quintrell's Admiralty orders, only one item needed to be attended to – that was to convey the barrels to the 74

'We will make the transfer to *Stalwart* this evening,' Oliver advised his first lieutenant.

'A responsibility off your hands,' Simon Parry commented.

'Perhaps.' Oliver was not entirely convinced. 'Until those chests are delivered onto English soil, I regard their care as my responsibility. They were entrusted to me by Captain Gore and I promised I would safeguard them.'

'But, you must surely concede, a 74-gun man-o'-war, being a larger ship with twice *Perpetual*'s metal and more than twice our men, offers greater security. A ship of the line is well equipped to withstand an attack should that happen?'

Oliver agreed and the pair stood in silence for a moment, their gaze fixed on the third rate warship across the water.

'Is Captain Liversedge familiar with the contents of these barrels?' Mr Parry asked.

'Until we met, a few days ago, and I mentioned *coins* and *Spanish silver* to him, he was totally unaware of the chests and certainly not cognisant of what they contained. However, I fear by the time the barrels have been transferred across the water and loaded into the third rate's hold, every man aboard will know as much as the captain. News penetrates the wooden walls of sailing ships as insidiously as shipworm and the dire effect is equally as devastating.' He turned back to his lieutenant. 'Do you trust this crew?'

Simon nodded. 'The majority of the hands are honest seamen but there are some whose colours can change in an instant if temptation is thrown their way.'

Oliver Quintrell valued his lieutenant's opinion. For the present, however, his mind was awash with conflicting thoughts. Could he trust his own men? Had word of the treasure already leaked from the ship? Is it possible an attempt to steal the chests would be made while they were anchored in the bay?

While his new orders had been written months earlier in Whitehall, the brief instruction, scribbled quickly on the page, seemed to reflect the inconsequential regard given to this matter in London. Yet for Captain Quintrell, his men and the captain and crew of the 74, the ramifications of carrying such a precious cargo ran as deep as the ocean that separated them. Even the question of Britain's legal rights to the treasure was something Oliver had spent hours mulling over while at sea. Yet he had accepted the responsibility and given his word. He intended to keep his promise.

'At what hour do you wish to ship the items across? It was dark and most of the crew were at supper when we received the chests in Gibraltar Bay.'

Gazing out across the bay, the captain answered cautiously. 'The conditions here are somewhat better than those in Gibraltar. If nothing changes, I suggest the delivery takes place at six o'clock with the start of the last dog watch when the men from the first dog watch will go below to eat.'

'It will be done.'

'I need not remind you that extreme care must be taken. The loss of one of the barrels would spell disaster.' Oliver continued, his mind still racing. 'Aside from having men operating the tackles, put away two boats to ship the containers across to *Stalwart*. Each boat is to carry only a single barrel and to make the journey twice. Utilize my boat and crew for one of them. I have already arranged for four seamen to assist in the hold.'

'What duties are they to undertake?' Mr Parry asked.

'They will work under the direction of the cooper.'

'Bungs?'

'Indeed. Having placed the chests into the barrels in Gibraltar, Bungs knows exactly where they are. Without him it would be nigh impossible to identify the particular ones without breaking them apart.'

'Can the cooper be relied on – considering his recent injury?' Simon asked.

'I have spoken with him and with the doctor and am satisfied he is up to the task. He has indicated the location of the specific barrels to me, though, I admit, with the vast number in the hold, I could not return and identify them with confidence.'

Simon Parry was still concerned. 'As you said, news of the treasure and its transfer to the third rate will travel round the ship faster than a rat along the rail. No threats or bribes will quell the tittle-tattle once tongues start flapping. However, the sooner it is attended to the better. I will attend to it personally.'

'Thank you. And I will speak with Mr Crosby and William Ethridge who will be assisting below decks. They are both trustworthy and reliable. Bungs also requested Ekundayo the Negro. He is both strong and honest. And Mr Tully has volunteered to lend a hand.'

'Can we trust them all to keep their mouths shut?' the lieutenant asked.

'I have faith in them,' the captain said. 'Let it be. Thus far, we have been particularly lucky that no attempt has been made on the coins. Once we sail from this bay with the barrels safely conveyed across and stowed, it matters little who knows their location as they cannot easily be removed. The only problem I foresee is if Captain Liversedge comes under enemy fire and his ship is searched.'

'What if he is sunk?' Simon asked.

'I will not allow that to happen,' Oliver retorted. '*Perpetual* will be sailing alongside the third rate for the entire cruise and will remain within pistol shot of her in Kingston Harbour. Besides that, Captain Liversedge has a company of marines aboard who, in his words, "are scratching their crotches bare for lack of something to occupy their time". Let us hope we do not have to call on them but, if the need arises, I am sure they will guard the barrels with their lives.'

'Sailing into the Caribbean will place us in the path of both Spanish and French ships.'

'I do not need to be reminded of that,' Oliver replied.

The newly risen moon cast little light across the steely water but the sailors preferred to adjust their eyes to the darkness than be distracted by the glimmer of flickering lanterns. The waist, however, was illuminated, and lanterns mounted in the bows of the two ship's boats. Manned by his own crew, the captain's boat was the first to be lowered to the bay and secured alongside ready to receive one of the containers. The longboat followed and waited its turn, floating a few yards behind.

Despite the feeling of excitement simmering on deck, it was tempered by the presence of the bosun's mate gripping a newly spliced starter in his left hand. Few words were exchanged.

The first barrel hoisted from the waist was enclosed in a web of cargo netting. It presented as any regular barrel containing pork or beef or water. No notches or stencil marks had been scratched or painted on it to indicate it held anything unusual. The only difference was that it weighed considerably heavier than most.

'Careful, men,' the midshipman called.

The ropes squealed through the blocks as the yardarm was braced round and the consignment was swung out over the water and lowered gently onto the thwarts of the waiting boat. As it settled, the waters of Guanabara Bay rose noticeably up the side of the boat's hull. In order to prevent the barrel from rocking, crushing the gunnels and rolling into the water, chocks were inserted under the curved staves and a rope fastened firmly over it. With the boat's crew limited to six oars it was a hard pull but the distance was less than a cable's length.

Oliver scowled at the burst of excitement and the cheer that went up on the deck of the third rate when the first boat touched alongside. To anyone observing, it was an obvious announcement that something out of the ordinary was taking place. Although the noise was quickly quelled by the officer on the deck of the 74, whispers spread that the barrels contained something other than victuals or water.

The second boat followed closely behind, while the captain's boat returned to receive the third item in the consignment.

When the final barrel was lowered to the boat from the frigate and lashed into position, the coxswain hauled the dripping line aboard and pushed off from the hull. Observing from *Perpetual*'s deck, the officers breathed a sigh of relief, but there was no excitement or euphoria evident in the faces of the boat's crew. They were hungry and weary and wanted to complete the task so they could return to the mess for a belated supper.

Hailing the 74, the coxswain coiled the rope in his hand and tossed it to the waiting seaman. Both bow and stern lines were quickly secured. Above the heads of the boat's crew, the yard arm was swung around with the line from the tackle swinging like a pendulum. Grabbing the iron hook, the web of netting was attached and the order sung out for the load to be hoisted. 'Haul away.'

All was going well, with the barrel lifted several feet from the thwarts, when a loud splintering creak was followed by a sharp crack.

'She's going!' a voice bellowed. 'Get the boat clear.'

The crew, knowing there was no time for that, threw themselves into the water to save themselves from being crushed.

Another loud crack and the weight of the load tore the tackle from the end of the yard arm sending barrel, lines and netting crashing through four of the boat's timbers. As it plunged, the sailors on deck were showered in a torrent of spray while the remaining sailors and oars catapulted into the water.

'Grab the netting!' a voice boomed from the deck. 'Get a hold before it sinks!'

Sailors scuttled down the ship's side like crabs. Others jumped into the water. For a moment the barrel, in its loose hempen wrapping, was visible on the surface and many hands grabbed for the ropes. But within seconds it went down with the lines trailing behind it. One eager salt held on but he, too, was dragged under. Those watching held their breath and witnessed only bubbles returning to the surface. The officers observed anxiously from the 74's caprail. When the sailor broke the surface, coughing and gasping for breath, he received a cheer from his mates.

'Silence,' Lieutenant Hazzlewood shouted.

'Who can swim?' another voice sang out. 'I need divers and attach a line.' The calls from the 74's deck to the men in the water floated across the bay.

'It's too deep,' one of the sailors cried. 'This harbour's got no bottom.'

'You there,' *Stalwart*'s lieutenant yelled across the deck. 'Cast the lead. On the last toss we had little more than three fathoms with a sandy bottom. With the low of the tide and no current, that barrel is going nowhere. I want a rope attached and this load hauled up right away. Look smart about it.'

From *Perpetual*'s quarterdeck, Oliver Quintrell watched the proceedings but showed little emotion. On the gangway, the cooper, the carpenter, Will Ethridge and Ekundayo exchanged glances but also remained quiet.

'No doubt you are pleased to see the back of them,' the sailing master, having just arrived on the quarterdeck, commented to Captain Quintrell.

'Pleased?' Oliver replied. 'At times I think it would be appropriate if the whole consignment was committed to the deep.'

'Surely not?'

'Consider,' the captain said, 'the amount of suffering associated with that loot. Consider how many slaves suffered unimaginable hardship to produce those Spanish coins. Taken from Africa, transported round the Horn to Peru then marched hundreds of miles to the silver mines of Potosi. Consider the men lowered into the bowels of the earth, never to see the light of day again. Consider those on the treadmills who replaced mules, because two-legged animals were cheaper to procure than four. Consider the slaves who turned the presses minting coins destined to fill the Spanish treasure ships. I wonder how pleased those poor departed souls would feel right now.'

Oliver looked directly at his sailing master. 'You ask if I am pleased. No, mister. I am not. All I know is that I have worried about my responsibility for long enough and am resolved to worry no longer. I have done what had to be done and now wash my hands of the matter. If Captain Liversedge wishes to lose sleep over this consignment, then that is his choice.' Turning his back on his officers and on the bay where voices were still being raised, and men and oars were splashing about in the water, he gazed instead to the outline of black mountains against the night sky.

'It seems ironical to me,' Simon Parry said. 'Perhaps that accident was meant to be. Perhaps the silver was destined to remain in South America.'

But any further discussion on the fate of the treasure was interrupted by a jubilant cry and huzzas reverberating from *Stalwart's* deck. The barrel, still wrapped in hempen netting, had been secured. Once it was hooked to a newly rigged tackle on the spar above, a dozen men grabbed the line and began hauling.

In the meantime, *Perpetual*'s damaged boat was grabbed by the sailors in the captain's boat before that too sank to the bottom. Bailed of water and with its broken oars retrieved, it was dragged over to the frigate with four of the boat's crew holding onto the gunnels. The other men were left to swim back where lines were lowered to help them climb aboard.

After their dunking, the two boat crews climbed aboard, relieved the chore was over. Surprisingly, no one had been injured in the unfortunate event.

With one additional item to be attended to, the captain ordered his boat to remain in the water and for the two women and the boy, Charles Goodridge, to be brought on deck.

Having waited patiently all day for confirmation of their transfer to the 74, the three parties were ready. The boy was eager and excited, whilst the women, though apprehensive, were pleased to be staying together and looking forward to having more space aboard the bigger ship. A small pile of dunnage preceded them from the carpenter's workshop, where they had been berthing, to the deck. On the gangway, Mr Crosby attended to his wife, talking quietly to her and reassuring her before leading her to the entry port and seeing her over the side. Climbing down with her skirt bunched between her knees was not an easy task.

Consuela Pilkington and Charlie Goodridge followed in silence and were shown off the ship by Lieutenant Nightingale. With their scant personal items stowed between the thwarts, the boat was shoved off before they had taken their seats. Mrs Pilkington almost lost her balance but was caught by her friend who prevented her from falling backwards.

'Be quick smart,' Mr Tully shouted to the coxswain who nodded his acknowledgement.

It was a short pull to the 74 with only the dip of the blades slicing the water and the growl of the oars breaking the silence. By the time they arrived, order had returned on the deck of the third rate.

As soon as the boat touched against the hull, Charles Goodridge hared up the ladder even before the boat was tied up, much to the ire of the coxswain. The women were assisted from the boat by one of the crew and handed aboard by several sailors. When he was satisfied they had been safely delivered, the coxswain headed the boat back to the frigate where it was immediately hoisted to the starboard davits.

That evening, Oliver shared a glass of Madeira with the doctor who appeared a little glum.

'No doubt you are relieved,' Jonathon Whipple said.

Oliver drained his glass and placed it on the table. 'To what are you referring, might I ask? The fact we are to sail from here in the morning?'

'No, I thought you were pleased they were gone at last.'

'Again I am not sure to what you refer. Who are gone? The Irishmen? The barrels? Or the women?'

'The barrels, of course,' the doctor said.

'I prefer not to speak of them,' Oliver insisted. 'But what of yourself? You appear quiet this evening.'

'I regretted being unable to be on deck to farewell the ladies when they left.'

'I assure you the women will be much more comfortable aboard the third rate. You do not need to concern yourself for their welfare.'

The doctor did not appear to be convinced. 'And the Wexford lads – you must have been glad to see the back of them.'

'They will not be missed aboard my ship.'

'Let us hope they do not come back to haunt us,' Jonathon Whipple said.

'Tosh! You need a drink, Doctor. You are becoming less than good company,' Oliver said. 'I have not been happy with the delay while waiting for stores and victuals. And I am not pleased knowing that our course takes us into the Caribbean. It is a hornet's nest of French and Spanish naval vessels, privateers and pirates, not to mention scheming merchantmen and slavers. However, I am obliged to follow my new orders and will make nothing more of it. Let us look forward to a smooth passage home and dwell on the positive side of the coin. England in early summer, which it will be when we step ashore. Nothing is more soothing to the soul. What say you, Doctor? A toast to an English summer?'

Jonathon raised his glass and mumbled into it, while Oliver tossed the contents down his throat and reached for the decanter to pour himself another glass.

'The women,' Oliver said, knowing the doctor's concern for them. 'They were, no doubt, happy to learn we are returning to England.'

'Delighted, though from my own point of view, I will miss them – particularly Mrs Pilkington for the assistance she has given me.'

'May I be so bold as to suggest you have become a little taken by her? She is indeed a fine looking person.'

The doctor flashed a disdainful look in response to the mention of the young woman – the widow of a shipwright – a person of no breeding or standing. As before, he became defensive. 'Mrs Pilkington has been a valuable asset in the cockpit, as has Mrs Crosby. They are fine, sensible and responsible females.'

'I don't doubt their qualities and behaviour but I am not the only one to notice the way you regarded the younger of the two.'

'If I regard her differently from her companion, then it is only out of concern for her. The abuse she suffered in Gibraltar was both injurious to her person and disturbing to her emotional and mental state. I have genuine sympathy for her. The insults she was subjected to should never happen to any woman.'

'I agree, Doctor and will say no more. In fact I have already said too much which I blame on myself for imbibing too much of this fine wine. But I still contend women are a distraction for most seafarers. That is the reason I will not have them aboard my command.'

'I believe you are the exception rather than the rule.'

Oliver was not inclined to indulge in an argument on this subject. Despite being buoyed by the reassurance all had been attended to in preparation for sailing, the celebratory mood he had been enjoying had now fallen as flat as the waters of Guanabara Bay. The sooner they departed this port, the better.

Early the following morning, the lookout on the foretopgallant yard gazed at the eastern horizon as the grey haze mellowed to mauve then pink. From his vantage point, he watched the leading edge of the sun's rim emerge like a gleaming gold coin from the grip of the horizon. As it lifted and grew, the sun's rays touched the frigate's masts and slid slowly down them, transforming the timber from tar-stained brown to warm amber, and the loosely furled canvas to gold thread. To the west, the sun's rays touched the tips of the mountains but the still waters of the bay were obliged to wait until it had risen sufficiently to bathe it in various shades of blue.

Captain Quintrell had been on deck since before dawn with his senior officers and several midshipmen. Everyone aboard was waiting for the tide to fill and to see the 74 weigh ahead of them. Despite only a light breeze, which barely ruffled the jack, the captain was confident the ebb would carry them out of the bay and once clear of the shelter of the surrounding mountains they would gain a wind to carry them out onto the ocean.

With the hatches and gunports sealed, the decks cleared and the larboard watch standing ready, the order was given to weigh and make sail. All eyes were on the 74 and a low hum of approval was shared when the third rate's anchor was catted.

With handspikes thrust into the holes in the windlass, the horizontal wooden drum creaked as it was turned, dragging *Perpetual*'s best bower from the silt. Dripping sand, seaweed and water, it was quickly secured to the cathead and, even before the jib was run up and the canvas rattled down, the frigate began drifting slowly seaward. With a tide of ten feet, the outflowing stream carried both the man-of-war and the handsome frigate from Guanabara Bay.

Eight bells rang out from *Perpetual*'s belfry echoing the chimes from the 74's bell half a mile ahead. Soaring to several hundred feet above the mast, a number of frigate birds circled the ship, their sleek black wings, tinged with a hint of purple, embracing the air. Their forked tails, now closed tight, appeared dagger-like while the breasts of the male birds revealed a hint of crimson, indicating the mating season was not far away.

Riding effortlessly on the warm tropical air, the man-of-war birds followed the two ships as they swam through the bay's relatively narrow entrance before entering the sparking expanse of the Atlantic Ocean. Being unable to swim, the massive sea birds dogged the ship, waiting for scraps tossed overboard and left floating on the surface. Their habit had gained them their name – pirate birds. With only a small number in attendance, they provided no evidence of bad weather at sea.

When the mountain peaks were but a haze of purple astern, *Stalwart* made its turn and *Perpetual* followed in its wake. With their bowsprits fixed on the north-east, the two fighting ships heeled gracefully to the wind and the coast slowly faded from view. Skimming over the south flowing Brazil Current, *Perpetual*'s deck received a spray of briny foam through the hawse holes. The foamy cutwater cascaded from her bow, creamed along the hull and left a path of white water in her wake.

With the moderate breeze filling the canvas and all lines coiled to the pins, the larboard watch relaxed. Arms, tanned with tar and sun, leaned against the rails. Everyone aboard, bar one, was pleased they were heading north to England.

'The deck is yours, Mr Parry,' the captain said. 'I intend to go below. I have correspondence to attend to. Have the men keep a keen look out. I expect we will encounter some shipping while we are on this course. Advise me if anything is seen. And stay within a mile of the 74.'

'Aye, Captain.'

Chapter 7

Gun Practice

While the joy of heading home had been the reason for the increased noise and merriment in the mess, as one week turned into two and the ship headed further into the tropics, the air became increasingly sultry and, with it, morale slowly dropped. The lackadaisical spirit that set in was followed by boredom in the men.

Having passed the most easterly point of Brazil's coastline, the two British ships were now heading northwest, assisted by the flow of the South Equatorial Current which would help carry them beyond the limits of the southern continent towards the islands of the West Indies. But winds and currents did not always work together and, if the wind dropped, ships faced the danger of being becalmed in the doldrums. When this happened the conditions became intolerable. With little call for sail handling, the days seemed long and monotonous, and with the sun burning down continuously, there was no relief from the oppressive heat even when sitting in the shade.

An occasional tropical storm delivered sudden torrential rain but was not always associated with the desired prevailing winds capable of carrying the vessels north. When such a storm approached, the band of rain appeared in the distance as a foaming white line stretching across the sea's surface travelling faster than any approaching ship. Closing on them, the pounding rain bounced up from the sea like grapeshot. The roaring sound thundered like a mob of galloping horses stampeding through the shallows. It turned the sea's surface into a seething cauldron of froth.

Yet, for the men aboard the British ships, the sudden downpours delivered some relief. The dancing water scoured the deck, cooled the burning hot pitch that wept from the seams between the planks and washed the sweat from those who wished to bathe under the waterfalls spilling from the sails. Queues and long locks of hair were shaken free under the deluge in an attempt to wash away the grease and tar that had built up over weeks and months. Rain provided a short break from monotony but, within minutes of it stopping, the clouds passed, the sun burned down, the decks steamed like a galley copper and the air the men breathed was more humid than ever.

On good days, the ships made seven or eight knots. If that rate could be maintained they would fetch the entrance to the Caribbean in less than three weeks. The trade winds would speed their passage but, until they reached that band of latitude, they were in the hands of the weather gods. With a horizon devoid of sails, clouds and even birds, the lookouts lashed themselves to the mast for fear of falling asleep at their posts.

The sight of a sail on the starboard bow brought every sailor to his feet. Others climbed up from below, eager for some distraction. The lookout hailed the deck and reported a brig heading towards them. As it closed on the two British ships, it was identified as a whale ship. Although it was sailing under Yankee colours, While *Stalwart* sailed by, Captain Quintrell took the opportunity to speak the ship to enquire what other vessels it had seen on its journey south.

After identifying himself with the use of a speaking trumpet, the master said he had encountered a fleet of French warships in the north, but they had not interrupted his passage. And apart from a packet boat off the coast of Virginia and a heavily laden merchant ship heading into the Atlantic from the West Indies, he had seen nothing else. When asked which port he hailed from and where he was heading, the master said he was out of Nantucket and bound for the whale grounds in the Pacific – one thousand miles to the west of Chile. Oliver Quintrell considered March late in the season to be heading around the Horn but made nothing of it.

As the sailors aboard the whaler had caught several sharks on lines the previous day, the ship's master offered two of them to Captain Quintrell. Having accepted, *Perpetual* and the whaler remained hove to, while words and fish were exchanged. As the master wanted nothing in return, Oliver thanked him and bade him God speed. The sizable carcases were quickly despatched to the galley with a request from the captain for a fish pie to share between himself and his officers. There was ample meat to make a tasty soup for the men's supper.

The encounter took no more than half an hour but it allowed the third rate to sail on alone. By evening, the distance had been made up and the frigate was back alongside.

The Equator came and went without need for the performances demanded on a southward voyage. Crossing the Line was entered in the log but was of no interest to the sailors. What was of interest to those who had not previously sailed along this coast was the nature and colour of the sea. Despite being one hundred and fifty miles from the coast of Brazil, the sea was murky and brown. Members of the crew who had visited Buenos Aires likened its colour and turbidity to that of the River Plate. Mr Mundy delighted in telling the midshipmen it was simply the discharging waters from the mighty Amazon River. Despite the distance from the river's mouth, the fresh water floating on top of the salty sea was potable. With this in mind, the midshipmen took turns hauling up buckets of water and sampling small doses, though some refused to swallow.

As the pair of British ships was now heading north-west, the captain suggested it was unlikely they would meet any vessels sailing from Europe as they would be unlikely to touch the Brazilian coast at this northerly latitude.

Having spent several hours of the cruise in his cabin, Oliver had written many pages of correspondence – mainly to his wife in answer to her letters. It was times like these when he pondered over his life, when not at sea, and his future. But he did not allow himself to look back. Nothing could be gained by that. Instead he looked forward. Being under orders to return to England, he resolved that when in Portsmouth, he would take better advantage of his time ashore than he had in the past.

With the war in Europe still waging and Napoleon's ambitions largely unchecked, he thought it likely his spell on the beach would be brief before he received a fresh commission. It was his fervent hope that he would be given command of *Perpetual* again or another similar sized frigate. He had served on larger ships as midshipman and lieutenant but, in his experience, he found the multi-decked warships reflected the many tiers of authority at play on them. A frigate, however, with only one gundeck, was more intimate as it offered the captain the opportunity to work closely with his officers and men and come to know them.

Being midway along the north coast of South America but with the fickle wind failing, Captain Quintrell called to Mr Tully: 'Send a signal to *Stalwart*. Advise the 74 that I intend to practice the guns. Tell me when you receive an answer.'

'Yes, sir.'

'Mr Parry, all hands to shorten sail, if you please. Let us fall back a mile or two. I don't want any loose shots landing on Captain Liversedge's deck.'

The acknowledgement from the third rate was almost instantaneous and while the crew of *Perpetual* was spilling wind from the frigate's sails, the third rate responded though it took *Stalwart* considerably longer to deaden its way. That suited *Perpetual* and allowed it to stand some distance behind the larger warship.

The order to prepare for action, accompanied by the bosun's calls, brought a rush of bodies surging onto the gun deck, the gun crews scattering to their respective stations. Gun ports were pushed open and secured, lashings were released from the gun carriages, tompions pulled from muzzles and barrels wormed of anything left from the previous firing. A dozen round shot were delivered to each gun while the powder monkeys hurried from the magazine carrying cartridges in a leather bag and announcing their presence with the familiar call: *make way for powder*. Inserting the rags, the canister and the round shot into the barrel completed the task. Having removed the sheet of lead, the gun captain checked his firing mechanism or reached for a slowmatch.

With eight or ten sailors stationed at every gun, all was in readiness and the crews stood waiting for the call to run out their guns. But, as this was only an exercise, any feelings of fear and apprehension were absent. There were no final words, admissions, wishes or handshakes. No will-making. No tourniquets delivered by the loblolly boy for use in emergency if a hand, arm or leg was blown clean off. Instead, there was a frisson of excitement and a crossfire of petty rivalry from one gun crew to another with caustic remarks and whispered wagers as to which gun would fire first and which crew would be the quickest to reload.

The banter was suddenly silenced by the booming voice of the third lieutenant reminding the gun crews that although this was only a practice, it was not a game and the lives of every man aboard would depend on their abilities when the action was real.

Being satisfied the frigate was at a safe distance from the third rate, Captain Quintrell gave the order to run out the starboard guns and for a full broadside to be fired. The ear-shattering explosive thunder of a dozen guns firing at the same time reverberated along the deck. The recoiling cannon rebounded on their carriage trucks causing the very fabric of the ship to shudder violently. Acrid smoke swirled up in clouds from the waist and spewed skyward belching out from the ship's belly like smoke from an industrial factory chimney.

Barely able to see their hands in front of them and with eyes smarting from the smoke, cheeks were quickly daubed in blackened streaks as the men attempted to rub the dust from them. When vision remained hazy, only the sound of the carriage trucks rolling across the planks warned them to stand clear of the next burst of fire and to be ready for the gun's deadly recoil. Between gasping and heaving to catch a decent breath, the heated muzzles were swabbed, wormed out, packed and reloaded ready for the call to fire again.

Apart from the smoke escaping from the waist, tongues of orange flame issuing from the gunports delivered a thick grey cloud that hovered above the water like a sea fret unwilling to evaporate. Each round of fire added to the density of the fog which billowed in layers like banks of cloud building on the horizon.

On the quarterdeck, the officers were alerted to the sound of shots being fired from the 74. After quickly checking the third rate to ensure it was not firing in anger, Quintrell decided Captain Liversedge had taken the opportunity to exercise his own guns at the same time. Having had both men and guns standing idle for several weeks, it was likely they were also in dire need of practice.

Shooting 18- and 24-pound shot from its heavy metal armament, flame and smoke spewed repeatedly from both larboard and starboard ports of the third rate. The sound, delayed by a few seconds only, followed the tongues of orange flame from its upper gundeck only. The ports on the lower deck remained closed.

From the quarterdeck, Oliver and his first officer observed the man-of-war being engulfed in a growing cloud that rose from the hull, swirled through the rigging and settled amidst the pyramid of spars and canvas. With the smoke increasing, the 74 disappeared almost completely until only the tips of its masts were visible.

Following three broadsides from *Perpetual*'s starboard battery, the order was given for the gun crews to transfer to the port side. Within minutes, the ports were opened, the guns made ready, hauled out and the exercise repeated.

'Begging your pardon, Captain,' the midshipman said, struggling to speak between fits of coughing.

'Not now, Hanson,' Oliver Quintrell replied.

'But I think it could be urgent, sir.'

Peeved at the interruption, the captain turned impatiently to the midshipman. 'What is it that cannot wait?'

'It's the foremast lookout, sir. He thinks the 74 has signalled but, with all the smoke about and at this distance, he says it's impossible to read the flags.'

Oliver expected it to be a message from Captain Liversedge, advising that the 74 was also going to practice its guns, but he could not take the chance. 'Mr Parry,' he called. 'Belay the firing and ask Mr Tully to go aloft. I need him to confirm this signal from the 74. Thank you, Mr Hanson,' the captain said. 'You did the right thing. Return to your station. Mr Tully will attend to the matter.'

The midshipman touched his hat, hurried forward and quickly vanished into the smoke billowing up from the waist.

Oliver observed his lieutenant sprint up the ratlines, rub his eyes and extend his glass towards the man-of-war. After a brief discussion with the man in the foretop and a second look to confirm his assessment, he returned to the quarterdeck.

'Signal reads: *Sail approaching. Dead ahead.*'

'Thank you, Mr Tully. Could you or the lookout see a ship?'

'No, sir. We could see nothing for the smoke. The 74's lookout has the advantage with the height of his masts.'

'Kindly go back aloft and report as soon as you see a sail or another signal. I need to know what the ship is. Let us hope it is just another whaler heading south.'

The captain turned to his first lieutenant. 'Mr Parry, have the men remain by their guns and bring us to half a cable's length of the 74 but keep us astern of her. As we cannot see that sail, it's likely she hasn't seen us either.'

Simon Parry agreed.

With the gun crews standing by but with no visibility from their open ports, they waited anxiously for fresh orders.

Fifteen minutes passed during which time the captain paced the quarterdeck screwing his eyes in an attempt to see through the veil of cloud.

'Deck there!' Mr Tully's voice carried from the royal yard on the main. 'Signal from the 74.'

'Report.'

'Two sail of ships both hull up on the horizon. Possibly French. Heading directly for *Stalwart*.'

'Thank you, Mr Tully,' Oliver called. Then turning to the midshipman he ordered a signal be raised to acknowledge the message.

With *Perpetual* swimming in the 74's wake, the captain waited for another signal from the third rate. On deck the feeling of excitement was now tempered with fear of not knowing the enemy they were about to face. But a third rate ship of the line and a frigate made a formidable team and, unless the two approaching ships had greater firepower, they would be fools to attack two well-armed fighting ships of the Royal Navy.

The next signal merely confirmed the sighting that two French ships were bearing down on the 74 and were directly in line with her. One was a French frigate. The other a three-masted vessel with squares on fore and main. 'Looks like a British sloop of war,' the lookout suggested.

'A French corvette, I presume,' Oliver commented. 'She'll be light and fast with only one gun deck and only a small crew.'

With the men already stationed for action, there were no drums or pipes – only the reminder to stand ready and wait for the order. Sailors and marines climbed into the rigging and took up their positions. A wave of apprehension swept over the ship. Hands chilled. Stomachs churned. Mouths and tongues ran dry. Yet the challenge also brought a burst of positive air. Every sailor knew that a captured French frigate would make a valuable prize even though it would be shared between both ships' crews. The small corvette would be an added bonus if that could also be taken.

'A bold move for the French pair to challenge a line-of-battle ship,' Oliver pondered.

'How many guns would you think?' the lieutenant asked.

'A big frigate – perhaps 38- or 44-guns. The corvette only 18- or 20-guns. A little over 60-guns when combined. Well short of the third rate's metal.' Oliver was puzzled as he squinted in an effort to see through the veil of gun-smoke. 'If I am not mistaken, because of the smoke, I contend the French captains have not seen us standing in *Stalwart*'s wake. I wager they are under the impression the 74 is sailing alone and that is why they have decided to take her on.'

The officers on deck liked the captain's suggestion and were in agreement.

'Let us remain behind this grey curtain for as long as possible.' Then he smiled. 'I should like to see the expressions on their faces when they discover they are taking on a British third rate and a frigate.'

'What action do you expect from Captain Liversedge?' Simon Parry asked.

'If the French bring the action to him, he will most definitely stand and fight. If, however, the French realise their mistake and veer away, the decision to make chase will be his. Whatever choice he makes, *Perpetual* will be with him.'

The sand in the hourglass slid through the neck painstakingly slowly from the time the ships were first sighted to them coming within firing range. As always, ships rising from the horizon appeared glued to the line and unwilling to part from it. However, once the hull was up and the ship freed from the horizon's grip, it sped from it as though the Devil's bellows was pumping air into its sails.

Standing only half a cable from *Stalwart*'s stern, the spread of the warship's canvas, combined with the smoke, meant *Perpetual* was completely obscured from the view of the two approaching ships.

Two shots fired from *Stalwart*'s forward carronades put everyone on alert. Even though the enemy was far out of range, they were followed by two more powerful shots. But the explosive discharges conveyed a clear message to Captain Quintrell. He read it as a signal from Captain Liversedge that he intended to bring the fight to the enemy. It also confirmed his awareness of *Perpetual*'s situation by adding smoke to the screen surrounding both vessels. Forward on the weather deck and on the gundeck, the gun crews stood ready for action.

'Deck there,' the lookout shouted from high on the mast. 'The Frogs have separated but are still heading straight for the 74. They intend to attack the third rate from both sides at the same time.'

The message had hardly been received when the ghostly outline of the corvette came into view off the 74's port bow. At the same time, the larger French frigate could be identified bearing down on its starboard side.

Moments of confusion aboard the corvette confirmed the opinion Oliver had expressed – the officers on the French deck had been oblivious to the British frigate hidden behind the 74's pyramid of cloth and cloud. Despite this realization, or because of it, as soon as the corvette's elegant bow was in line with that of the 74's there was a deafening roar as fire shot from the gunports of the small French vessel. *Stalwart*'s response was to release a barrage of shot from both upper and lower decks on her port side. By the time the gun crews on both ships had reloaded, the damaged corvette and the 74 were beam to beam. It was an extraordinarily uneven fight.

Captain Quintrell ordered more sail to bring him up from the 74's wake and put him in a position to launch his own attack on the corvette. With the helm over, *Perpetual* veered towards the smaller French vessel with the intention of sailing across its bow.

On the far side of the 74, the roar from the warship's starboard guns and the response from the French frigate were deafening but the officers on *Perpetual*'s deck were unable to see what was happening. But everyone aboard was conscious that a well-timed broadside from *Stalwart*'s twin decks was capable of blowing the French ship out of the water.

By coming up on the corvette with the intention of forcing it between *Perpetual* and the 74, Oliver Quintrell was placing himself in danger of being hit by the man-of-war's round shot as it flew across the French deck. He had faith in his fellow captain, though, and was confident that when Liversedge saw his manoeuvre, he would cease firing on his port side. But there was no guarantee.

With the bow of the corvette bearing down, Oliver ordered his bow chasers to aim for the corvette's foremast. The second shot hit its target. The timber creaked and cracked. Lines whipped away wildly, blocks thudded on the planks and severed ropes' ends swung above the deck. The mast leaned perilously but did not fall.

Another deafening shot rang out from *Perpetual*'s forward carronade, blasting the bowsprit and taking out the forward stay. As the taut line snapped and flew off with the speed of a bullet, the foremast fell slowly back, collecting the main and topgallant yards before lowering a blanket of salt-hardened canvas across the bodies already writhing on the deck.

'We have her,' Oliver cried, as *Perpetual* swung under the corvette's damaged bow and came up on her vulnerable beam. Sailing to within biscuit-throw of the small ship, *Perpetual*'s starboard guns were ready for action when the corvette swam between her and the third rate. The order was given for the crew to aim for the hull betwixt wind and water.

As the French corvette had not been expecting to encounter a second British ship and had been firing at the 74 through its larboard ports, its starboard ports had remained closed and its guns were not ready to fire. Because of this, *Perpetual* suffered little damage but inflicted much on the French vessel.

'Aim low,' Oliver ordered. 'Don't hit the 74. Captain of Marines, have your sharp shooters take out the men in the tops.'

The confused French soldiers balancing in the corvette's remaining rigging had been concentrating their attention on the 74 and did not expect musket fire to come from behind them. Now, under fire from both sides, they were incapable of swinging their muskets around without hitting each other or becoming caught up in the tangle of lines and swinging ropes surrounding them and making themselves easy targets.

With the ships passing at a speed of three or four knots, the time available to place accurate shots and reload as they sailed by was limited. But *Perpetual* delivered two full broadsides into the corvette's hull, pummelling the French ship and sending splinters flying skywards. A constant roar of cannon fire from *Stalwart*'s starboard batteries indicated the action was still continuing against the French frigate.

Besides the thunderous noise issuing from beneath the smoke, chaos had erupted on the corvette's deck. The screams and yells were not of pain or victory but cries of panic. It was the sound of men in mortal danger and typical of an undisciplined rabble such as that which made up the majority of French crews.

When the smoke lifted sufficiently, Captain Quintrell could see the mortal injury the corvette had suffered. Along the waterline, its hull had been holed in several places. But it was the unseen damage below the surface that had sealed the ship's fate. Taking water, it was going down fast. Men scrambling to escape from below were hindered by fallen spars and canvas. The few that managed to crawl from beneath the raffle headed for the rails and launched themselves into the water.

'Cease fire!' Oliver shouted. 'Helmsman, steer clear. That ship is going down. Let us not get tangled up with her.'

While, thankfully, there was no firing from the 74's port side, a battle was still raging off the warship's starboard beam. With round shot spewing from the third rate's red-hot muzzles, the large French frigate had kept her distance and managed to run the gauntlet without appearing to suffer major damage and sail clear of the action.

Despite the captain's order, an occasional musket shot rang out from *Perpetual*'s rigging, the marines aiming at the wounded French sailors scrambling to reach the rail. They made easy targets for the redcoats.

'Cease fire!' Oliver yelled again. His order was echoed by the sergeant of marines.

When *Perpetual* cleared the stricken corvette, the sea quickly invaded its hull causing the deck timbers to explode with the popping sound of canister and grape, turning the planks to matchwood. The ship was going down by the stern, and the *tricolor*, which was spread on the surface, was caught on the spinning wheel of a whirlpool before being pulled down into the vortex.

Suddenly there was a complete lull in firing. The guns on the three remaining ships were silent. From *Perpetual*'s quarterdeck Oliver Quintrell was anxious to see what damage the third rate had suffered. Then he caught a glimpse of the French frigate making a run to the south. Despite receiving some decisive shots, it had sailed beyond the reach of the 74's stern chasers. Its topmast had gone but otherwise it appeared sound and it was obvious to everyone it had no intention of staying around.

'Should I put away the boats and take on the corvette's survivors?' Mr Parry asked.

For Oliver Quintrell there was no decision to make. 'Leave the survivors and wounded to Captain Liversedge. He will pick them up.' Then he looked across to the man-of-war. '*Stalwart* is in no position to come about and give chase. Mr Mundy, mark our position on the chart. Mr

Parry, give the order to bring us about with all haste. Bring me up on that impertinent Frenchman. He will not escape.'

Turning the frigate's head, *Perpetual* made a broad sweep of the ocean to a position where he could see the French ship heading away. With no time to signal the 74 to advise his plan, Oliver decided it was unnecessary. His course of action would be obvious to Captain Liversedge.

Sailing south, with a distance of five miles separating him from the French ship, Captain Quintrell was relieved when he received word from the carpenter that *Perpetual*'s hold was not only dry but the hull was virtually unscathed. News from the doctor was also reassuring. During the fight, only a few men had received minor injuries. All had been attended to and not a single man was occupying a cot in the cockpit.

Oliver was relieved *Perpetual* had suffered only superficial damage and felt sympathy for the crew of the smaller French ship. The corvette had been unprepared for the action and the decision to attack a 74-gun British naval third rate had been ill-conceived and foolhardy. It had been an unevenly balanced fight and the corvette had stood no chance from the outset. As a result, many of the corvette's sailors had paid with their lives. Such was the cost of sea war.

'More sail!' Oliver ordered. 'Let us make that frigate ours.'

On deck, the hands responded with renewed vigour, hoisting every inch of canvas they could muster, dowsing the canvas with water and bracing the lines as taut as harp strings. For the men, a successful chase meant a prize-of-war and a guarantee of money in their pockets. And, if they were away from the 74 when they took it, the prize would be all theirs and would not have to be shared.

However, up ahead was a vessel that was larger than *Perpetual* and carried more guns. Studying it through the lens, Oliver and his officers estimated 38- or 42-guns as against their own 32. And, as every foremast Jack knew, recently-built French frigates were sleeker and faster than traditionally-built British ships. But the Frenchman had suffered some damage which evened the chances of catching it. Despite that, Oliver was puzzled by the French captain's actions. By heading away, he had demonstrated he had no concern for the fate of the corvette and its men.

On the quarterdeck, Captain Quintrell and his officers considered the challenge ahead. With no indication from the French captain that he was prepared to stand and fight, or haul down his colours and heave to, it was obvious he intended to try to outrun *Perpetual* and would aim to extend his lead even if the chase lasted several days.

With a following wind and despite the damage the Frenchman had suffered, the gap between the two vessels changed little. For half a day, all eyes in the tops, on the quarterdeck and from the forecastle were fixed on the fleeing ship, anxious for any sign of it dropping off. The main worry expressed by the officers was that they might lose sight of the enemy when night fell and in the morning find only an empty horizon. Then unexpectedly, after six hours of chasing, a call came down from the foretop.

'The Frog's heaving to,' the lookout shouted.

Telescopes snapped open but even without a glass it was obvious the helmsman was having difficulties maintaining a straight course. The broad white wake left by the French frigate was drawing a serpentine line on the surface of the sea.

Having pursued the vessel for only forty nautical miles, *Perpetual*'s crew cheered when the French captain struck all sails and hauled down his colours. But despite the air of jubilation around him, Captain Quintrell approached the enemy with caution. He knew the French to be cunning.

As they sailed closer, another call from the masthead identified the name painted on the transom: *Flambeau*.

'What is that Frenchie up to?' Mr Mundy asked. He received no answer.

Leaving the quarterdeck rail, Mr Parry accompanied the captain as he went forward with a glass. The sailors standing by the lines moved aside to let them pass.

'She's listing off to starboard, Capt'n,' came a familiar voice from the foretopsail yard. 'I reckon she's taking water.'

'Thank you, Smithers,' Oliver Quintrell replied, closing the telescope and returning to the quarterdeck. It was just as the sailor had suggested. The French frigate was listing noticeably to starboard and appeared to be in danger of sinking.

Chapter 8

Flambeau

As the distance between the two frigates narrowed, Oliver ordered a shot to be fired from one of the starboard guns. It was aimed wide and low and well clear of the enemy's side. The iron ball skimmed the water, bouncing three times before splashing into the sea. Everyone waited to discover what response it would raise from the Frenchie but there was none. Oliver remained cautious.

With the enemy frigate hove to, *Perpetual*'s sails were backed.

'All hands, Mr Parry. Have the men stand by the guns. Helmsman, bring us up to within musket shot of her starboard side.

As *Perpetual* swam towards the foreign frigate, the extensive damage it had suffered became obvious. Round shot had pockmarked its hull and shattered the starboard gunnels from stem to stern. Aloft, every square foot of canvas had been peppered with holes from grape and chain, and the once handsome frigate had lost its main topmast. Much of the running rigging had been severed leaving frayed ropes' ends dangling and swaying to the rolling swell. Oliver was amazed the main shrouds and stays had held and the fore and main had not come down. Until it was closely examined, it was impossible to assess the extent of the damage to the hull below the waterline. As for the rudder, it had split vertically with half of it shot away. The part remaining was hanging from the sternpost and in danger of being ripped from the stern by the next large wave. Only the preventer chain had saved it from being lost completely. How the frigate had made the speed it did when *Perpetual* was in pursuit was remarkable. Oliver had to commend the helmsman for steering the ship in the condition it was in.

Yet, equally disturbing was the apparent state of confusion and disorganisation on deck. Men were running this way and that, sails were left unfurled, lines hanging loose, blocks swinging like pendulums over the deck and orders being called but not heeded. Cries of panic were coming from every quarter of the ship.

As the two vessels came alongside, a heavily accented voice hailed *Perpetual* through a brass trumpet. 'My, ship is hit. He is sinking.'

Despite the French captain having struck his colours and the obvious confusion and chaos on deck, Oliver was still cautious. Grabbing the speaking trumpet from his lieutenant's hand he called out: 'I am Captain Quintrell of His Majesty's frigate *Perpetual*. I wish to speak with your captain.'

'I am *le capitaine*. My name is Moncousu. My ship is sinking. I must abandon him. You must take my men.'

Oliver returned the trumpet to Mr Parry. 'Inform the captain I intend to board and will accept his sword.'

Receiving no answer from across the water, Oliver ordered two boats to be lowered.

'I want sharp shooters in the rigging and half a dozen marines to accompany me. I require Mr Crosby and three of his mates to come also. I will need an urgent assessment of the damage. Perhaps the hull can be patched and the ship saved.'

'She'll make a tidy prize,' the sailing master said.

That was the least of the captain's considerations.

Within minutes, Captain Quintrell, accompanied by his second lieutenant, the carpenter and his mates, and six marines were heading across the short stretch of chop between the two vessels. A second boat carrying more marines and several able seamen followed behind.

From the sternsheets, Oliver had the opportunity to study the frigate rising up before him. It was relatively new displaying much evidence of skilled craftsmanship and pride in its finish. It would take weeks of work if it was ever to be restored.

Like many French ships, the transom was ornately carved although bombardment from the 74 had caused extensive damage. Unfortunately, the close-quarter pounding it received from the third rate's 24- and 18-pounders had destroyed its rails and punctured its sails with massive holes and tears.

Boarding was not easy as the gangway entrance was crowded with French sailors convinced the ship was going down and eager to escape in the approaching boats.

Mr Tully discharged his pistol into the air and yelled for the men to stand back. With muskets levelled at them from the marines in *Perpetual*'s tops, the Frenchmen reluctantly understood and moved back, allowing Captain Quintrell and his men to climb aboard.

On reaching the deck, Oliver looked around. His main interest was in the number and configuration of guns on the weather deck, the state of the frigate's masts and top hamper and the amount of damage the sails and rigging had suffered. His first few steps up the sloping deck confirmed that the ship was indeed listing badly.

From a group of men gathered in the forecastle, Oliver caught sight of gilt buttons and braid flashing in the sun. The French captain presented himself in full dress uniform but the greeting he extended was curt and ungracious. With his limited English, the unmannerly officer identified himself as *Capitaine* Moncousu. He said his frigate, *Flambeau* was out of Brest though Oliver doubted that Brest was the port he had just departed from and considered a French island in the Caribbean more likely. He did not state where he was bound.

No sooner had that formalities been observed than the Frenchman repeated the information he had delivered earlier. 'My ship is sinking. He is taking water. I have lost many men and have many more whose lives are in danger. You must take them into your ship.' Then, he continued in French, speaking rapidly and, at times, raising his voice along with his hands and arms which he swung in violent gesticulations.

Oliver stood, watched and listened, somewhat bemused, as the captain repeated himself twice over. Despite not fully understanding what was being said, Oliver followed the gist of the one-sided conversation, but was not interested in the French captain's lamentations. More importantly, he wanted to know the amount of damage the ship had suffered. He had no desire to have it sinking from beneath his feet.

'Where is the damage?' Oliver asked bluntly.

'Forward. Starboard. A lucky shot from your man-o'-war,' he said sourly. 'The water has filled the hull. *Mon Dieu*, do you not understand? *Flambeau* is sinking.'

With that, *Capitaine* Moncousu unbuckled his sword and thrust it at Captain Quintrell's chest. He then grabbed the English commander by the cuff and started pulling him towards the bow to show him the problem.

Knocking the Frenchman's hand from his sleeve, Oliver handed the sword to Mr Tully, and turned to his carpenter. 'Mr Crosby, be so good as to go wherever *le Capitaine* indicates and report back to me with all speed. I must know the extent of the injury to the hull and the possibility of plugging the hole or holes. I also want to know how much water the ship has swallowed and how much time we have left before she founders.'

'Aye, Captain.'

Accompanied by two sailors both shouting at him in French, Mr Crosby hurried forward ignoring them. William Ethridge followed closely behind with another of *Perpetual*'s carpenters.

Retreating to the relative calm of the quarterdeck, Oliver took time to consider the damage to the ship. Looking aloft, the damage to the topmast was obvious. Underfoot, a raffle of lines was waiting to be coiled. On the deck, belaying pins turned in circles with the motion of the ship, and loose grape shot that had bounced down onto the deck rolled back and forth along the scuppers. Walking in any direction without stepping on something was almost impossible.

In their eagerness to leave the ship and get into the boats, the undisciplined French sailors continued to challenge the marines on the gangway, their behaviour typical of the landsmen pressed into service by the French navy.

Further forward, a group of sailors squabbled and abused each other while attempting to swing a boat from the davits. The words they uttered, while not understood by the British crew, spoke of frustration and anger.

Amidships, another group of French seamen argued as they tried to right an upturned boat they were attempting to get over the side. Desperate to save their own skins, the sailors showed no inclination to save the ship. The frenzy was uncontrolled. The presence of *Capitaine* Moncousu had no effect.

'Belay!' Oliver shouted. 'Stop what you are doing.' But his voice failed to carry over the din.

Conscious of his limitations with the language, Oliver turned on his heel and beckoned to the Negro who had just climbed aboard. It was not be the first time Ekundayo had served as a translator. 'Tell these men to stop what they are doing and move to the stern.'

When the deep Caribbean voice boomed out with the French accent spoken on the island of Saint-Domingue, the sounds were suddenly stilled. The marines were then able to force the mob aft and collect the weapons still in their possession. During this time, a few more heads emerged from the hatches. Being desperate to escape the flooding hull, some were unprepared to wait for the boats and headed straight for the rail and jumped into the sea.

'Fish those idiots out,' Oliver called, before turning and questioning the French commander. 'What measures have you taken to save your ship?'

The French captain was taken aback. 'The damage is too great.'

Oliver shook his head and repeated his question only to receive the same answer. At that moment, Mr Crosby returned and Captain Quintrell was able to direct his question to his carpenter. 'Tell me what you found. Has any effort been made to stop the sea engulfing the ship?'

'It's like the French captain says,' the shipwright explained. 'The damage is severe. There's a great cleft in the starboard bow that extends from the gunnels down to the waterline. I understand an attempt was made to fother the hole, but the pressure of water, while the ship was sailing, would have made it impossible. At the moment, being hove to, the sea is only lapping in but I imagine when she was making eight or nine knots the bow wave would have been cascading through like water from a burst dam.'

'Can anything be done to save her?'

'I think the hole could be plugged if the starboard bow could be raised a few inches.'

Oliver nodded. 'Have you sounded the well and examined the hold?'

'I stuck my head down below but what I saw was not good. Empty barrels are floating freely. I didn't measure the depth but, even if the damage is repaired, I fear it will take days to pump the water out.'

'We do not have days, Mr Crosby. Perhaps hours only. I will arrange for you to have more help, but for the present, you and your men must do the best you can. Kindly check the rest of the hull. The starboard beam received all the fire, so I imagine the port side is unscathed. In the meantime, I will see if we can lift the bow very slightly to make the repair work possible.'

The carpenter dried his hands on the cloth he was carrying and knuckled his forehead. 'I wouldn't recommend sailing her until the level's down and the ship is back on an even keel.'

Oliver agreed. 'In the interim, we will pray the sea does not come up on us. You have forty-eight hours, Mr Crosby, otherwise the 74 will head north without us.'

Armed with the facts, Oliver turned to his men. 'The hold is flooded. As you can see, the ship is listing badly and if she goes over by more than a few more inches, we will lose her. There is no time to waste. Will,' he said to the young shipwright, 'check the gun deck. Make sure all the ports on the starboard side are tightly sealed. I want no more water coming in.'

'Aye, Captain.'

'Mr Tully, pass a message to my coxswain. I need more hands from *Perpetual*. Return the boat forthwith. Have it return with twenty strong men and two more of the carpenter's mates.'

The lieutenant nodded.

'You four,' Oliver called to his men waiting by the bulwarks. 'Get some help from the Frogs and man the windlass. Unseat the best bower from the cathead on the starboard side, swing it clear of the hull then cut the cable. Let it go. We must lighten the bow. Leave the larboard anchor for the present. Next, move the bow chasers as far aft as possible. Muster some of the French sailors to help you.' Glancing up at the forecourse yard, he quickly assessed the enormous weight of canvas furled to it. 'Unbend the forecourse,' Oliver ordered. 'Lower it down, smartly as you can, and drag it aft. Rest it across the quarterdeck. When that is done, head down to the gun deck. I want the four forward guns on the starboard side rolled back to the waist. They should move fairly easily on their carriages.'

Satisfied with his efforts to lessen the weight on the injured hull and heel it over slightly, Oliver considered there was little more he could do in a short time. Looking aft, he recognised anger and frustration in the faces of the French sailors facing the loaded barrels of the marines' muskets. 'Push those Frenchies as far aft as possible,' he ordered the sergeant of marines. 'Let them sit on the deck and be silent. They will add weight to the stern.'

Looking forward, he could see the prostrate bodies of two of his carpenters on the deck. Lying flat on their bellies, they were chipping away with chisel and hammer at the splintered gunnels. He could hear similar sounds rising from the deck below where Mr Crosby and the other wrights were also working on the hull.

'I trust these small measures will bring her head up sufficiently,' Oliver said to his lieutenant, before addressing the French commander.

'With the help of my carpenter and his crew, it is possible the hole can be plugged and *Flambeau* will be saved.'

Moncousu threw his head back and laughed. 'It is not possible,' he replied sharply.

'Nothing is possible unless we try,' Oliver answered, refraining from saying more. 'Captain Moncousu, do you have men working the pumps?'

'*Naturellement*, my men are on the pumps this moment.'

Without the familiar rhythmic clanking associated with men working hand-pumps, Oliver was not convinced. 'I trust they have not deserted their posts,' he said cynically. With no reply, he inhaled deeply, the air hissing through his teeth. 'Mr Tully, kindly check the pumps. Make sure the men are not shirking their duty and have them rotated regularly. *Capitaine*, do you have more than one pump.'

'No. *Flambeau* has one pump only.'

'Mr Hanson, send word for a hand-pump to be ferried over from *Perpetual*.'

'Aye aye, Captain,' the midshipman replied and hurried away.

Though the French captain's eyes were flashing about from one place to another, he appeared unwilling or unable to offer any useful suggestions.

'Captain, I want two dozen of your men to go below with buckets, open the hatches to the hold and start bailing water. You will need a further two dozen men to hoist up the buckets and empty the water over the side.' He leaned forward and glared at the Frenchman. 'You do have buckets, I presume?'

'You cannot empty a ship's hold with buckets,' the French captain argued.

'Then what is your proposal, sir? Shall we stand here twiddling our thumbs and wait for the ship to sink?'

Without responding, Captain Moncousu turned his back and hurried away to instruct one of his men to organise the bailing.

Over the next few hours, Oliver Quintrell checked regularly on the progress Mr Crosby and his men were making replacing the smashed timbers on the ship's hull. With the starboard bow raised slightly and only an occasional wave splashing over, he monitored the level of water in the hold. Apart from praying, there was little else that could be done.

Despite near exhaustion from constant labour, few on board slept well that night. The repetitive clanking of the pumps was constant as was the sound of hammering from the team of carpenters. The companionways creaked under the comings and goings of the bailing teams and the jolting and jarring of the damaged rudder was unnerving. Throughout the night, the complaints of the Frenchmen continued, though they were no longer consumed with the fear of drowning but of being overworked. Some slept on the warm deck content in the knowledge their ship was not going to sink.

Apart from other concerns, Oliver was eager to rejoin the 74 as early as possible. If he delayed too long, he feared Captain Liversedge would proceed north without him under the impression *Perpetual* had been sunk during another encounter with *Flambeau* or was continuing to chase the French ship south towards the Horn. It was imperative to return to the rendezvous as quickly as possible before any change in the weather added to their problems.

After dozing for an hour, Oliver was woken with the news the worst of the frigate's wounds had been sealed. Having successfully removed the damaged timbers and replaced them, Mr Crosby was confident no more water would enter the ship.

With the level in the hold reduced considerably, the French seamen were reluctantly forced below and a grating secured above them. The accommodation was far from ideal, even to keep prisoners in, but as they were only two weeks from Jamaica and it was the only area large enough to confine the mob of eighty French sailors, it would have to suffice.

The following morning, with the pumping and bailing continuing non-stop, preparations were made for the two frigates to sail. A heavy hawser was brought up from *Flambeau*'s cable tiers and secured to her bow. A boat was lowered and the cable was hauled across to *Perpetual* and attached to her stern.

Fortunately the wind was in their favour and only small wave tips ruffled the otherwise smooth surface. The ocean swell rolled lazily in long slow heaving troughs typical of the Atlantic. With the point where the engagement had taken place having been charted at the time, conditions were favourable to meet up with the 74.

Now that the prize's hull was sound and the ship seaworthy enough to sail under tow, all that remained was for *Perpetual* to take up the cable and proceed slowly in a north-westerly direction. Sailing north in this manner promised to be both slow and tedious.

With Mr Parry in command of *Flambeau*, Captain Quintrell returned to *Perpetual* with Captain Moncousu. For the present, the Frenchman was placed in a cabin below deck. It was Oliver's intention to transfer him to the 74 when they reunited with the third rate.

Having headed south for six hours chasing the French ship, Oliver estimated the return voyage, with the foreign frigate in tow, would take twelve hours or more. This estimation proved fairly accurate, no thanks to the wind or the sailing skills of his men, but to the ocean current flowing along that section of the South American coast.

Unfortunately, that same gulf of water had carried the third rate one hundred and fifty from the position Mr Mundy had charted, so when the man-of-war was not sighted where it was expected to be, the sailing master insisted Captain Liversedge had not waited for them and had headed north alone. Oliver was not convinced and argued that the third rate had merely drifted. A few hours later, when the lookout reported a sail on the horizon, his opinion was confirmed.

Seeing *Stalwart* off the larboard bow brought a round of huzzas from the British sailors. The rendezvous offered relief to Captain Quintrell. He intended to relinquish the task of towing the damaged frigate. Being far larger and stronger, it was logical that *Stalwart* would assume that duty.

But the atmosphere aboard *Flambeau* was not as positive. Of the British sailors and shipwrights who had been put aboard the prize and had agreed to remain there to sail her north, there were mumblings of discontent. Most of the hands had eaten little over the past three days, Apart from that, they had laboured non-stop and many had caught little sleep over the past seventy-two hours.

There was only a minimal number of hands to work the French ship and despite the ship being under tow, the men were kept busy with constant sail handling. As predicted, the helmsmen's job was a struggle. With the damaged rudder hanging loose from the stern post, the ship had a will of its own. But the captain had not been prepared to wait for a new rudder to be constructed before getting underway. He was optimistic the shipwrights could replace it once they were re-united with the third rate.

Chapter 9

Reunited

The return of the British frigate and its French prize was welcomed with the firing of an 18-pound gun from the deck of the 74. *Perpetual* acknowledged the signal with a shot from one of its 12-pounders. With his ship heaved to, Captain Liversedge and his officers were on deck awaiting the reunion.

With Oliver Quintrell eager to share his reports, the frigate was brought alongside the 74 so a message could be conveyed across. Apart from wanting to present details of the events of the past three days, he was anxious to learn what had transpired aboard the third rate since they last spoke. What of the survivors from the corvette? How many were there? What damage had *Stalwart* suffered in the encounter? But the hour was late and darkness was almost upon them. The last few days had been draining, both physically and mentally, and as the captain climbed the companion steps from the waist, he was conscious of a great weariness in his legs. On the quarterdeck he listened to a message being delivered through the trumpet to the 74 advising Captain Liversedge that he would visit him in the morning.

At dawn the next day, despite a restless sleep, Oliver felt fresh and alert when his boat conveyed him to the third rate. After an official welcome, William Liversedge was quick to congratulate his friend and invite him to his cabin for refreshments.

'Well done, Oliver. A nice prize,' he said.

'We caught her just in time. Another few hours and she would have been lost.'

'A fine effort. But what of *Perpetual*? You look largely unscathed. Did you suffer any serious damage during the encounter?'

'Nothing significant. But what of you?'

'Surprisingly little. The hull is thick. The encounter was very short and soon after you departed, the carpenter and his mates commenced their repair work to the planking that was damaged. The sailmaker assures me the canvas can easily be patched and the bosun's mates have finished splicing lines and re-reeving the blocks. Thankfully, there was no major damage. And your special barrels are safe.'

'I had forgotten about the barrels!' Oliver said.

William Liversedge smiled and continued. 'I trust there is nothing to prevent us from proceeding to Jamaica.' Then his expression changed. 'I was sorry to see the corvette go down. It was a pretty craft. It never sits well on one's conscience knowing one is responsible for the deaths of many innocent men who were merely following orders.'

'I carry as much blame as you. In war many things happen which we prefer not to dwell on.'

'That is easier said than done.'

'I agree,' Oliver said, 'but in this case, the French pair made the foolish decision to attack. You had no alternative but to defend yourself.' He paused. 'Were there many survivors?'

'Some. As you saw, the corvette went down very quickly. Many were trapped beneath her fallen canvas and unable to make the deck. Of those thrown into the water, most could not swim. By the time the boats were lowered there was nothing but flotsam and floating bodies to collect. My men plucked twenty-five survivors from the water. They are now secured under guard. Regrettably a large number were killed in the action or drowned, including the corvette's captain.'

The pair sat in silence for a moment. The cold lantern suspended from the centre beam swayed gently. Through the window, a vast dome of pale blue sky rested on the sea. Within the cabin, the fine furnishings reminded Oliver of a reception room at the Admiralty – a far cry from a captain's quarters aboard a fighting ship just after a battle.

'How are the conditions for your prisoners?' Oliver asked. 'I enquire because I have the eighty French sailors from *Flambeau* locked in their own hold. While the majority of the water has been pumped out, the area is exceedingly damp and unhealthy. For these and other reasons, the men cannot remain confined there for long. It also concerns me that between us we are carrying a considerable number of French prisoners.'

'Fortunately my hold is dry and *Stalwart* has adequate provisions to see us through to Jamaica. Presently, I have a group of marines guarding the prisoners. I agree this situation would not do to continue but I intend to offload all the prisoners in Port Royal. It would be impossible to carry them back to England.'

'That is good to hear,' Oliver said.

'As to your prize, I am sure the agent in Kingston will award a good price for the French frigate. It is the second prize you have delivered into that harbour in the last two years, is it not?'

'Indeed,' Oliver said. 'And from the chatter I hear bandied about by the men, I believe they are already planning how they will spend their share.'

'Is the French ship seaworthy?' William asked.

'After much pumping and patching, the carpenter assures me she will not leak and will make it to England if necessary. However, I would be grateful if you would take her in tow to the Caribbean.'

Captain Liversedge was happy to oblige but when asked if any injuries were suffered by his men during the action, his expression changed. 'My surgeon has his hands full. The cockpit is full with men suffering mortal wounds. Grapeshot is lethal on an open deck.' He took a long sighing breath. 'Also, at the time, I lost a dozen good sailors and a boy and sadly, a very promising young midshipman. The surgeon did all he could to save him but his wounds were too great. I was informed this morning he had died during the night. He was a young gentleman from a notable family. A midshipman in whom I saw a lot of potential.'

'I feel for your loss,' Oliver said. 'What was his name?'

'Algernon Biggleswade Smythe. Though he preferred to be known on board as Mr Smith.'

The news shook Captain Quintrell. 'Algy,' he muttered. 'He was certainly a fine young man and, I agree, he had the essential qualities to make a good officer in the King's Navy. Kindly add my condolences when you write to his father. I shall forward my own letter of sympathy in due course.'

'I am sorry, Oliver,' William said. 'I had quite forgotten that he served under you aboard *Elusive*.'

'Yes, when he first entered the service. It was at the same time Lieutenant Hazzlewood joined my ship also serving as a midshipman.'

'Thank you for telling me.'

'What happened?' Oliver enquired. 'Was he cut down on the quarterdeck?'

The third rate's captain shook his head. 'No. It was not enemy fire. Number four gun burst. The gun captain realised it was overheating and yelled a warning. Those nearby were able to take cover but, with the thunderous noise all around them, few heard the call. It claimed the life of every man in the gun crew, including the gun captain, and a powder monkey who was passing by. His head was blown clean off.

'Even on the quarterdeck, the explosion was deafening. It shook the ship and blew a hole in the deck directly beneath it. It was a wonder the gun didn't drop through to the deck below. Pieces of metal and splinters of wood shot the length of the gundeck and impaled themselves in the bulwarks at the far end. Unfortunately, Mr Smith was standing nearby and was blown across the deck. The crew of that gun was part of his division.'

Oliver shook his head. 'An inglorious end for a young man with a promising career ahead of him.'

'The service he gave to his country will be acknowledged,' Captain Liversedge said. 'He was loyal and never questioned his orders or flinched at the duties he was given and, though he was killed by one of his own guns, he died during a battle. That makes him a hero in my eyes and his service will be remembered as such. Time will tell if the other men injured on that day will survive. Presently, they are in the hands of the ship's surgeon and the Almighty.' William reached for his pocket watch. 'I will be conducting the burial service at ten o'clock. Would you care to stay aboard and pay your respects?'

'Without question,' Oliver said.

Casting off the gloom, Captain Liversedge's tone changed again when he turned his attention to a more pressing matter. 'I see no point in dilly-dallying here. If you are in agreement, I propose we make sail in the afternoon. The sooner we reach Kingston the better.'

'*Perpetual* is ready. However, taking the prize has caused me a minor problem. I have placed twenty-five of my men aboard *Flambeau* to sail her, along with a lieutenant and a middie. Apart from those men, my carpenter and some of his mates have agreed to remain with her and continue the repair work during the onward voyage. Unfortunately this has left me very shorthanded.'

'I understand,' William said.

'If you are in a position to replace my men with some of yours, I would be beholden to you.'

William Liversedge was happy to oblige and said he would also arrange for a squad of his marines to guard the French prisoners. Finally, in accordance with Captain Quintrell's earlier request, the towing cable presently attached to *Perpetual* would be transferred to the man-of-war.

'Your men will be shipped back to you as soon as I can arrange for a new crew to replace them.'

'I am much obliged,' Oliver said. The pair further agreed that when they arrived in Jamaica, the prize would be returned to Captain Quintrell to arrange its delivery to the agent after the French prisoners had been removed from the hold and handed over to the authorities in Kingston.

An hour later, Captain Moncousu and his only surviving lieutenant were ferried across to the 74. They were immediately conducted to a small cabin below deck and a guard placed outside the door. Oliver insisted the French captain should receive no special treatment.

'How many prisoners are there aboard the prize?' Captain Liversedge asked.

'About eighty men,' Oliver said. 'A similar number were lost during the action.'

'An expensive butcher's bill.'

Oliver agreed. 'Unfortunately, the surviving Frogs are far from happy. You can probably hear the hullabaloo they are making from here. Having inspected their accommodation in *Flambeau*'s hold, it comes as no surprise. Although the pumps are manned continuously day and night, the well still measures a foot of water. Despite that being a vast improvement on what is was, the air below deck is stale. Even the walls weep. The sooner we can bring up our destination in the Caribbean the better.'

'I estimate one week,' William said, 'but that depends entirely on the wind.'

The estimation was as Oliver had predicted.

Two hours later, HMS *Stalwart* stood motionless on the ocean, her topgallant yards aback and tipped at an angle to the deck signifying that a burial at sea was taking place. *Perpetual* stood alongside with the French frigate a short distance behind.

On the deck of the third rate, the crew assembled to witness the service. After shepherding the men around the deck, the bosun gave the order: 'Ship's company. Off hats.' At the same moment, the bell in the belfry sounded and the 74's crew, along with the visiting officers of the British frigate, stood in silence as Captain Liversedge conducted the burial service for the young officer who had died as a result of the accident on the gundeck.

Sewn within a canvas hammock and having a pair of cannon balls resting at his feet, the body was placed on a wooden bulwark close to the entry port. The British flag was draped over it.

Captain Liversedge spoke of the death of Midshipman Biggleswade Smythe, not yet seventeen years old, and commended his service to his country. After which, the company joined together in reciting the Lord's Prayer before the captain turned to the committal, repeating the words that he had spoken many times before:

'We commit his body to the deep, to be turned into corruption, looking for the resurrection of the body, when the Sea shall give up her dead...'

With the timber beneath the corpse raised to an acute angle, the enshrouded body slid from beneath the flag and plunged into the deep.

A lump formed in Oliver's throat.

Lifting his eyes from the now vacant area on the deck, he glanced across to Lieutenant Hazzlewood, the friend and fellow officer who had served alongside Mr Smith from the start of their naval careers. Tears were streaming freely down the officer's cheeks.

Algy had been like a younger brother, a son and a mentor to the older man and the best friend he had ever had. Oliver knew that for the lieutenant no one would ever fill those vacant shoes. Mr H would miss everything about his friend – his voice, his appearance and his elegant manners but, above all, he would miss the youth whom he had watched grow into a man. No loss could be felt more acutely than within the confined walls of a wooden ship.

The tears that flowed brought no shame.

Chapter 10

The Signal

As the cloudless skies continued, the sun bore down on the ships' decks melting the pitch and loosening the oakum pressed between the planks. In the rigging, the lines sweated tar making the rope slippery to grip on. The sailors climbed with care. With the fickle winds, every attempt was made to harness the smallest zephyrs no matter what direction they blew from. Constant calls to adjust the braces and trim sails had kept the watches busy and, after several days, the patience of officers, crew and the prisoners confined below was wearing thin. Tempers were short and frayed but the situation was beyond anyone's control.

From *Perpetual*'s quarterdeck, the sight of a jolly boat being rowed across from the 74 came as a welcome distraction. The midshipman aboard carried a sealed envelope addressed in an elegant hand to Captain Quintrell, R.N. Under normal circumstances, when making such a delivery, the boat would wait for a reply, but in this instance the crew shipped their oars for a few moments only. No lines were tossed and the boat did not tie up. When it bumped up against *Perpetual*'s hull, a sailor hanging from the steps accepted the letter handed to him, turned and climbed back. On reaching the deck he glanced over his shoulder and was surprised to see the boat already heading back to *Stalwart*.

From the gangway, the envelope was handed to the officer-of-the watch who, in turn, handed it to one of the midshipmen who delivered it to Captain Quintrell. Oliver thanked the young man and indicated for him to deposit it on the table. Having been told the boat had not waited for a reply, Oliver saw no urgency in opening it. He had been expecting a message from Captain Liversedge with confirmation the *Perpetual*s he had placed aboard the French ship would be returned and that members of the 74's crew would replace them to man the prize vessel. Also, the captain had promised to transfer some marines from the man-of-war to the prize vessel to guard the prisoners. Oliver was also hoping for news that he would be receiving a few extra hands to assist on *Perpetual*. Captain Liversedge had indicated he had plenty of men and while relatively calm conditions prevailed, now was an opportune time to conduct the transfers.

For the moment, however, Oliver Quintrell was engaged with Mr Parry. The pair, sitting together at the table in the captain's cabin, had been studying the chart calculating the distance to their destination in the Caribbean. Presently they were occupied with pen and paper, deliberating over the total number of French prisoners confined in *Flambeau* plus those survivors from the corvette being held in the third rate.

Unfortunately, because of the preoccupation with the fear of *Flambeau* foundering when the prize was taken, the French prisoners had never been counted and names and rates had not been recorded. That situation would need to be rectified before the convoy reached Kingston, as an inventory would be required when the prisoners were handed over to the British authorities.

Simon Parry glanced down at the unopened envelope on the corner of the table. 'Do you want me to leave,' he asked politely.

'No, please stay,' Oliver said, slightly perplexed, as he examined the seal before breaking the wax. 'A rather formal letter from William seems somewhat unusual.'

'Perhaps it is an invitation to dine aboard the 74,' Simon Parry suggested with a grin.

Oliver smiled back, took out the single sheet of paper and opened it. On noting it only contained two lines of script, his expression changed and, after reading the message, his brow furrowed. The correspondence was not what he had expected. 'I do not comprehend,' Oliver said, handing the note to his lieutenant. 'Captain Liversedge is requesting I send thirty able-bodied seamen to serve on the 74.'

'That is ridiculous,' Simon said. 'Didn't you speak with him about being short-handed and come to an agreement about him sending men to assist us?'

'Indeed, I did.' Oliver insisted, reflecting on the conversation he had had only two days earlier. 'I was expecting the return of Mr Crosby and his mates, and the twenty-five sailors and officers I stationed on the prize plus a few extra hands besides. Now, I am being asked to supply the third rate with thirty of my men.'

'But we cannot spare thirty men,' the lieutenant blurted. 'We barely have enough men to work the ship and man the guns. As it is, the watches are extremely shorthanded. Imagine the situation if we meet with more action. The gun crews would be—'

Oliver interrupted. His tone was abrasive. 'That is the result of sailing from Portsmouth with only two hundred men. Did I not state at the time that it was hardly an adequate number?'

Simon Parry reiterated his previous argument. 'Under most circumstances two hundred men is sufficient for a frigate of our metal.'

'Circumstances change, Simon. I remember pointing that out at the time. After losing men in Gibraltar and the Azores, what are we left with? A complement of only one hundred and forty men. One of His Majesty's frigates would normally carry two hundred and fifty.' Oliver felt his blood beginning to boil but reminded himself that a verbal outburst would serve no purpose.

'What do I do?' The question was rhetorical. 'I am obliged to assist my fellow captain – after all, the prize he is towing is mine. But, if I transfer another thirty across, I will be putting my command at risk. The French frigate's hold is bursting with rampant young French seamen who are ill-disciplined and unruly and have not taken kindly to being locked in a stinking damp hold without fresh air or sunlight. One can hardly blame them for that. But it means these prisoners require constant monitoring and must be guarded day and night. Add to that, the fact *Flambeau* is a ship that needs careful handling and is obliged to remain in tow until it is delivered into Kingston harbour. I suggest that is the reason for the request.'

Simon Parry was perplexed. 'I see no reason why a third rate with a full crew cannot cope with that situation?'

'I am at a loss also,' Oliver said, shaking his head. 'This is one contingency I had not considered. However, when I spoke with William in Guanabara Bay, he advised me he had lost several men, deserters who had preferred to sign on merchantmen, American packets, West Indiamen, anything that was leaving the harbour. Yet he had been optimistic he would be able to sign or press extra sailors in the town. However, when the time came to up-anchor, his officers had brought in only two dozen men – mainly landsmen and the dregs of the dockyards. And recently, he lost a complete gun crew and several men. With every cot in his cockpit occupied by the sick and wounded, he is probably short of about a hundred active seamen.'

Simon Parry awaited the captain's resolution.

Oliver referred to the figures they had been assessing. 'From our present location, we calculated the distance to Jamaica is over 1,500 nautical miles. Depending on the wind and weather, providing we can sail without interruption or misadventure and can average six or seven knots, we should fetch Kingston in ten to twelve days or thereabouts.'

Simon Parry was concerned about the French frigate in tow slowing the 74's progress but reluctantly agreed.

'Then it is my duty to oblige Captain Liversedge,' Oliver said.

Simon Parry reminded him that by releasing that number of men he would put *Perpetual* at serious risk. But the captain was not to be swayed.

'Then let us pray this leg of the cruise is uneventful,' Simon said.

'Hmm. We must manage as best we can, as we always have done in the past. I suggest you muster the crew as soon as possible. Nominate thirty sailors to transfer across. If there are volunteers, so much the better. Let's attend to this matter immediately and get the transfer underway while we have the benefit of a calm sea.'

With all hands assembled on *Perpetual*'s deck, the response to the call for volunteers surprised Mr Parry and the other officers. Getting men to volunteer for anything was usually a thankless task. On this occasion, however, twenty men immediately jumped to the call. Strange. What had prompted that response? Was it the chance to serve on a 74? Or was it perhaps the thought of better rations and accommodation that attracted the hands? In Mr Parry's opinion, there was nothing to complain about on *Perpetual* and there were certainly no rumblings of dissatisfaction. If the men who volunteered thought they might receive better pay, the lieutenant was quick to dispel such ideas? Perhaps they felt they would be safer on a ship of the line should they come under attack from a French or Spanish convoy. That was a matter of conjecture. But with no answers forthcoming, the officer could draw no conclusion.

The remaining ten sailors, to make up the total, had to be selected and their names added to the list. The old hands who had served with Captain Quintrell on both *Perpetual* and *Elusive* were reluctant to move.

Once completed, the names of the thirty men were recorded and they were sent below to collect their personal items. Two boats were lowered and within less than an hour of the demand having been received, the boats were being rowed across to the man-of-war.

That evening, the two young midshipmen on deck commented on the clamorous noise and raised voices coming from the French frigate. Despite the distance between the ships, they were able to observe increased activity on the deck of the third rate and a boat being ferried back and forth between the 74 and *Flambeau*. The pair joked about the changing of the guards even the possibility of a party being held on deck but decided the noise was coming from the unruly, malcontent prisoners in the hold. As darkness descended quickly in the tropical latitudes, the two vessels soon dissolved into the black of night. The disturbance lasted less than an hour and before the watch ended, all was quiet again.

Following Captain Quintrell's compliance with the request and the subsequent despatch of the additional men, Oliver was not expecting thanks, but considered that a signal acknowledging the transfer would have been appropriate. At first he dismissed the omission but, when nothing arrived the following day or the day after that, he thought it strange, even rude, although he accepted that Captain Liversedge and his officers had much to contend with. His main concern was for the crew he had placed aboard the prize and for the French prisoners being held below. He wondered about his carpenter and mates and the progress of the repair work they were undertaking. A sound ship would bring a better valuation and financial return from the prize agent. As neither of those matters had been reported to him, he presumed that all was well.

With the first blow from the trade winds, the convoy of three ships was guaranteed good sailing as it headed north. But the danger of meeting French or Spanish squadrons was heightened, as they neared the most southerly islands of the West Indies. Some complaints were reported to the officer-of-the-watch due to the shortage of hands in each division. Oliver had warned his lieutenants that this was to be expected and, until they reached Jamaica, the crew would have to contend with the additional demands and duties. He assured them it would not last for long.

The following morning, a series of signal flags was hoisted on the 74's halliard. The message was delivered to Captain Quintrell in his cabin.

'Are you sure you read the flags correctly, Mr Lazenby?'

'Yes sir,' the middie said. 'Mr Tully was on deck. He can confirm it.'

Oliver turned to his first lieutenant, nonplussed. 'I am instructed to proceed to Portsmouth.

Simon inclined his head. 'What? Portsmouth!'

'That is the order I have been given.'

'Does that mean *Stalwart*, with the frigate in tow, is no longer bound for Jamaica? Or does she intend to sail into Kingston alone and deliver our prize herself? I fear the men will not take kindly to that proposal,' Simon said.

Oliver was bewildered. 'It is unlike William to send a brief signal, such as this, without no prior discussion or explanation. So, why has he suddenly shied away from sailing into the Caribbean? Surely not the fear of meeting enemy ships? Why has he chosen to stand to the Atlantic and return directly to England? What has prompted him change his mind?'

Simon Parry was equally as mystified. 'And what of his *supercargo* – the exile he is charged with delivering to Kingston? Has he forgotten about that order? And what of our barrels stowed in his hold?'

'Damn the *supercargo*. Damn the barrels,' Oliver yelled jumping to his feet. 'I do not care about either. What I do care about are the members of my crew including a lieutenant and midshipman, plus my carpenter and his mates.'

He looked questioningly at his first officer. 'Whatever the reason, I do not intend to be separated from our prize so easily. Send a signal to the 74. Acknowledge the message and ask *Stalwart* what her heading is.'

'Aye aye, Captain.'

'And maintain a safe distance behind the pair.'

The block on the preventer tackle swung pendulously over the deck, as Oliver Quintrell listened to the creak of the braces being stretched under pressure on the belaying pins. Standing at the starboard rail of the quarter deck, he watched the sea hurrying by. Sailing close to the wind, the frigate was making nine knots. Then, after staring for too long at the two black shapes half a mile ahead, his eyes became bleary.

As the sea streamed from *Perpetual*'s hull, patches of bright light burst on the surface. The brilliance shone like plates of polished silver before disappearing and reappearing a few yards away. The sea's luminescence was a phenomenon which never failed to captivate his attention. Though he had witnessed it many times before in these latitudes, he could not help but be amazed by its magic.

Distracted, Oliver shook his head in order to concentrate. First, he considered the number of knots they were making and the distance *Perpetual* was standing from the 74. Then he considered the absence of communication and tried to discount it as not being unusual. He had his orders – to accompany the third rate. The weather was fine, the sea calm, the wind holding. Now they had entered the band of the trade winds, it was likely to blow consistently and carry them to the Caribbean. In these circumstances he would have no occasion to signal the 74 until they neared their destination.

But as the hours and two full days elapsed, with no reply to his signal, Oliver was perturbed and slightly anxious. Pacing the quarterdeck, he surveyed the third rate through narrowed eyes. Standing approximately half a mile ahead, the 74 was sailing easily with the French frigate trailing behind on a nautical leash.

Turning to one of the midshipmen, Oliver ordered another signal to be sent at first light. 'Will proceed to England on return of carpenter and men. Advise.' The midshipman headed off to rummage through the bunting in the locker for the necessary flags.

From the belfry, *Perpetual*'s bell rang out eight times. It was time to set the first watch of the night. Though Oliver waited and listened hard, there was no corresponding echo from the third rate.

'There is something wrong,' Oliver said.

Mr Parry, standing beside him, agreed. 'With our present speed and the sea conditions, it would be impossible to sail a boat across. We could attempt to come up alongside her which would allow you to speak her.'

'I need to think,' Oliver said. 'As night is almost upon us, there is nothing we can do at the moment. Until I discover the 74's intentions, If the wind holds, I will stay with her and, in a day or two, she will reveal her course by making a turn into the Caribbean or bearing north and east if she intends to head across the Atlantic.'

'And if the wind drops?'

'Let us deal with that when we need to.'

'Perhaps Captain Liversedge is ill,' Simon suggested gingerly. 'Perhaps there is fever aboard the ship.'

Oliver stared at his first officer whose face was illuminated by the lantern swinging above the binnacle stand. His expression was grave. 'I fear control of the 74 has been taken out of Captain Liversedge's hands. If that is so, I would like to know who is in command.'

One thing was for certain, Captain Liversedge was not a turncoat. He was a British officer through and through and Oliver would stake his life on that fact. Perhaps one of his lieutenants had taken control.

'The French captain perhaps?' Simon Parry suggested.

'Moncousu? That nincompoop! How could that be possible?'

'Who else could it be?'

Oliver shrugged. 'What I do know is that there are more than fifty of my men spread across those two ships, one being a prize-of-war that my men won fairly in battle and deserve to receive a reward for. As to the third rate, if my assumption is correct and it has been taken, it is my sworn duty to wrest it back. No matter what the cost, we must rescue our men, retrieve our prize and save Captain Liversedge and the 74 at the same time.'

Chapter 11

Across the Pond

With his mind awash with conflicting thoughts, Oliver Quintrell gazed across the ebony sea searching for the line where the world ended and the sky began but he was unable to locate it. Concealed behind the soot-black curtain draped from the heavens, the horizon, which had been visible only a few hours earlier, had disappeared completely. Now, only minute moth holes of light pricked the backcloth of night and, with the moon not yet risen, darkness obliterated the frigate's rigging and spars though they rose only a few yards from where he was standing. Very occasionally the flaccid canvas luffed, the flapping sound reminding him of the wandering seabirds of the Southern Ocean that occasionally circled a ship at night.

Scanning the sea in the direction he had last sighted the third rate, Oliver Quintrell strained his eyes before calling for a glass. As the lieutenant retrieved it from the binnacle, the reflection of the glim flashed on the brass tube.

'She's still there, Capt'n,' Mr Tully said.

'I have confidence in your eyesight,' the captain said, but on saying that, he still wanted to satisfy himself. Holding the lens to his eye, he slowly swept along the black divide. Twice over, he repeated the sweep till eventually he settled on two spots of pale amber light and hovered over them. *Too low for stars*, he decided. Then, putting down the glass and allowing his eyes to adjust to the darkness, the black shape of the warship and a smaller vessel behind it emerged. 'She is indeed still there,' he confirmed. 'Not as far distant as I thought and, like us, going nowhere. Unless she is washed by a different current to that which we are sitting on, I think she will not drift far during the night.'

The lieutenant nodded, though his gesture went unnoticed. 'Shall I send the signal in the morning?'

'Call me before daybreak and run up the signal at sunrise.' He snapped the telescope shut. 'It is unlike Captain Liversedge not to respond. Surely the earlier signals were seen and would have been reported to him. On this flat calm, I doubt he was too busy to reply.'

No knowing if the captain was speaking to him or expressing his thoughts out loud, the lieutenant agreed with the captain's final observation. Those concerns and speculations had already been whispered around the table in the wardroom.

'I am going below. Good night, Mr Tully. Call me if there is any change.'

'Aye aye, Capt'n. Night, sir.'

The air was warm and there was not a breath of breeze. The lieutenant loosened his stock, took a few paces back and listened for the ship's heartbeat. It slept as soundly as the men below cradled in their canvas cocoons. Absent were the familiar shipboard noises – the hissing lines; the creaking timbers; the grind of a rusted pin revolving in a block's sheave that demanded the bosun's attention; the gurgle of water curling from the bow scouring the length of the hull; even the occasional flop and flutter of a flying fish as it misjudged the distance between the wave-tips and landed on the deck. The hum of voices; the clatter of dice or bones on the wooden deck; the resounding clang of a copper dropped on the galley's stone floor and even the patter of footsteps had died with the onset of the night's stagnant air.

The lieutenant gave an involuntary shudder. It was not cold but the tropical night air was clammy and held as still as a graveyard. Only the smell of tobacco and occasional glow from the bowl of a pipe being lit in the forecastle assured the officer-of-the-watch that he was not alone. The helmsman, only a few paces away, was slumped against the wheel, one arm hanging between the spokes, his head resting in the crook of his other. It was going to be a long night.

Every half-hour, the ship's bell rang, barely disturbing those dozing on watch. They coughed, stretched their legs from under the boats, rolled over and farted. The teak planks made for a hard bed. A bundle of teased oakum stuffed into a pillow helped a little.

Mr Tully listened to footsteps approaching the scuttlebutt. The lid creaked as it was lifted. The dipper splashed and dripped as it scooped water. A moment later, the lid dropped back and the footsteps retreated to the forecastle. The sailor's thirst had been quenched without his identity being known.

Two hours passed and moonrise was a welcome sight. It revealed the silver staircase leading to the luminary body. The surface of the sea heaved slowly in its slumber, rising and falling almost imperceptibly like a sleeping serpent. As the heavens changed from black to pewter-grey and the sea to shades of slate, a misty halo outlined the shy moon allowing only a crescent-shaped sliver of its actual shape to be seen. With the addition of several brightly flickering stars, the spots of amber that had indicated the position of the 74 faded. Mr Tully was unconcerned.

For several minutes, he was distracted by the gliding flight of a broad-winged seabird circling the ship as if searching for a suitable place to nest. After a while, it swooped low almost glancing the sea's surface with its wing tips before sheering off and peeling away. The cat's cradle of rigging wrapping the ship offered no inducement.

Young Mr Hanson, having completed his regular round, reported that all was well and with nothing of interest to say, excused himself from the quarterdeck and returned to the companion steps that led down to the waist. Resuming the spot he had previously occupied, he closed his eyes and dozed.

'What was that?' Mr Tully said with some urgency but not raising his voice unduly.

'What was what?' the helmsman replied, straightening his back and shaking the sleep from his head.

The lieutenant did not answer but cupped his hands around his ears and swung his head slowly from side to side, scanning the sea for sounds.

'What was what?' the helmsman repeated.

'Be quiet and listen.'

The helmsman copied the actions of the officer-of-the-watch. 'What did you hear?' he whispered, spreading his feet and returning both hands firmly to the wheel.

For a while the pair stood in silence.

'There it is again,' Mr Tully proclaimed.

'I didn't hear nuffin',' the helmsman complained.

'Then you must be deaf.' Not only had Ben Tully excellent eyesight but his hearing, despite the loss of part of one ear, was also keen. His years spent serving before the mast had taught him to miss nothing, no matter how insignificant it might seem.

'There it is again,' he called and moved over to the rail. The tone of his voice indicated he was confident about what he had heard. Sometimes, during the late hours of the night watch, dreams competed with wakefulness and played tricks on the imagination but, on this occasion, he was convinced that was not the case. 'Mr Hanson! On deck!' the lieutenant called briskly.

Shaking his head, the middie stumbled up the steps to the quarterdeck.

'Lively now. Stand by the rail and tell me what you hear.'

The young man was a little befuddled but knew better than to argue.

It took several minutes of concentration for all three men to arrive at the same conclusion.

'It's the peep of a bosun's whistle,' the midshipman announced.

'It's faint, but I believe that is what it is,' Mr Tully said.

The helmsman claimed the calls were coming from the ship. 'Perhaps from an open gunport,' he suggested. 'But why would one of the bosun's mates blow his whistle in the middle of the night?'

'It's coming from the sea,' the middie argued, though sounding unconvinced of what he had said.

'It can't be from the 74. That's too far away.'

'Wake the watch,' Mr Tully ordered, 'but do it quietly. It's possible there is a boat within hailing distance but we are unable to see it. Then go below and notify the captain of my suspicions. Apologise for the disturbance but ask if he would come on deck immediately.'

The midshipman hurried along the gangway to the forecastle to alert the sailors in his division and for them to pass the word to the other members of the watch. He then headed down to deliver the message to the captain.

Within minutes a line of sailors was leaning against the rail while others were hanging in the shrouds scouring the sea for a ship. Whilst most agreed that they could hear the occasional faint sound of a whistle, none were able to see a boat on the water.

'More light,' the captain ordered when he stepped up to the quarterdeck. 'If we cannot see the vessel, it is likely the vessel cannot see us either.'

The shrill of the occasional call was becoming clearer. It was drawing closer and, after several minutes, every man on deck heard it and commented about it to his mate.

'Silence there! I want to know the direction those peeps are coming from. Surely we are not all as blind as bats? Next time you hear the sound, reach out your arm in the direction it came from.'

The next shrill peep surprised everyone. It came from a distance of only twenty or thirty yards from the frigate's side. Immediately, every sailor on the gangway leaned forward with his forefinger pointing down to the water.

'Mr Hanson, lower a boat but keep a line on her,' the captain ordered.

'There!' someone shouted. 'There's something in the water. Over there,' he yelled again.

Everyone looked.

'There's a man in the water. He has something shining in his hand.'

'A bosun's whistle, no doubt,' Oliver said.

'From a wreck, do you think?' Mr Tully asked.

'If so, there may be more unfortunates in the water. Prepare to assist this one aboard,' he ordered, 'and make a thorough search of the sea for survivors, debris or bodies.

Call the doctor and have blankets brought on deck. And have the galley prepare some hot fluids as quickly as possible.'

'Aye aye, sir.'

With all hands hanging over the side to get a view, a line was thrown to the man in the water. There was a gentle cheer as the swimmer grabbed it and allowed himself to be hauled around to the wooden steps on the ship's side. A diminutive figure climbed slowly and, by the time he made the deck, he was exhausted.

Captain Quintrell thought his eyes were deceiving him. 'My God – Charles Goodridge – what on earth were you doing in the water?'

Unable to speak coherently, a blanket was slung around the boy's shoulders and another thrown over his head. Under the added weight, his knees buckled and he sank to the deck. Sea water dripping from his hair and finger tips formed tiny rivulets that ran along the black lines of caulking on the deck.

'Stand back, all of you, let the lad get some air.'

As the members of the watch shuffled back, a bosun's silver call dropped from the boy's hand and rolled into the scuppers. Oliver wondered how he had acquired it but that was the least of the questions he wanted to ask and it would wait till later.

'If this is some boyish prank you are playing,' the captain said, 'it is the most foolish game I have ever seen. I trust this wasn't done as a dare or for a wager and another idiot, as foolhardy as you, is still out there in the water.'

Charlie Goodridge shook his head.

'Don't you know there are sharks in these tropical waters?' Oliver continued. 'Didn't you consider that a wind could blow up and the ship would move from its present position? Do I have to remind you we are in the Atlantic Ocean and land is hundreds of miles away? Or were you intending to drown yourself?'

The doctor interrupted politely and spoke quietly in the captain's ear. 'I would caution you to allow the boy to catch his breath before you question him any further. His face is rather grey and his lips almost blue.'

'The reflection of the moonlight,' Oliver claimed.

'In my opinion, the lad has overexerted himself to the extent his body has been deprived of oxygen. Right now, he needs rest and quiet in order to recover.'

Though angry with the boy's dangerous exploit yet anxious to discover the reason for it, the captain had no option but to bow to Dr Whipple's recommendation.

'A stretcher or a hammock or a volunteer to convey the boy below,' Oliver ordered.

'I can walk,' Charles said, rising to his knees.

'Take care,' the doctor advised.

But there was something burning inside the boy and it had to come out. He grabbed the captain's arm and pulled him down toward him. 'They have taken the ship,' he whispered, his voice rasping, his words almost incoherent.

'Who?' Oliver demanded, leaning his ear towards the boy's lips.

'The Frogs and some others.'

'Say no more,' Oliver replied. 'Mr Tully, clear this rabble off the deck. Take the boy below to the cockpit.' Then he turned to the doctor. 'I will join you there shortly.'

From the entrance to the cockpit, usually covered by a curtain, Oliver stepped inside speaking his thoughts out loud. 'What in all Heaven has happened? For pity sake, let this not be true.'

Jonathon Whipple beckoned the captain to the cot in which the boy was lying. Swaddled in several rugs and with a hot brick wrapped in a towel near his feet, Charles Goodridge had regained his breath and composure, and was eager to speak.

'There is nothing wrong with me,' he protested trying to raise himself. 'I'm not sick. I want to get up.'

'Not yet,' the doctor advised, turning to the captain. 'I recommend a sedative to calm him. It will allow him to sleep and you can question him later.'

'No!' Oliver was adamant. 'Let him sit up. It is imperative I speak with him immediately.'

'He is very excited and overwrought,' Dr Whipple warned.

'From what the boy told me on deck, he has good reason to be so. Kindly allow me a few moments to speak with him in private. There are questions I must put to him and it is possible he has an important message to convey to me. Should I need your assistance, I will call on you.'

The doctor was not pleased.

'Trust me, Jonathon, these moments, while his memory is fresh, are vital.'

Though unwilling to leave his patient and fearing a relapse from the boy, the ship's surgeon stepped away from the cot and repaired to the small cabin that housed his apothecaries' chest and surgical instruments. Inside the room was a chair and desk with a slanting lid. Taking a ledger from the desk, the ship's doctor tried to occupy his time thumbing through the leather-bound book to the entries he had been making earlier in the day.

Satisfied the doctor was out of earshot, Oliver Quintrell leaned towards the boy. 'Charles, you know who I am, don't you?'

'Of course I do, Captain.'

'And how did you get here.'

'I swam from the 74.'

Oliver cocked his head to one side, his eyes still fixed on the lad. 'Are you sure you were not carried by boat part of the way?'

'No sir, I sneaked off the ship when no one was looking. I climbed down the steps and slipped into the water. I'm certain no one heard me or saw me go. Then I swam.'

'That is quite a distance, young man.'

'I'm a good swimmer,' Charles said.

'You would need to be. That was either a very brave venture or a very foolish act. Many things could have prevented you from succeeding.'

Charles ignored the comment as he pulled the blanket from his shoulders and pushed the brick away from his feet. 'I'm too hot,' he complained.

Oliver lifted the covers from the cot. 'How did you find the ship? The night is black outside?'

'I knew where *Perpetual* was because I was on deck when the sun was going down. There was no breeze and the sky was clear so there was no chance of a wind blowing up.'

'Most boys your age have little interest in the wind and weather.'

'My father often took me with him in his boat. It was a small clinker-built one that he made in the shipyard. That was before the fever took him. He'd made the boat so we could catch fish on the bay.' He gazed at the deck beam overhead and reminisced. 'I wonder where our boat is now.'

'Forget about the boat,' Oliver said.

The boy's cheeks appeared hollow and his bottom lip began to quiver.

'You say you swam all the way. Were you alone or did you have company?'

'I had porpoises for company,' he answered in all seriousness.

'That is not what I meant.'

'No, sir,' the boy replied. 'I told it like it was. I dropped into the sea and swam. I judged the distance to be less than half that of the New Mole to the beach at Algeciras and I had swum that twice and against an incoming tide. Pa said Gibraltar Bay was five miles across so this was no distance at all. And the water was warmer than the Mediterranean.'

'We are not on Gibraltar Bay now,' Oliver reminded.

'Too right,' Charles's face brightened. 'The sea was flat calm and there was no tide to fight against and no fish to speak of.'

'And what if a wind had sprung up and I had given the order to make sail.'

'But there was no wind, Captain, and no sign of one coming, so how could you?'

It was a bold statement from one so young but Oliver could not argue with it. 'Then, I think you were fortunate to have succeeded, but my concern now is for what you told me on deck. Say again. Are you telling me that *Stalwart* has been taken and the captain is being held prisoner? Is this a tale or were you telling the truth?' If it was true, the news confirmed Oliver's worse nightmare.

'God's honour, Capt'n,' the boy cried out, 'it's the truth. The French officers took Captain Liversedge and the lieutenants and locked them in the midshipman's berth below deck.'

In response to the boy's sudden outburst, the doctor emerged from his storeroom and stood for a moment watching the pair. It was not difficult for Oliver to read the expression on his face.

'The doctor is concerned for your welfare,' he said fairly loudly, 'but my concern is for the welfare of the men aboard the 74.' Lowering his voice, Oliver turned back to the boy. 'What you are saying is that the 74 is now in French hands. I cannot believe that. But what of the French sailors we locked in the hold of the French frigate? Where are they now?'

'They were freed and brought over to the 74 in boats and I heard tell that the sailors from *Perpetual* are now locked up in the hold in their place.'

This revelation was astounding.

'But how could a handful of Frenchmen overcome the British crew of the third rate? Surely they must have put up a fight?'

'I don't know what happened,' Charles said. 'But I know that half of *Stalwart*'s crew are now locked in the 74's hold. The other half are on deck keeping watch like nothing ever happened.'

'That makes no sense,' Oliver said. 'Are the French officers standing over them and threatening the seamen?'

'No,' the boy said confidently. 'The sailors seem quite friendly with the Frenchies.'

'How do you know all this?'

'Because I was in the midshipman's larder when Captain Liversedge and the ship's officers were brought down and locked up. I heard what was said and kept quiet as a mouse. But after a while one of the guards noticed me under the table and told me to scram, so I took off and hid somewhere else.'

'Who was guarding the captain when he was brought down? Were they French sailors?'

'No, there were French soldiers and ordinary English seamen.'

Oliver was perplexed. 'These *ordinary seamen* – do you know who they are?'

'Yes. I'd seen three of them before aboard *Perpetual*.'

'What? Who? Which men?'

'They said they were English but they spoke the same as all the other Irishmen on the ship.'

'You are talking about British sailors.'

'Yes, Captain. I heard tell that three-quarters of the crew are Irish.'

'And the men you recognised?' the captain asked.

'They left the ship in Rio. They had first come aboard in the Western Isles – off a shipwreck, or so I heard.'

Oliver threw his head back and raked his fingers through is hair. 'Damnation!' he cried, 'Incredible! How could this possibly came to pass?' His oath prompted the doctor to hurry to the boy's cot-side but the captain held out his arm to stop him approaching.

'It's all true what I've told you,' Charles swore. 'That's the reason I swam over. It was the only way to get word to you.'

'Did one of the officers send you?'

'No, sir,'

'This was your idea?'

'Yes, Captain. I thought if I asked anyone they would laugh at me and call me a fool, like you did. So I thought to myself, no one will miss one of the ship's boys – at least not right away. And if and when they did, they'd think I'd fallen overboard and drowned.'

Oliver was dumbfounded as he tried to absorb all the ramifications of what Charles Goodridge had told him. At the same time, his mind was attempting to digest the awful predicament faced, not only by the captain and crew of the 74, but by himself and his own men. Then a frightful thought suddenly struck him: What if the two ships – *Stalwart* and *Flambeau* – mounted a combined attack on *Perpetual*? What chance would his ship stand?

His thoughts were racing. What action should he take? Should he allow his frigate to drop from the horizon as though the current had carried it over during the night? Or should he launch a surprise attack on the 74 before the enemy was aware their secret had been uncovered. But to attack a British ship – a third rate man-of-war mounting 74-guns – plus a French frigate of 38-guns making a combined battery of at least 112-guns – would be a recipe for disaster.

Such a move would be impossible for an undermanned frigate of 32-guns no matter who was in command of the other two vessels. Furthermore, whatever course of action he decided on, it had to be more constructive than merely giving the order to fire.

Perhaps a boat, carrying two dozen men, could be sent across before the sun rose. Providing they were not seen, they could climb aboard and release some of the British officers. But it was already too late. Through one of the cockpit's open gun ports, he could see the colour of the horizon changing. In less than half an hour the rays of morning would emerge from the horizon to open up like a gilded fan.

'Jonathon,' Oliver said, allowing the doctor to approach his patient. 'The boy is well and needs no sedative. However, a warm drink and a good breakfast would be appropriate after his strenuous exercise. For the present, I request you keep him here, at least for a few hours, and do not let him speak with anyone.'

The doctor's frown dissolved. 'I will do what I feel is necessary.'

'Thank you. I trust you understand. The story the boy has related to me is troubling and I must discuss what action to take with my officers. I will speak with you later.'

'Whatever you say,' the doctor replied. Evidently, there was little that could surprise the ship's surgeon.

Chapter 12

Proposals

In the pre-dawn light, the captain's cabin remained gloomy. The glim in the lantern, swaying above the table, flickered. After taking a sip of water, the captain regarded each of his men as they entered, the younger ones rubbing sleep from their eyes. The doctor and the officers on watch were not in attendance.

'Come in, gentlemen. Quickly, if you will, and be seated.'

'Thank you, Casson,' Oliver said and waited for the door to be closed. Only then did he address the company. 'I am sure, by now, you have heard something of the events that occurred on deck only a few hours ago.' Without waiting for their confirmation, he briefly outlined the facts surrounding the boy's return and related, in detail, the information he had uncovered about the situation existing aboard HMS *Stalwart*.

The startling revelations were greeted with shock and disbelief. In response to the officers' indignation, the captain invited them to offer their ideas as to the best course of action that should be taken. The discussion was heated and brought a raft of alternative proposals. The captain held his counsel until the others had spoken.

'We could reduce the enemy's firepower by sinking the French frigate or setting fire to it,' Mr Tully suggested.

'How could that be achieved?' Oliver queried. 'We would first have to get men aboard.'

'They can swim like the boy did and lay charges.'

The sailing master was not impressed. 'Last evening, the sea was flat calm and there was no wind.'

'Exactly as it is at the present,' Oliver exclaimed and turned to Mr Parry for his opinion but having once lost a ship under his command, resulting in the deaths of many good men, the first officer was reluctant to commit to the argument but offered an observation. 'Fire is our worst enemy at sea. It quickly gets out of hand and if it reaches the magazine the consequences are catastrophic. We would gain nothing by taking such action.'

'I agree, Simon,' Oliver said. 'It would be foolish to scuttle a good ship.'

The pair of midshipmen boldly suggested launching a surprise attack on both the 74 and the frigate. They argued that although the King's officers might be under lock and key there would be plenty of other hands on the ship loyal to the Crown. They argued that the *Perpetuals* who had been left to man the French frigate would stand and fight.

'But are they free or are they being held prisoner as the boy suggested?' Oliver asked.

The argument against a surprise attack was a matter of numbers. There were well over four hundred British sailors and more than one hundred Frenchmen across the water. Of the several hundred British sailors serving aboard *Stalwart*, it was not known how many were in league with the French captain or the Irish rebels. Furthermore, on boarding the 74, how could they distinguish between the different groups? Englishmen and Irishmen looked the same. Ginger hair and green eyes might indicate Celtic blood but that did not automatically mark those men as being mutineers.

The youngest midshipman, Mr Hanson, timidly suggested sailing to Kingston and leaving the shipload of Irish rebels and French sailors to sort out their own differences. The idea had some merit. If *Perpetual* sailed to Kingston and returned with a convoy of ships to retake the 74, the problem could be resolved. But, the captain argued, there was no guarantee of finding fighting ships of the Royal Navy in that port willing or able to assist. Another alternative was to sail to Portsmouth for help. But England was half a world away and any assistance could take months to arrive by which time *Stalwart* and the frigate could have made port anywhere in Europe or even sailed north to America and offered their services to the Yankees.

Mr Tully took the view that a stealthy attack on the 74 at night, launched from boats by a boarding party armed with cutlasses, knives and pikes, could disable some of the crew. In a short period of time, they could do significant damage to the ship's running rigging and rudder and temporarily disable the vessel. With his fervour fired up, the lieutenant and several of the others were eager to jump into a boat that very moment and head across the water.

The problem confronting Mr Tully's enthusiastic operation was the likelihood of being seen. A daylight attack was impossible and, even at night, moonlight would not hide a boat loaded with sailors and marines. If not spotted by the lookouts, the splash of a blade or grind of an oar in a thole pin would announce their presence.

Oliver looked to his officers to judge their reactions. The facial expressions varied from disbelief to thrill to abject fear.

'The boy said the French prisoners had been released from *Flambeau*'s hold and indicated our men have now taken their places beneath battened hatches.'

'Surely our mates would have put up a fight. I cannot imagine them surrendering quietly. Wasn't this exchange of men seen or heard by our lookouts?' Mr Parry asked.

The two youngest midshipmen glanced guiltily at each other.

Oliver pounced. 'You saw something and didn't report it?'

'We heard a disturbance,' Mr Hanson said reluctantly. 'And saw movement on the 74's deck and a boat ferrying back and forth to the French frigate.'

'And you thought nothing unusual in that?' the captain growled.

The pair did not admit to what they had thought.

Oliver glared at them. 'I will speak with you two later.'

Turning from the midshipmen, he addressed his senior officers. 'I intend to question the boy again,' he said. 'I need to find out if Captain Liversedge had any indication of a conspiracy brewing before this happened. I trust we do not have any such mutinous rumblings among our foremast Jacks?'

Simon Parry shook his head. 'There was some discontent before we made Rio, but presently all is well.'

He turned to Mr Tully. 'The men converse with you quite freely. Has there been any worrying tittle-tattle in the fo'c'sle?'

The second officer shook his head. 'The men are pleased to be heading home, and apart from the heat, the lack of wind and being becalmed, there has been nothing for them to grumble over. When we were about to leave Rio, their tongues wagged about the barrels sent over to the third rate. Any mention of treasure soon sparks murmurs. But since we sailed, the whispers have ceased.'

'The damned treasure comes back to haunt us,' Oliver sighed. 'I had not given any consideration to that. Perhaps that is another reason the 74 was taken. Would the French have known about the treasure chests?'

'If they didn't know before they took the ship, I imagine they do now,' Mr Parry commented.

Oliver looked out through the windows spanning the width of the cabin. The sea was as smooth as quicksilver but warmed to the colour of amber. There was not a cloud on the horizon and the deck beneath his feet had no inclination to sway. Mr Mundy had warned him that these conditions could persist for days.

The sailing master interrupted. 'Where do you think the 74 will be heading?' he asked.

'That depends on who has command. If it is Captain Moncousu, then I would suggest Martinique or one of the French islands of the West Indies. However, he may choose to head across the Atlantic taking the third rate as his prize and make for Brest or Toulon or any other port on the French coast. If, on the other hand, Irish rebels have taken the ship, they will make for a secluded harbour on the west coast of Ireland – or possibly head for Cork where they will find sympathisers.'

Mr Mundy was scornful. 'The Irish uprising was quashed in '98, yet here we are, seven years later, talking of rebels and sympathisers.'

Oliver recounted the words Dr Whipple had spoken when they first discussed the Irish situation. *Once a rebel, always a rebel.* In the doctor's opinion, the Irish had long memories. At the height of the Irish uprising, they had waited in vain for a promised French force of forty ships carrying forty thousand troops to support their cause, but that had never arrived. Two navy ships – with only sailors and a handful of soldiers and marines aboard – did not make an invasion force.

'I must speak with the doctor to gain some insight into the temperament of this rebel crew. And as an Irish-born gentleman, I need to know where his loyalty lies.'

'I beg you tread carefully,' Simon advised quietly. 'Loyalty is a sensitive issue in Ireland which many men prefer not to commit to.'

'I will tread as carefully as I deem necessary,' Oliver replied, unable to curb his exasperation.

'Ah, but with a cache of Spanish silver beneath their feet,' the sailing master reminded.

'What in tarnation has that to do with our situation?' Oliver growled across the table. 'Let me be clear, we must do nothing to provoke an attack on *Perpetual* and, for now, whatever course the 74 charts, we will escort her according to the orders I received from the Admiralty.'

The officers agreed.

'In the meantime, gentlemen, consider the problem and let us reconvene here at noon.'

Before he left, Mr Tully had a final question. 'What of the signal I was to send this morning?'

'Belay that message,' Oliver said. 'I now know why Captain Liversedge did not respond. However, when it is daylight, send the following signal: Awaiting sailing orders. Advise.'

The lieutenant acknowledged the request.

'It will be interesting to see if we receive a reply and what the response is.'

The early morning meeting with his men had raised new questions in Oliver's mind and made him more anxious than ever to return to the cockpit. It was frustrating that the only person he could question was a ten-year-old boy. Respecting the doctor's wishes, he allowed time for the lad to eat, rest and refresh himself.

The events the youngster had related were extraordinary, yet Oliver Quintrell had no reason to doubt the boy's veracity. What the lad had done had been incredibly brave yet doubly unwise and extremely foolish. So many factors could have led to his failure, and failure would have resulted in only one thing – death. However, working entirely alone, Charles Goodridge had succeeded in bringing the unwelcome news across the water. Oliver now needed more information before he could act.

On returning to the cockpit Oliver found the boy sitting with the doctor, both eating bowls of porridge. After offering the captain his chair, Dr Whipple politely offered to leave them to talk privately but, this time, Oliver invited the doctor to stay.

After listening to the boy recounting the events of the previous night, Oliver was satisfied his story had not wavered. But he was still puzzled over what had happened aboard the 74 and how command of the ship had been taken from Captain Liversedge. Usually, he had little time for sailors' tall tales but in this instance, knowing the boy's inquisitive nature, his keen intuition and eye for detail, he hung on every word he uttered.

'Before this happened, did you notice anything unusual?'

Charles thought for a moment. 'There was a lot of whispering among the men.'

'Did you hear what they were speaking about?'

'I tried,' Charles said, 'but it sounded like Chinese to me. One of the other boys said that was how the Irish talked.'

'Irish – Gaelic?' the doctor offered, exchanging glances with the captain.

'They never bothered you?' Oliver asked the boy.

'They were too busy collecting names and having each man make his mark or sign on a sheet of paper.'

'Sounds reminiscent of the days of the rebellion,' Jonathon Whipple commented.

'Is there anything else you can tell me,' Oliver asked.

Charles swallowed the last mouthful of porridge and thought for a moment.

'On the day I was in the middies' berth and Captain Liversedge was brought down, I heard the tall fellow called Murphy boasting to his mates. He said he had the Frenchman in his pocket and that if they trusted him, he would have them back home in Ireland in no time.'

Oliver was astounded. 'How on earth does a lubber like Murphy take control of a 74 and manage to have the French captain wrapped around his little finger.' Though the opinion he had formed of Captain Moncousu was poor, it did not detract from the enormity of the situation. It was worse than Oliver had imagined. 'It makes no sense at all,' he sighed. 'And throughout all this you heard nothing unusual?' he asked young Charles.

'There was some shouting but there were no shots fired.'

'You were not held or injured in any way?' the doctor asked.

'No one was interested in me or the other ship's boys except when we were needed for fetching meals and running errands. The rest of the time we were free to go almost anywhere in the ship. I wanted to go to where Mrs Pilkington and Mrs Crosby were being held.'

The doctor looked anxious and was about to speak but allowed the boy to continue.

'Trouble was, there were guards posted on the companionways and I couldn't get through to the aft cabins. I didn't know what to do or who to talk to, so after thinking on it for a while, I decided to swim over and tell you.'

'How grateful I am that you came to that decision,' Oliver said.

Wood shavings curled from the plane as it was driven along a length of cedar, a pin hammer tapped a repetitive tune and the saw's teeth rasped as it bit into a length of knotted wood. They were familiar sounds in the carpenter's workshop but when Charles Goodridge entered the lantern-lit workshop, it felt empty.

Hopping up onto the lid of the sawdust barrel, he looked around. The narrow space against the central bulwark, where Mrs Crosby and Mrs Pilkington had slung their hammocks, had been dismantled after the women had been transferred. It had never been a real cabin – not even a substantial structure – but merely a quickly erected frame with sacking curtains draped around it to create an area long enough for the women to sleep in. The space had now been taken up with a pile of sawn timber and several cases of nails heaped on top of each other. Absent too were Mr Crosby and three of the most experienced shipwrights. Along with them, the air of congenial banter that usually bounced back and forth across the workbenches throughout the day was missing.

This morning the workshop was occupied by two of the carpenter's mates and an apprentice. Though they were performing their duties in a regular fashion, not a word was being exchanged until Charles interrupted them.

Fred Purvis, the oldest tradesman on board, looked up. 'Watch out,' he said in a broad accent, 'Here comes trouble.' The others stopped and looked up in surprise.

A voice called out: 'I thought you was across on the 74.'

'He was. What's up?' Fred demanded. 'Has Mr Crosby come back? Where is he?'

Charles shook his head.

'Well, don't keep us in the dark,' the Yorkshireman continued. 'How come you're back? Spit it out, lad.'

'It's a big mess over there,' Charles said.

'What d'ya mean?' Fred asked.

'The Frogs have taken over the 74 and Mr Crosby and his mates are prisoners.'

Fred dropped his plane and moved around the bench to where Charles was sitting. 'That's not possible. How do you know?'

'I know. I was there. I heard talk. Then at night, I slipped overboard and swam back here.'

'God's truth?' Fred said, while the others gathered around the boy to hear his full story.

'I want to know what we can do,' Charles said. 'How can we get Mr Crosby and the others back?'

'Egad and little fishes, that's a fancy pickle,' Fred said.

'Does Captain Quintrell know?'

Charles nodded. 'He was as surprised as you lot when I told him.'

'What of Mrs Crosby and Mrs P? How are they faring?'

Charles couldn't answer as he didn't know. He was worried and wondered if perhaps he shouldn't have left in such a hurry.

'Have a word in Bungs's ear,' Fred said. 'He likes having something to chew on. Besides, he's been around a long time and knows a thing or too.'

Charles screwed his nose. 'Me and Bungs don't get on too well of late.'

'Don't worry,' the carpenter said, 'Bungs don't get on with everyone at times – or so he says. Go tell him what's going on and ask what he thinks. It'll give him something to mull over and, you never know, he might come up with an idea.'

At noon, Charles joined Bungs, Eku and young Tommy Wainwright at the mess table. Eager to hear what the boy had to say, the men on the nearby tables gathered around to listen to the lad's story first hand. For fifteen minutes, all ears were glued on Charles Goodridge.

'The Frogs and the Irish have got together and taken control of the 74 and the prize, and the rest of our men have been locked in the hold.'

'Well I'll be darned,' Bungs exclaimed.

'But there are hundreds of men on those two ships,' Smithers called from the next table.

Charles nodded. 'I heard tell that a third of them are French, another third are Irish and the rest are regular hands like us. Then there's the officers, of course, but they don't count for much.'

'Fine kettle of fish,' Bungs said, scratching his bristly crown. 'A length of slowmatch in a barrel of gunpowder would quickly solve that problem.'

Ekundayo turned to the lad. 'If you want to swim back and pass a message that help's on the way, I'll swim with you.'

'Me too,' one of the hands from another table added. 'I can swim good.'

'I suggested that idea to Mr Tully but he said Captain Quintrell wouldn't hear of it. He said I'd likely be spotted in the water and shot.'

'No one will see my black pate in the water at night,' Ekundayo added.

'Too right,' Will Ethridge said. 'But what could the pair of you possibly do on your own?'

'Who knows?' Bungs asked. 'Anything is better than sitting here on your arses doing nothing. I reckon you should go direct to Captain Quintrell. Forget the lieutenants. Trust me, the captain'll listen.'

As soon as they had finished eating and before the bell sounded for them to go on watch, the Negro and the boy headed to the captain's cabin.

'Begging you pardon, Captain.'

'What it is Casson?'

The steward stood in the cabin doorway. 'There are two sailors here asking to speak with you. They say it is urgent and you will want to hear what they have to say. One is that imp of a lad, Charles Goodridge.'

'Send them in and kindly shut the door.'

Ekundayo looked uncomfortable as he bowed his head to the deck beams. 'Begging your pardon, Captain but young Charlie, here, and me's been talking about what the lad said was happening over on the third rate.'

Oliver looked questioningly at the pair. 'Continue.'

'The lad wants to go back and I volunteer to go back with him,'

'I have already considered the idea and said it is out of the question.'

Charles Goodridge didn't wait to be asked for his opinion. 'But I'm the only one who could climb aboard and go about the decks and no one would question me. They've all seen me running around the ship and I've spoken with many of them. You know me, Captain always asking what's what and why and wherefore.'

'And I guarantee, if I was seen,' Eku said, 'no one would question me either. There are several blacks on the third rate and a handful on the French ship and the officers claim we all look the same.'

Without being drawn into that aspect of the argument, Oliver admitted the pair presented a good case. Most other sailors from *Perpetual* showing their faces aboard the third rate would be stopped and questioned and any plans the captain had set in motion would fall in a hole. He thought about the proposition for a while. 'Do you think you can swim to the 74 and get aboard without being seen?'

'Yes, Captain,' the unlikely pair replied in unison.

'If both wind and weather were in your favour, how would you get aboard?'

Eku was quick to reply. 'We'd climb up between the preventer chain and the rudder to the great cabin and get in there. One of the stern windows is bound to be open.'

Oliver turned to the lad. 'Was there a guard posted in that cabin?'

'There were two outside. I saw them,' Charles said. 'But we shall climb inside.'

'And what then?'

'We would help the officers escape. And swim back with them.'

'What if they cannot swim,' Oliver asked. 'Very few officers swim well, and it is quite a distance between the ships.'

The pair looked dejected.

'I admire your spirit and enthusiasm,' Oliver said, 'but you said yourself the captain and his men had been confined in the midshipmen's quarters. Therefore, I presume when Moncousu took command he claimed the great cabin for himself. It would be foolish to enter the ship from that point.' Oliver stood and paced the cabin. 'At the moment, I am unsure what course of action to take without jeopardising the lives of everyone aboard those two vessels across the water. I believe it would be impossible to take a boat across without being seen. I note your idea but, for now, your suggestion must be shelved.'

'But the boy did it,' Eku insisted.

'Indeed, he did and I applaud his bravery,' Oliver said, 'but on flat calm water, with no wind and under a black night sky. While this unnatural calm persists for the present, and at this latitude has been known to last for weeks, we cannot guarantee the conditions will last until tomorrow. The barometer indicates a change is coming and if a squall blows up, we will be lucky if the ships can stay within sight of each other. Swimming or even taking a boat across will be impossible. Now, return to your watch and don't do anything foolhardy. If I need your help, I will call on you.'

Disappointed, the pair turned. The Negro touched his black knuckles to his temple and, with a gentle shove in the back with the flat of his hand, prompted the boy to move out.

Chapter 13

The Plan

As arranged earlier, the officers reconvened in the great cabin. This time the doctor joined them. When invited to speak first, he expressed his concerns for the two women who had been transferred on the pretext the 74 was a safer environment. Oliver showed little concern.

'Do you have no care as to what becomes of them?' the doctor demanded.

'Sir, I am fully aware of the situation. According to Captain Liversedge, the 74 has several women aboard, including the two females transferred from this ship but, at this moment, they are of little interest to me. What concerns me is the fate of a senior post captain, his officers and five hundred men who make up his crew, not to mention the fate of members of my own command aboard *Flambeau*. These matters are foremost in my mind and I will beg you not to burden me with trivia.'

Dr Whipple shifted uncomfortably. He had no recourse. His thoughts were for the welfare of Mrs Crosby and Connie Pilkington.

Oliver shuffled in his seat, flicked a moth from the table and mellowed. 'Although the French Captain may use deceit and lies against his enemies, I believe, from the cut of his cloth, that Captain Moncousu is of noble birth and therefore, I envisage no harm coming to the womenfolk while he is in command. However, an unruly mob of irate Irishmen are more of a worry.

'I pray you are right on that score,' the doctor said.

Despite the slightly tense atmosphere, Dr Whipple continued. He volunteered to go to the 74 alone if a boat could be made available to him. By that means, he argued that he would be able to assess the situation and return with news. He also stated that he would attempt to pass word to Captain Liversedge advising him that *Perpetual* was aware of his plight and assuring him that help would soon be at hand.

The plan was audacious and was quickly shouted down. Everyone agreed that as soon as the doctor stepped aboard the 74 he would be restrained. Furthermore, if the true investigative nature of his visit was uncovered, his life would be in danger. Either way, he would not be returning to the frigate and no one would be any wiser about the situation aboard the third rate or the fate of those being held prisoner.

Oliver had no intention of putting the doctor's life at risk. 'There are many sea miles ahead of us before we reach the West Indies,' he advised. 'If, however, we can take back the French frigate, we will reduce the odds against us. Then, with two frigates we can consider making our move against the 74.' He looked around for objections. He received none. 'What choice do we have other than turning our backs on our fellow officers and heading to Jamaica as Mr Hanson suggested?'

The answer was a resounding *No!*'

'Gentlemen, at least we are agreed on one score. We must fight to regain control of both ships. We have the lives of those aboard the 74 to consider and if we do not act soon the opportunity will be lost. The boy proved it is possible to swim across the water. But sending one boy or even one man would serve no purpose. To achieve any degree of success it will require at least a dozen armed men.'

There were nods and murmurs of agreement.

'I propose that a dozen volunteers shall swim across the pond and board *Flambeau*. This must be executed with extreme stealth and caution. My plan has various facets. The first is to board the frigate and separate the two ships by cutting the tow line uniting them. Currently, as the hulls are sitting on a millpond, I presume the hawser has dropped well beneath the surface. If a swimmer can dive underwater, he can cut through the cable from below the waterline without being seen by the lookouts.'

'Wouldn't it be easier for someone to climb aboard and unhitch the line?'

'I agree, but that man would be spotted on the deck by the French sailors on watch. Severing the cable will not be easy. It is the thickness of a man's wrist. And the sailor chosen will need to be a strong swimmer, carry a sharp blade and keep his head down so as not to be seen. Once the rope is cut through, if a breeze of wind arrives or if the swell or current stirs beneath its keel, the French frigate will drift free of the 74, hopefully without anyone taking immediate notice of it.

'Secondly, if a dozen good swimmers can make it across the water undetected, their task will be to climb aboard, dispatch the sentries and sailors on watch without making any noise then release our men from the hold.'

The sailing master shook his head. 'That is not possible.'

'Might I ask why?'

'The slightest squeak out of just one man, a knife or musket dropped on the deck, any unusual noise would echo in the darkness and the cries of pain or alarm would carry across to the 74 and alert them. Consider, also, when the mob of *Perpetual*s are released from the hold – they are not going to emerge in silence and any sounds they make will carry and the 74 will know the ship has been boarded.'

'I don't agree,' Mr Tully said. 'Those aboard the 74 won't give a thought to that happening on the French frigate.'

'Be that as it may,' Oliver said. 'We must first get men aboard.'

'But who is capable of swimming for half a mile?' Mr Mundy asked, doubting any response.

'I, for one, can,' the captain admitted, 'and I intend to go.' Being aware his first lieutenant was not a swimmer, he added, 'Mr Parry, you must stay and take command of *Perpetual* in my absence. I want no one to volunteer who will be begging for help because he's in danger of drowning.'

'Who'll go with you?' the sailing master asked.

'I know of several men aboard who are strong swimmers,' Oliver said. 'William Ethridge can swim. He repaired the hull at the horseshoe island when it was damaged in the Southern Ocean. And the Negro can swim also. He spent hours in the water when we launched the diving bell off the coast of Peru. And we still have a couple of lascars aboard – pearl divers.'

'I swim like a kedge anchor,' Mr Mundy announced but the captain was not amused.

'I swim like a fish,' Mr Tully said. 'I'll go along and I know half a dozen other men who will go with me.'

'Good. That is settled. Speak to them immediately. This calm will not last and, when the weather gods decide to breathe again, any chance we have of boarding in this manner will be lost.'

'It will not be easy,' the captain reminded, 'and every man must carry a cutlass and knife. Pistols are too heavy, too noisy and the powder will get wet.'

'I have another suggestion,' the sailing master said. 'If a sailor climbed through an open gunport onto the lower gundeck, and had a pocket full of large nails, he could spike the guns and render them useless.'

'That would be impossible without being seen or heard,' Mr Parry contended. 'Apart from that, the gunports will be tightly fastened.'

The captain agreed. As far as he was aware, the French knew nothing of the boy's adventure or that word of what had transpired on the 74 had reached *Perpetual*. He thought it unlikely they would open fire on the British frigate.

Feeling reasonably satisfied with the proposal he had presented, Oliver turned to his senior officer. 'Bring us to within half a chain's length of *Flambeau*, if that is possible. That will reduce the distance for the swimmers.' The danger from sharks in the tropical waters crossed his mind but he chose not to mention it. 'If we succeed in regaining the French frigate, we again make it our prize.'

That suggestion brought satisfied smiles all around.

Oliver nodded. 'First we must surprise the Frogs on night watch and dispatch them silently. Then release our men held below deck and retake control of *Flambeau*. After slipping her from the 74 we will have evened up the metal – a 32- and a 38-gun frigate against a 74-gunner.'

The idea met with almost everyone's approval. 'Are you going to attack the British warship, Captain?' the wide-eyed midshipman asked.

'She is no longer British, Mr Hanson. She has been captured and is being commanded by a French captain or a group of Irishmen and is therefore an enemy of His Majesty. My aim is to win her back and return her to Captain Liversedge.'

A sound of feet tapping rattled around the cabin. Oliver held up his hand. 'Hush, gentlemen. Sound carries easily on the sea.' Then he turned to Mr Tully. 'Gather your volunteers together and bring them here. I do not want to discuss this matter on deck.' Then he addressed the other officers. 'Advise your divisions to be silent but to be alert and remain at their stations. Hopefully, if all goes well and the French frigate drifts sufficiently, we can get it and *Perpetual* a good distance away from the 74 before they wake. As you all know, a third rate ship of the line is neither as fast nor or as manoeuvrable as a frigate, so if a wind blows up, we will have a distinct advantage.'

'But she has bigger guns than ours,' the youngest midshipman added.

'Thank you, Mr Hanson. That is why we need to drop back and stay out of range of her stern chasers.'

'When do you intend to put these plans into place?' Mr Mundy asked.

'This evening. Before the moon rises.'

The murmur of agreement rose to a clatter of voices as each man turned to the man next to him and shared his views. The doctor, seated next to the captain, took the opportunity to speak privately.

'A word in your ear, Captain,' the doctor said. 'Regarding the Irishmen aboard those ships: are you aware of the enemy you are about to confront? I doubt you witnessed the fighting in Ireland in '98 or before that?'

Oliver admitted he did not.

The doctor's expression was grave. 'It was fighting like you have never seen before. Men fought with pikes and sticks, fence posts and sharpened plough blades – killing, maiming and burning everything before them. They fought like men possessed with the Devil at their heels. I heard accounts of those who died stating that their wounds were more horrific than those I would have witnessed on the corpses brought in from the backstreets of the London Boroughs. Throats cut. Eyes gouged out. Disembowelled. I warn you, Oliver, the spirit and commitment in the Irish heart cannot be dowsed no matter what you do. I only hope you are not facing that sort of fight when the enemy is stirred.'

'Thank you, Jonathon. We will be ready,' he said, turning his attention back to the assembly and raising his voice. 'Let me remind you all – we are fighting for King and country and whatever the colour or design of the flag raised against us, we will cut it down.'

His words drew cheers from the group.

'Gentlemen, let us save our ship, reclaim our prize and fight with our last breath to wrest the 74 from the hands of the enemy.'

The low rumble of commitment echoed around the cabin.

'I take it we are resolved?'

Oliver glanced to the cabin window. 'There is no time to waste. In a few hours, the sun will be down and darkness will be upon us. When the moon rises, I expect the sea to shine like quicksilver and anything seen floating on the surface will be a target. Time is of the essence. I pray those clouds gathering in the east are not the harbingers of a sudden squall. Remember, we do not want to alert the watches on either the frigate or the 74, so there will be no boats lowered and no grappling irons tossed over the rails.'

'It is a daring scheme, Oliver,' Simon Parry said. 'Do you believe it will work? You are sending only a handful of men against hundreds of sailors, soldiers and marines aboard the 74.'

'I have faith in my men. Besides, there will only be small number of men aboard the French ship and they will not be expecting an attack. Aside from that, what is the alternative? Do we turn our backs and sail away and allow the French to keep our fighting ships as their prizes?'

With no more suggestions or questions, Oliver concluded. 'I have put great faith in the boy's story. I pray to God he has spoken the truth.'

When the sun had gone down, night drew in rapidly blanketing everything in darkness. The moon was not due to rise until nine o'clock.

Taking a final look over the pond of water stretching between the ships, Oliver contemplated his plan and considered the many dangers that lay ahead. Gazing at the ebony water while listening to the soft hand-clapping of the wavelets teasing the hull, his attention was drawn to a pale brown mass of tangles. It floated by no more than a dozen yards from the ship's side. At first glance, it resembled a mop of unkempt ginger hair and he mistook it for the head of a swimmer. Strolling along the deck, he observed its slow passage and kept pace with it until it reached the stern and gently drifted away. Very quickly he had realised it was merely a bunch of seaweed – the type that grows on the surface in this region of the world's oceans. Yet not one of the lookouts at the mastheads had noticed it, nor had any of the sailors reclining against the bulwark rails. The fact it had drifted by unobserved convinced the captain his plan would succeed.

Having attended to the requirements of the men preparing to swim, Mr Parry had the deck, and following the plan he and the captain had discussed, he ordered the helmsman to steer closer to the French frigate. While there was no wind he had to rely on the helm to gain some response from the swell plus occasional drafts of light air. In answer to the rudder, the frigate drifted across very slowly.

Sitting on deck leaning their backs against the bulwarks, the volunteers had waited for the final remnants of day to fade and the sky to assume the colour of charcoal. Not a word was spoken. The sailors and officers had their instructions and knew what was expected of them. The last pair to join them was Charles Goodridge and Ekundayo. Having reconsidered the request put to him, the captain had conceded the pair had attributes that could be put to good use.

When the order to embark on the mission was given, the men climbed down the rope ladder and slid silently into the water on *Perpetual*'s larboard side so they were hidden from the view of lookouts on either of the other ships. Holding onto the handlines or treading water, fifteen swimmers waited until a large canvas sack had been lowered to them. In it were cutlasses, knives and hangers. Each man took a pair of weapons. There were no pistols or muskets.

When Captain Quintrell gave the signal, one-by-one each swimmer relinquished his grip and swam around *Perpetual*'s stern. Being in the low latitudes of the tropics, the sea was not cold. Silently and seemingly effortlessly, the volunteers, including the captain, spread out across the water and headed toward *Flambeau* not more than one hundred yards away. The 74 stood motionless a further hundred yards ahead of that, the heavy hawser, uniting the pair, submerged in the waters between.

Though the men had been told there was no sea running, there was a slight pull from the Equatorial Current as it flowed north but the men were swimming across it so it had little effect.

The progress of the swimmers was observed discretely from lookouts in *Perpetual*'s rigging, together with topmen on the yardarms and Mr Parry and the other officers on the quarterdeck. Familiar with how clearly sound carried over water, those on deck were under strict instructions not to shout encouragement or make any sounds that would draw attention to the men in the ocean.

Swimming across the pond towards *Flambeau*, the heads glided with the ease of a barge hauled by a boat-horse along the still waters of a canal. Every stroke drew them closer to the French frigate.

In the west, the last vestiges of day had been obliterated by dark clouds piling up on the ocean's rim.

'That will give the men better cover,' the midshipman commented quietly to the helmsman in an attempt to sound positive. But the helmsman was wary. He knew what a sudden change in the weather could mean.

Having overheard the conversation, Mr Parry echoed a similar view. 'If those clouds deliver rain, they will also bring wind. And if the wind arrives before the men reach the ship, all three vessels will drift. Retrieving the swimmers will be nigh on impossible. If the wind arrives after the cable is cut, once the order is given to set sails, the 74 will immediately notice the Frenchie is no longer trailing behind it. Who knows what will happen then?'

The young man looked from the leaden sky to the heads bobbing in the sea. 'Pray to God they make it,' he said.

'Have faith,' Mr Parry replied. 'The rain is not yet upon us and there is no wind. The men have already made half the distance. Now they are faced with boarding and taking the sailors on deck without alerting anyone.'

'Is that possible?'

'The captain believes it is, and I have faith in his judgement.'

Kicking noiselessly, the group closed on the French frigate. When they reached the hull, Oliver tapped the Negro on his shoulder. 'Wait here and mind the boy.'

Eku nodded. The mismatched pair was aware of what had been asked of them and swam around to the plaited cable and waited there each with one hand resting on the heavy hawser. They were to await word that the boarding party had been successful in taking the ship before they headed across to the third rate.

The sounds that followed came from the deck. There were several dull thuds, a faint smothered gurgling cry, a rasping growl and suddenly a high-pitched squealing miaou from the ship's cat. Having been curled up sleeping in the scuppers, the black feline had been invisible in the darkness. Unfortunately its tail lay directly under the feet of one of the boarders when he dropped onto the bow. The screech the animal let out was enough to raise the dead and carried across the water to the other two ships. Heads popped up, sailors turned and stared. Questioning voices were heard. Everyone froze.

From the waterline, Eku cried clearly and loudly, '*C'est le chat*!'

For a long moment, everyone held their breath fearing a rush of crew onto the deck or voices hailing from the 74 to know what was happening. But the spontaneous explanation served its purpose and, with no further interest excited by the ear-piercing sound, everyone resumed what they had been doing.

To the half a dozen French sailors and couple of soldiers on the French frigate's forecastle, the sudden appearance of men tumbling over the rail was totally unexpected. One of the soldiers picked up his musket from the deck, but before he could level it and pull the trigger, it was snatched from his hand, drawn across his throat and held tight until his windpipe was crushed and his legs collapsed beneath him. A sailor sleeping against the pin rail received a fatal puncture from a hanger in the centre of his chest. His mouth fell open before he had even opened his eyes. Mr Tully leapt on the back of a French sailor who in turn tried to swing the lieutenant off him. When a cutlass blade sliced across his opponent's calves, he dropped then gurgled after the same blade sliced across his throat. As other French sailors climbed out of the hatch, they were dropped on the deck and silenced.

With more than a dozen men dispatched, Captain Quintrell waited for a frenzied response from below, but none came. So far his plan was going well. With two of his crew left to dispose of the bodies and three more to go aft, Oliver lead the others down through the forward hatch to the mess where another group of young French sailors was relaxing.

Without weapons and lacking courage, they were quick to surrender. Mr Tully then conducted a search of the other decks rounding up several more surprised French soldiers and seamen. Heading deeper into the ship, the captain located the locked grating beneath which his own men had been secured. He was pleased to learn that Mr Nightingale and the prize crew, plus Mr Crosby and all his men were safe and in good health. There was an immediate outburst of jubilations from the men when they realised they were to be released. The captain quickly stifled the noise.

While two of his sailors searched for an axe or crowbar to free those in the hold, the captain addressed his men through the holes in the grating telling them what was afoot and advising what he expected of them. A marlinspike was used to lever the lock from the hatch coaming and the men were pulled out one by one. They immediately headed to the weather deck with the instruction to stay silent. All that remained for the boarders to attend to was to round up the remaining Frenchies from within the ship, push them down into the hold, secure the hatch cover and station a pair of armed guards over them.

Confident *Flambeau* was now in British hands, a signal was passed to the two swimmers, Ekundayo and Charlie Goodridge, waiting in the water. They had been assured by the captain that the cable would remain in place until they returned. If all went well a new hawser would be floated over to *Perpetual* so she could again take on the task of towing the French prize. Much was dependant on a breath of wind blowing up during the night lifting the two frigates' sails sufficiently to carry them away from the third rate before they were missed.

With the French sailors locked up once again below deck, the *Perpetual*s were divided into two watches to man the prize frigate. Sailing would not be easy as repair to the rudder had not yet been completed. Mr Crosby assured the captain that he and his mates would stay aboard and continue the work to ensure the prize was made seaworthy.

Chapter 14

Mischief aboard the 74

Having received the long-awaited signal that all had gone ahead as planned, Charles and Ekundayo swam slowly along the tow cable attached to the 74. Cautiously and slowly, their hands loosely cupping the heavy hawser, they pulled themselves along it. With no waves to contend with, the pair glided silently in the darkness. As they neared the stern of the warship, they dived beneath the surface and swam alongside the submerged rope coming up only once to take a breath. With the moon not due to rise until later that evening and the sea and sky as black as coal, it was unlikely they would be seen.

Ahead of them, the hull of the British warship rose up from the water like an overhanging cliff face. Standing as motionlessly as one of the prison hulks set in the silt of Portsmouth Harbour, the 74's hull was equally as daunting. Apart from the stern lights, a yellow glow streamed from the windows of the great cabin and from the smaller windows of the cabin below it. Several were open. Above the windows, painted in large letters and embellished in gold, was the ship's name: STALWART.

When the pair was within a few feet of the rudder, Eku beckoned Charles to follow him to the larboard side. If they climbed the preventer chain attached to the rudder, as they had originally planned, there was a chance they would be seen from the great cabin and, for the present, it was not known who was occupying it.

With little choice available, the pair kicked for the steps leading to the entry port. Their hope was that no one would see them climbing aboard – a concern they had spoken of with Captain Quintrell. The Negro's wet skin, being the colour of polished jet, was disguise in itself but there was nothing to hide the pale pink hide of the ten-year-old boy.

Eku climbed first with Charles at his heels. When he reached the gangway, he glanced forward and aft to check all was clear then reached down, grabbed the boy's hand and hoisted him bodily onto the deck. The couple stood motionless for a moment, the water running down their legs pooling on the planks then, without a word, Ekundayo tiptoed forward, through the darkness, staying close to the rail. Charles followed one stride behind. The line of wet footprints quickly dried on the warm deck.

'Hey,' a voice called out sharply.

The pair froze, turned and leaned nonchalantly against the bulwark.

'Is this your watch?' the voice asked.

'No, Massa. Just came up for a breath of air. Mighty hot below,' Eku replied with his best plantation accent.

'Well, you ain't got no business here. Get below and don't let me see you on deck 'til you hear the bell.'

'Yessa, Massa,' Eku replied, putting his hand on Charles's shoulder and shepherding him toward the main hatch. As he had served on a ship of the line, and as the boy from Gibraltar had spent a short time aboard *Stalwart*, finding their way around the third rate was not a problem for either of them.

Captain Quintrell had eventually conceded that the boy had a good chance of getting aboard the third rate without attracting attention. Plus, with his inquisitive eye he would be more observant than most other sailors. But the captain had refused to allow Charles to go alone and Ekundayo was a good choice to accompany him. Apart from being educated and alert, the Negro was strong and almost twice the size and strength of the average able seaman.

The job the pair had been charged with was to check the situation that existed on the gun decks and to report back on what they saw. The captain was anxious to know if the guns were being manned throughout the night and, if so, by how many gun crews. It was also important to learn if the guns were ready for action, but more importantly, who was in command of the ship?

Before leaving *Perpetual*, he had warned the pair not to do anything foolhardy or dangerous and, above all, to avoid getting caught. They were ordered not to venture any further than the gun decks and when they had completed their reconnoitre they were not to dilly-dally before slipping into the water and swimming back to join the others.

Oliver's concern was that if his plan to take the French frigate failed and his men were discovered, the 74 would immediately turn its guns on *Perpetual* and a single broadside could blow it to matchwood.

During the time they had spent in the water waiting for the boarders to take the frigate, Ekundayo and Charles Goodridge had occupied their time conceiving a plan of their own.

'We'll start on the lower gundeck,' Eku said.

Charles remembered what the captain had told him. He was to follow the Negro's orders and not argue or ask questions. 'Aye aye,' he whispered.

While the weatherdeck had been black and silent, as they descended to the upper gun deck, the flood of light from the lanterns and rumble of voices were unexpected and unnerving to the lad. Apart from the refit crews, the warships he had roamed over in the Gibraltar dockyard had all been empty – the only sounds being those of hammers, chisels and saws. Ekundayo, however, was more familiar with the gundeck sounds and the congestion.

Apart from the blast of noise that greeted the pair, there was a near-suffocating smell that met them. It was heavy with sweat, residual acrid powder smoke and tobacco fumes together with the glutinous odour of congealed fat burning in the slush-lamps and cooking smells drifting up from the galley. While the gundeck was almost twice as long and broad as that of *Perpetual*'s, it was impossible to see beyond the first few cannon, as hammocks belonging to the gun crews were slung from the overhead beams between each gun and groups of sailors were huddled together along the gangway throughout the full length of the deck. Some seamen were sitting on sea chests, benches, stools even half barrels. A few even straddled or lazed on the cold guns' barrels.

Charles hesitated but Eku grabbed him by the elbow and directed him to the steps leading down to the lower gun deck where they were met with a similar scene. While the sound of voices was slightly subdued, the shrill notes of a penny whistle drew an accompanying beat slapped on the side of a barrel. A chorus of voices sang in a language neither man nor boy understood. Snoring came from within some of the hammocks where some men slept, scratched, coughed and cursed.

For the pair of intruders, confronted with this scene of normal seagoing behaviour, it was difficult to believe that this was a ship of the line that had just been seized and was in enemy hands. Even Charles wondered if the story he had told Captain Quintrell was true or had been a dream. But it was the truth. With his own eyes, he had witnessed Captain Liversedge being bundled away under guard

At the bottom of the steps, the boy and man parted company and set off on their own missions.

Eku headed to the ship's starboard quarter while Charles moved to the port side and searched for a hempen sack or piece of netting. When he could find none, he grabbed a swab bucket from beside the half barrel where the mops and brushes were kept. Starting at the first gun on that side of the ship, he looked at the beam above his head where the equipment for handling the gun was hanging – a rammer, a sponge and a wormer. Hanging directly above the square of lead covering the gun's powder bowl was a curved horn and with it a short length of quill cut from a goose's feather. Charles reached up as far as he could but, even standing on his toes, he was not tall enough to grasp it. With a pained expression on his face, he called to the nearest group of sailors.

'Borrow yer stool, mister?' he asked.

'Bugger off. Find your own.' The Irish accent was very obvious.

'I only need it for five minutes. Please, mister. The gunner sent me to collect the powder horns and quills. I have to take them down to the magazine so he can check them. Then I have to fill the horns and made sure all the quills is clean.'

The man sneered. 'What sort of chore it that at this hour of the night?'

His mate, perched beside him, laughed. 'I'll wager he dropped an eight-pound shot on the gunner's toe!'

'Or spilled powder on the magazine's floor,' another suggested. They all laughed.

'Here,' the sailor said, pulling the three-legged stool from under him. 'Take this but mind you bring it back in five minutes. Any longer than that and I'll have your guts for garters, and I ain't jesting.'

'I promise,' Charles said, grabbing the stool and stepping cautiously onto it so as not to overbalance. He was thankful the deck was not swaying. Reaching up, he lifted the horn and quill from the hook in the beam. Stepping down, he placed them carefully in the swab bucket before advancing to the next gun, taking the stool with him.

At every third of fourth gun, he was cursed by the sailors and asked what he was doing. One of the gun captains argued that his horn was full and didn't need checking and said he cleaned his quill every time his gun was fired. Charles was quick to defend himself saying he had his orders and there would be hell to pay if he didn't return with the correct number of horns. Grumbling, the gunner reached up and handed the items to the boy who thanked him and moved along the deck. By the time he had reached halfway, the bucket was already heavy – wooden pails were weighty even without water or anything else in them.

When he reached the end of the gun deck, he had fourteen horns in his bucket and two under his arm. Eku was already waiting in the gloom at the end of the deck, the whites of his eyes and flash of his white teeth highlighted by the nearby lantern. Eku took the load from the boy and went straight to the end gunport.

'What you doing?' a voice boomed.

'Need to empty a pail and draw some water to swab the deck.'

'Deck was swabbed this morning and it'll be swabbed again tomorrow. It don't need no more swabbing.' The accent was definitely Irish.

'The third lieutenant said there was powder and sand in the cracks between the deck timbers and I'm to make sure every grain is scrubbed out.'

The sailor didn't argue with a punishment set by one of the lieutenants. He'd known far worse duties set at the whim of a disgruntled officer. The sailor had probably forgotten the ship's regular officers were locked away below decks. 'Get about your business and make sure you lash the gunport when you're finished. I'll be round to check it later and you'll be in trouble if you don't.'

'Yessa, Massa,' Eku replied, turning his bare back on the Irishman and winking at the boy.

With the sailor showing no more interest in what the presumed ex-slave was doing, Eku unlashed the gunport, pushed it open and fastened it securely.

Using both hands, Charles lifted the wooden pail and swung it across to his friend leaning out over the water. Quickly upending the bucket, Eku discharged its contents into the sea. There was a splash and the pair looked at each other, but the sound had not carried to the men close by. The only evidence that remained was a handful of featherless quills, resembling short straws, floating on the surface. Ignoring them, the Negro returned the bucket to the boy, closed the port lid and lashed it tightly so there would be no complaints. After nodding to his accomplice, the pair parted company again. This time, Eku headed down the ship's larboard side, while the boy crossed the deck and went about his business on the opposite side.

Armed with a bristle brush in his hand, Ekundayo collected the leather fire buckets that were hanging from the deck beams above the gun ports – one for each cannon. When asked what his business was, he said he had been told to scrub every bucket and fill it afresh with water before returning it to its position. As he worked his way along the deck, the sailors, whose games he interrupted, cursed and swore at him but, because of his powerful build, he attracted no real abuse. Having opened another gunport, he emptied each bucket of the residual water in it then returned it to its hook – empty. No one checked his work or noticed the difference.

When the pair completed the lower gundeck they reunited and moved up to the upper deck where their jobs were made more difficult by the number of sailors occupying that area.

Boosted by their convincing performances, whenever stopped and asked what they were about, they brazenly repeated their stories and succeeded in achieving the mischief they had planned. Furthermore, when Eku found guns unattended, he slipped the quoins and prickers under his arm and dispatched them to the sea through the open ports.

It took the pair a little more than half an hour to complete the work they had decided upon and to meet up again at the hatch where they had started.

'Up you go,' Eku said. The lad led the way swinging an empty bucket in his hand. Once out on the weather deck, they made for the entry port but were stopped on the gangway before they had time to climb over.

'Who goes there,' a marine officer called.

'Jem and a boy,' Eku replied. 'Come to empty the lieutenant's night-water bucket. It weren't emptied this morning.'

The marine took a step back. 'Well, make good and sure you don't spill it down the hull or you'll be out there with a brush scrubbing it off.'

'Yessa, Massa, sir.'

Satisfied, the soldier faded back into the darkness allowing the two mischief-makers to clamber down the outside steps and slip back into the sea without anyone seeing them depart.

Swimming around the ship's stern, they were careful to bear away from the lights shining from the cabin windows before heading back across the water to where the French frigate was standing. Halfway across, Eku noticed the boy was unable to keep up to his pace. Placing Charles's hand on his shoulder, he supported the lad for the remainder of the swim. After covering three-quarters of the distance, the pair located the cable floating only a few inches below the surface. Grabbing hold of it, they hauled themselves along it until they were beneath *Flambeau*'s bowsprit.

'Welcome back,' Oliver whispered, leaning from the rail near the heads. 'How was it?'

'It was fun,' Charles replied with a big grin on his face.

'Come aboard,' the captain called quietly, 'and dry yourselves.' He had a rug waiting to swing around the boy's shoulders.

'I trust all went well. You can report to me later,' Oliver said, looking at the Negro who stood several inches taller than himself.

'Yes, Captain. I just wish we could have done more. I wanted to fill the powder bowls with damp sand, but I would have been noticed.'

'Indeed you would have. Now you are safely back, it's time to release the cable and detach us from the warship. We have taken the deck and freed our own men from the hold and replaced them with French crewmen. However, there are still some officers sleeping undisturbed in their berths below unaware of what has happened. It is time to rouse them and put them with the rest of their countrymen. Then, with the helm over, I am hoping *Flambeau* will slowly drift in the night. All we need is a breeze of wind and we will be over the horizon before the 74 stirs and realises we are gone.'

'Let us hope so,' Eku replied.

As they spoke, cries came from the upper gundeck of the 74 and grey smoke could be seen billowing from the furthest larboard gunport.'

Oliver looked at the Negro: 'What did you do?'

'Nothing to worry about, Captain. It's not a big blaze, just enough to keep them traitors occupied for a while. A few handfuls of teased oakum, a pinch of powder and a length of lighted slowmatch under one of the guns.'

'I trust it will not set the ship alight.'

'No sir, I had no intention of doing that. But I doubt anyone aboard will be taking much notice of the French frigate for the next half an hour.'

Oliver scowled. 'I invited you to use your initiative, but I'm not sure I approve of your tactics. For now, however, go below and help Mr Tully.'

Eku winked at his young friend before heading off.

On deck, Oliver frowned as he gazed across the water where a mixture of sounds was carrying from the 74. Cries of panic, shouts and orders were being screamed above the peeps of a bosun's whistle and the beat of the drums calling all hands to stations. From deep in the man-of-war's hold came the muted sound of banging. Battened beneath the hatches were one hundred and fifty British sailors desperate to escape a ship they feared was on fire.

As the Negro had said, no one was paying any attention to the damaged frigate floating some distance away and the distraction provided ample opportunity for the tow cable to be cut and for Oliver's men to swim back to *Perpetual* unnoticed.

In *Perpetual*'s mess, the sailors gathered around the Negro and the boy. Everyone was eager to hear what had happened across the water. Eku was happy to oblige and relate the deeds he and his young friend had got up to.

'What on earth did you do that for?' Bungs asked scornfully. 'There's plenty of extra powder horns and quills in the magazine and any idiot can fill a water bucket in no time.'

'Me and Charles thought it a good idea,' Eku said. 'The captain said he didn't want his command to come under fire from the 74 fearing it could have blown us out of the water. Charles and I decided that if the gun captains had no powder for the bowl we'd have enough time to swim back before they launched a broadside at us.'

Bungs was unimpressed.

'Young Charles was ambitious. He wanted to have the blaze running the full length of the lower gundeck. That would have been impossible and I told him it was too dangerous. We could have burned her down to the waterline and that would have been a catastrophe. But a small fire and nothing but empty water buckets on hand would keep them sailors on their toes for a while.'

'So what happened after that?' Bungs asked.

'The towing cable was released and *Flambeau* started drifting – only slightly at first, but drifting. When it had dropped back sufficiently, a new hawser was run across from the Frog to *Perpetual*.

'Why didn't you cut the cable when you were on the third rate?' Bungs asked.

'We couldn't do that without being seen. Besides, if we'd cut it close to the ship, the cable's end would have hung slack instead of stretching out to the ship it was towing.'

Bungs sniffed.

'The captain reckons we are drifting with the current and hopes that by morning the gap will have had widened to twenty miles.'

Chapter 15

Martinique

The tropical heat was oppressive. The sailors' shirts stuck to their backs and arms. Perspiration ran down their legs and dripped from their brows onto the bleached planks. Every man's hair was as wet as if he had just come from under the pump – the only cool relief the men could find.

Even the captain had his steward sling a hammock for him in the great cabin because his inner berth was too hot. With waves of tiredness overcoming him, Oliver desperately needed some sound sleep but, because of their location, he was loath to quit the deck. Mr Tully had assured him he would call him if anything was sighted, be it either the islands of the West Indies rising from the horizon, or a sail. Oliver eventually accepted the offer and was asleep a few seconds after his head had sunk into his down-filled pillow.

Certain he had only closed his eyes for a fleeting moment, he was startled by the sound of a musket being fired. It was distant but it was definitely the sound of a shot. It was the signal he had prearranged with Mr Parry aboard *Flambeau* if he needed to reduce speed in order for a message to be conveyed across.

As the captain rolled from his hammock, Mr Tully was at the cabin door.

'Musket fired from the bow of the frigate, sir.'

'Return the signal and reduce sail. Allow *Flambeau* to swim up alongside. I'll be on deck directly.'

After splashing some water on his face, fastening four of the buttons on his shirt and tucking his shirt tail into his trousers, Oliver stepped up to the quarterdeck. He was met with the sound of the musket being fired from *Perpetual*'s stern. Above the deck, the sails luffed and the main topsail yard creaked as it was braced around, slowing the frigate's progress.

From the quarterdeck, he could see that a similar order had been given by Mr Parry on the deck of *Flambeau*. Under reduced sail and still under tow, the recaptured French frigate drifted to within pistol shot of the slightly smaller British frigate.

Six bells sounded simultaneously on the two frigates' decks informing the captain he had slept solidly for two hours.

'What news, Mr Parry?' Oliver called across the water.

'I would speak with you, Captain. Is it possible you could come aboard?'

A little surprised at the request, but having full trust in his first lieutenant, Oliver did not question why the request had been put. Instead he ordered his boat to be put away and the crew to stand ready.

Mr Tully, having just returned from the bow, closed the telescope he was carrying and returned it to the cupboard beneath the binnacle.

'What did you see, Mr Tully?'

'The 74. She's heading away, hull-down on the horizon with a full head of sails billowing like a cloud on the ocean's rim. She'll be gone before dark.'

'What direction?'

'She's standing to the north-east. Definitely bearing away from the Caribbean and making for the Atlantic.'

'Then we shall let her go,' Oliver said.

Mr Tully showed no concern. 'Aye aye, Captain.'

'The deck is yours while I speak with Mr Parry but get the lookout to keep a keen eye all around.'

The lieutenant touched his temple in his usual manner.

From the rail, while awaiting his boat, Oliver studied the French frigate. Dents the size of dinner plates, punched into it by the 74's round shot, decorated her hull. Smaller holes peppered her gunnels as though she had been set upon by a flock of giant woodpeckers. Her rails were absent in parts, having been smashed to splinters. Her second and third gunports had been blown out leaving a large gaping hole which fortunately was well above the waterline. The damage had been temporarily boarded up by the carpenter. The elegant tracery of carvings around her bow, demonstrating a remarkable degree of skill and artistry, had also been shattered. Surprisingly, the carved and painted figurehead of a woman holding a flaming torch at arm's length was still intact. The large section beneath the empty cathead, where raw unpainted timbers reached down to the waterline, was the result of the work Mr Crosby and his mates had done to prevent the ship from sinking. Had Captain Moncousu failed to surrender his ship when he did, *Flambeau* would have sunk within the hour, in Oliver's estimation.

Mr Parry greeted his captain when he climbed aboard the prize.

'I trust all is well,' Oliver said, glancing about the ship. The possibility he had been wooed aboard by an officer under duress had crossed his mind but the idea was quickly dispelled. But what greeted him was the disturbing sound of men wailing. It was coming from below.

'Join me in the cabin,' Simon said. 'I need your opinion and advice.'

Oliver nodded and followed Mr Parry below to the cabin that Captain Moncousu had previously occupied.

When taking the ship, Oliver had failed to appreciate the fine accommodation the Frenchman had enjoyed. Though only a little bigger than his own cabin in *Perpetual*, this area was furnished in the manner of an elegant French drawing room. Velvet drapes hung at the windows, hand-stitched tapestries covered the chairs, turned legs supported the highly polished walnut table and a multitude of mirrors reflected light on every wall.

'I'm surprised the cabin wasn't raked when she ran from the fight. Quite extraordinary,' Oliver commented.

'I have no complaints about the accommodation,' Simon Parry said with a slight grin. 'But the prisoners do. No doubt you heard them when you came aboard.'

'How long has this been going on?'

'Every minute and every hour from morning till night since we placed them there. They complain about the water lapping back and forth beneath their feet. They claim their situation is worse than being in a British prison hulk. They swear that the heat, damp, mould and cockroaches will be the death of them.'

'I think those are French cockroaches which we cannot be blamed for.'

Simon Parry was not amused. 'Three men were dragged out today almost dead. Only brandy and fresh air saved them from expiring completely. The problem is the water. It is not deep but the liquid that remains in the hold is foul and the stench takes your breath away. It's a combination of seawater, filthy bilge water and now night water.'

'Are you using the pumps?'

'Constantly. Though the level is low, the walls and beams weep brine and the air has taken on a foul smell and it is getting worse. I would invite you to sample it for yourself, but I dare not have the hatches opened as the prisoners are becoming desperate and would rush the guards if they saw any chance of escaping.'

'What about a wind sail to send some air below?'

'I have had one rigged each day but with little breeze and the air of these latitudes so humid it is insufficient to alter or improve the conditions.'

'So what do you suggest, Simon?'

'In my opinion, it is inhumane to leave the prisoners below for much longer. At the speed we are currently making, it will take us eight weeks to cross the Atlantic, by which time, I will have a hold filled with dead Frenchmen or will be tossing bodies over the side every single day on our voyage to Portsmouth. My suggestion is that we make for Jamaica as was Captain Liversedge's original plan. By doing that, we can deposit the French sailors at Kingston, leave the prize with the agent and then return in *Perpetual* to England.'

'I agree something must be done,' Oliver said. 'And quickly. I will speak with Dr Whipple and get his opinion then inform you of my decision. I am sorry you have had to bear this situation and I understand your concern. In the meantime, how go the repairs?'

'The carpenter and his mates continue to work from dawn to dusk with the help of some of the other hands. There was far more damage than was at first thought.'

'Please thank Mr Crosby for his efforts and encourage him to continue. Do you have spare spars to rig up a topgallant mast on the main?

'Yes, that will be done very soon. For the present he is concentrating on a new rudder. I would not want to head across the Atlantic until it has been fixed. How the French captain had steerage, I do not know. The rudder was almost shot away.'

'Thank you, Simon,' Oliver said. 'Maintain your lookouts and signal me immediately if you need assistance. We are nearing the West Indies and, according to my calculations, I expect to have the southernmost islands in sight tomorrow or the next day. I will speak with you again in the morning. I agree something must be done to improve the lot of the prisoners.'

First light brought a call from *Perpetual*'s foremast lookout. Land was sighted off the port bow. Having studied his charts the previous evening, it was as Oliver expected.

'Martinique, I believe,' he said to Mr Mundy.

The sailing master studied the rugged outline through his telescope.

'That's British, isn't it, Captain?'

'Ceded to Britain as part of the Treaty of Amiens three years ago.'

'If that's the case, couldn't we take these Froggies into the port there?'

Oliver took the glass and lifted it to his eye. 'Those French islands are regularly contested and have a habit of changing hands unexpectedly. Having been away from England for so long, I am not sure where they stand at the present.'

'British still, I think, Captain. There's Diamond Rock right on the southern tip. The Royal Navy built a fort on the top of it, hoisted 18-pounders up the sheer cliff face and set up 24-pounders in several natural embrasures. It's said to be invulnerable.'

'Indeed' Oliver laughed. 'I wonder what the lookouts would make of us. Two frigates – one British-built sailing in convoy with a French-built ship. Despite the colours flying at our masthead, I would not wager money on their correct assessment of our nationality. Nor would I attempt to navigate the strait between the rock and the island with round shot raining terror down on us from the top of that monolith. It's a stone frigate, Mr Mundy. Commodore Hood commissioned it a sloop of war with the name, His Majesty's ship *Diamond Rock*.' It is indeed invulnerable and I, for one, will not take it on.'

'I would wager it's still ours, though,' Mr Mundy added.

'Captain Liversedge informed me our spies have wind of a French plan to attack it.'

'Best we head for the protection of the island then,' the sailing master said.

Perpetual's officers who were standing nearby nodded in agreement and offered their own views on the situation. But Oliver excused himself and strode to the lee rail where he took several turns up and down the deck pondering on the rugged peaks rising from the translucent blue water.

When the soft breeze died, the canvas flagged. The tips of the gently rippled surface sparkled in the sunlight burning his eyes even though he shielded them with his hand. For a moment, he was distracted when a large turtle broke the surface only twenty yards from the ship's side and swam by, quite oblivious to any threat or danger.

When it disappeared, Oliver turned and rejoined his officers.

'I have reached a decision. When we have some wind, we head north standing away from Martinique and the Island of Dominica that lies to the north of it. In a little over twenty-four hours we will make La Désirade and Guadeloupe.'

'They are definitely in French hands, are they not?' the sailing master reminded.

'That is correct and exactly what I want. To the best of my knowledge, the small strip of land known as La Désirade is neither well-populated nor fortified. It has been home to slaves, pirates and peasant farmers for years. That is where we will head for to land the French prisoners.'

'You are going to hand them to the French authorities?'

'I doubt there is either a port or naval establishment on that strip of rock.'

The sailing master was bewildered. 'Do you intend to let them go free?'

Oliver turned and looked across the taffrail to the French frigate being drawn in its wake. 'If the prisoners remain battened down under *Flambeau* hatches, they will be dead within a week. If, on the other hand, we attempt to sail into the Caribbean Sea, we will be inviting an attack. We will come under threat from land batteries on the French and Spanish islands and will have to dodge the broadsides of any enemy ships we encounter. By charting such a course, I will be putting the life of everyone aboard at risk. Consider also the pirates and privateers who are familiar with these waters and claim them as their own. For those villains of the seas, we present an easy target – one good frigate with a lame duck tagging along behind, and we only have enough crew to handle half the guns on each vessel. Because of that, I am not prepared to enter the Caribbean. Nor am I prepared to jeopardise my rights to *Flambeau*. The men fought hard to take her and, for their efforts, they deserve to return home with at least one prize-of-war.'

'But surely,' the sailing master remonstrated, 'you do not intend running *Perpetual* into a French harbour with the tricolour or white flag flying at the peak?'

'I have no intention of making port, Mr Mundy. When La Désirade is clearly in sight, Mr Parry will have *Flambeau*'s cutter put on the water. Of the thirty or more sailors being held in the hold, I am sure there will be enough able seamen amongst them capable of sailing a small boat.'

'But, without our men, how will the cutter be returned?'

'It will not be returned. It is a French boat and the sailors are entitled to it. I will ensure it is supplied with water and biscuits. It will be cast off when we are ten miles from the island. If the prisoners wish to sail onto Guadeloupe, which is only another five miles to the west, I will furnish them with that information.'

'That is very generous of you,' the sailing master said critically.

Oliver ignored the remark. 'I must convey the message to Mr Parry so he can make the necessary preparations.'

'And what then?' Mr Mundy asked bluntly.

The captain's patience was wearing thin. 'As soon as we dispense with the French sailors, we point our beak to England. Hopefully, by then, *Flambeau* will be capable of sailing independently and, if both ships can make good speed, there is a fair possibility we can catch *Stalwart* before she reaches Europe.'

'It's a big pond out there, the 74 is in good condition, has ample crew and quite a head start on us.'

'So much more reason to put my plan into effect as soon as possible.' Oliver turned from any further questions. 'Mr Tully, a signal shot to Mr Parry, please. I need to speak with him again.'

'Aye aye, Captain.' The lieutenant immediately relayed the message to the midshipman who in turn delivered it personally to the marine sergeant who stepped smartly up to the taffrail and discharged his musket into the air.

Late in the afternoon of the following day, Oliver Quintrell and Mr Parry watched from the quarterdeck of the French frigate as the prisoners were brought up from the hold. British seamen stood by the bulwarks, cutlasses in hand, while half a dozen marines balanced in the rigging with their muskets pointing towards the deck.

Dishevelled, dirty, stinking and half-blinded by the sunlight, the French sailors, mostly young men, emerged from below, rubbing their eyes in an attempt to adjust to the brightness. Their condition and appearance was far worse than Oliver had expected. Though they had been fed and watered, they looked gaunt, their faces were the hue of a pale moon and their joints appeared as stiff as those of old men.

With news of their release and imminent freedom delivered to them in their own language by Oliver's translator, some wept while others appeared stunned. But on sighting the lush green hills on the distant islands, a frisson of excitement ran through the group. One sailor looked over to the captain and thanked him. He said most French seamen had heard rumours of how terrible the British prison hulks were and, while incarcerated below, they had considered that if their time in the hold was a taste of what lay ahead, they would rather die than be subjected to such a fate. To be granted their freedom on a French island was more than they could have wished for.

As soon as the painter was tossed from the boat's bow, the cutter fell away from the frigate's hull and a jubilant cheer was raised from the Frenchmen.

Standing by the rail, Captain Quintrell and Simon Parry watched the sailors step the mast, clear away the cutter's sail and set it to catch whatever breeze was blowing.

'Did you learn anything new from those prisoners?' Oliver asked of his first officer. 'I am anxious to know how their captain took a man-of-war from the British officers in charge of her. I would also like to know who the Irish political prisoner is that is being carried aboard. Is it he who has fired up the insurgents? Is he the man now leading the Irish rebels?'

'The prisoners said nothing to me,' Simon said, 'and, as they weren't aboard the 74 after it was taken, it's likely they didn't know. Perhaps they should have been questioned before being given their liberty.'

'Too late, now,' Oliver said. 'We will, no doubt, learn the truth before too long.'

With the tiller hard over, the loaded boat turned and headed west. The volcanic islands covered in lush green vegetation were surrounded by turquoise blue water and edged with a rim of sparkling white breakers.

'They are the lucky ones,' Oliver mused. 'Now, let us pray for a favourable wind so we can catch up with their mates aboard the 74.'

'And when you catch them?' Simon Parry said.

'I will not be so generous next time.'

Over the next two days, with every spare hand that could swing a hammer or handle a chisel assisting the carpenter, good progress was made with the repairs aboard *Flambeau*. The new rudder was completed and attached to the stern post. A replacement topgallant mast was hoisted aloft, yards crossed and sails bent. Mr Crosby declared the frigate's hull sound. She was in danger of sinking. More importantly, under her own wind and steerage, she no longer required a tow.

With her elegant lines and a brightly coppered bottom, which she flashed when she heeled to the wind, *Flambeau* was capable of out-running *Perpetual*, if sailed to the best of her ability. Having delayed their sailing, in order for the repairs to be completed, it was now time to depart from the gateway to the Caribbean and head across the North Atlantic.

'Just in time, by the looks of it,' Mr Tully said, handing the captain the glass and pointing. 'Hull up on the south-eastern horizon. Looks like banks of clouds gathering.'

Oliver studied the rim of the sea. 'Pyramids of sail?'

'Yes, sir. A fleet of warships, I'd say. Twenty or more.'

'What are they, Mr Tully?' the captain asked.

'From the flashes of colour I could see, I'd wager they are French and Spanish combined.'

'What do you make of their heading?'

'West-north-west. Martinique, I suggest. Perhaps it's the French force sent to take Diamond Rock that you spoke of.'

'Let us hope that is their business and that they do not deviate from their present course. We would be blown to pieces if that fleet came within gunshot. Mr Hanson, raise the French colours and send a signal to Mr Parry to do likewise. Let us pile on every inch of cloth we have and get out of here, and hope we meet no other enemy ships along the way. North-east, if you please, helmsman.'

The watch quickly responded to the sound of the bosun's peeps. Sailors swarmed round the lines at the pin rails. Others climbed aloft and slid along the footropes to shake the reefs out of the topsails and topgallants. The booms were rigged for the studding sails both alow and aloft. Under Mr Parry's orders, the French frigate received similar treatment.

'In Heaven's name, how do you hope to find the 74 in the Atlantic?' the sailing master asked pointedly.

Oliver looked up to the royals and watched as they were unfurled. 'If Captain Moncousu is in command, he will sail the most direct route to France. How fast he travels will depend on the winds but, I guarantee you, before he reaches Europe, I will catch him.'

'But, as you said yourself, we have only one hundred and forty men divided between two frigates.'

'Mr Mundy,' the captain said, looking directly at his sailing master. 'I have one hundred and forty British seamen who are eager to return home. In the meantime, it is up to you and the other officers to make sure every man aboard both ships, whether he be cook or servant, landsman or loblolly, is capable of taking his place in a gun crew. That applies to topmen and marines also.'

'You intend to attack the 74, if we find her?'

'Yes, if necessary,' Oliver relied curtly. 'While I have no desire to attack a British man-of-war, I do not intend to see her handed over to Napoleon Bonaparte as a prize.'

'But there may be five hundred sailors aboard.'

'I am quite aware of that, thank you. However, one quarterdeck is not big enough to accommodate three captains. The question remains: who is in command right now and who will be at the helm by the time they raise the coast of France? Will it be the Frenchman – Moncousu, the leader of the Irish rebels – Murphy, or the British captain – William Liversedge? Much can happen in a month's time. Ask me that question again when the time arises but for now, let us concentrate on making way and going about the business of overhauling the third rate.'

Chapter 16

Eku's Tale

Hurrying along the mess deck, Charles Goodridge's arm was grabbed by the cooper.

'Hey, you! Where are you off to in such a hurry?'

'I'm going to eat,' the boy said.

'Well,' Bungs said, 'what's wrong with eating with me?'

Charles looked around. 'Nothing, I suppose.'

'Now ain't you a bright lad. So, if there's no one else sitting here, why not come and sit your arse down opposite me and keep me company.'

Reluctantly Charles agreed.

'I gave you good advice last time, didn't I? Without a word from me you'd not have been allowed to go across with the others. Now, do as I say and sit your body down. I ain't got no one to chatter with, so if you can put a bung in that barrel-mouth of yours and not let it out too often, we can have a sensible conversation and you can tell me about that bit of mischief you and Eku got up to on the 74.'

The boy shrugged. 'It wasn't anything special and you've probably heard about it anyway.'

'I want to hear it from you,' the cooper said.

Despite feeling disinclined to be sociable, Charles slid along the wooden chest that served as a seat. Folding his arms across his chest, he straightened his back and looked directly at the old man but said nothing.

'So what's matter with you today? Cat got your tongue?'

Charles didn't answer, dropped his eyes to the mess table and stared at the stains impregnating the timber.

'I know what your problem is,' Bungs said. 'You're worrying over that Mrs Pilkington, aren't you?'

'Maybe I am,' Charles murmured.

'And what are you going to do about it?' Bungs asked.

'I can't do nothing now the 74's headed away.'

'So if you can't do nothing about it, what's the sense in moping about it? Have a bit of faith in Captain Quintrell. If anyone's going to find that ship in this Atlantic, it'll be our captain. You mark my words.'

The light from the overhead lantern was shaded for a moment when the West Indian arrived and stood over the pair.

'What cock-and-bull story are you telling him now?' Eku asked, flicking his wrist at the boy. 'Move over,' he said.

'Where's Will?' Bungs asked.

Eku studied the cooper's face. 'Is your brain double-reefed again? He's helping Mr Crosby again. The Frog ship might be sailing, but there's still plenty of repair work to be done.'

Leaning forward till he was little more than a few inches from the Negro's face, Bungs growled. 'There's nowt wrong with my brain. Never was. Never will be.'

Eku leaned back but the rant continued. 'The boy's saying nothing, but I reckon you know something and you're not letting on. You was over there and I heard you went down into the French ship's hold to parley with the prisoners.'

'Aye, but only because I can speak their language,' Eku said, 'and the captain ordered me to do that.'

'You edging for special favours, are you?' Bungs said with a sly grin.

'Don't be daft,' the Negro said.

'So tell me, who did you speak to and what did you learn?'

Eku lowered his voice. 'I weren't sent down for idle talk. I was sent to tell the prisoners they were to be put ashore on the island.'

Bungs kept digging. 'Aye, but you must have had a yarn while you was with them Frogs.'

Eku glanced over his shoulder to the next table where Smithers and his mates were sharing a joke. 'Between you and me and the lad here, I spoke with one of the sailors. He wasn't black like me, but he was dark-skinned. A mulatto. He said he was a steward on the French ship and served the officers – delivered their meals, washed their clothes, polished their shoes – you know. He said he'd been at sea for ten years. Told me he'd grown up on a plantation in the Indies and run away to sea when he was a lad – like me.'

'Rats arse!' Bungs hissed. 'Tell me something I want to hear. I'm not interested in how many times he took a piss.'

Eku continued unperturbed. 'He was happy to talk and asked about *Stalwart* and *Perpetual* and where we were bound.'

'Crafty sod. Spying he was.'

'No, he wasn't,' Eku argued. 'You should have seen his face when I told him that he and his mates were to be put ashore on that French island. At first he thought I was jesting.'

'More than them Froggies deserved, I reckon. I could have told the captain what to do with them.'

'I'm sure you could,' Eku replied.

'So did he say what had happened aboard the third rate and how they'd managed to steal the 74 from Captain Liversedge?'

'He did, and I told Mr Hanson and asked him to pass word to Captain Quintrell.'

'And?' Bungs said.

'He said it wasn't important now the 74 had sailed away.'

The old man growled. 'Some of them middies are idiots, I tell you. What would he know? Now you tell me what you found out, and I'll decide if it's important or not.'

Eku glanced around the mess again. He didn't want his story being overhead and spread around the ship. Juicy tales spread faster than rats running round the railings. 'It wasn't the French responsible for the 74 being taken. It was the Irish.'

'What?'

'Shh! You heard me right. Remember them Irish lubbers that demanded to be paid off in Rio – five of them, there were. Well, after picking up their pay and bits of dunnage and leaving *Perpetual*, the very next day they signed to serve on the third rate. And, once on board, they wasted no time in spreading word among the hands that they were going to take the ship to Ireland and launch a new rebellion against the British.'

Bungs laughed. 'The crew must have thought them barmy.'

'Perhaps some did. But not all. Within a few days of boarding they had taken down names of every loyal Irishman aboard. By all accounts there were hundreds of Irishmen aboard *Stalwart* who had signed a year ago in Cork.'

'Hogwash!'

'It's true as I sit here. Not only did they get their names, but they had them swear a hand-written oath pledging loyalty to Ireland. I don't know what they were promised in return.'

'Same as what the French wanted – liberty, equality, fraternity.'

'That's right. That is what the French sailor said.'

'What was the name of the rebel rouser?'

'Murphy. Joseph Murphy.'

'Scab,' Bungs cursed then bethought himself. 'It's a mighty big step up from spewing your voice box on deck to taking a 74. How could that be? I'd heard it was the French captain who'd taken the ship.'

'I know it's hard to believe, but I'm telling it like it was told to me. He said Moncousu – the captain – was placed in a cabin on the 74. Because he had surrendered his sword he was not treated like a prisoner. But he did have a couple of marines keeping an eye on him. Only problem was – the guards were Irishmen and Captain Liversedge didn't know that. It was the guards that let Murphy talk with the French Captain.'

'And?'

'And the story is that the Irish rebel offered the French captain command of the warship with a crew of two hundred Irish-born sailors, on condition he sailed the ship to Ireland. Stands to reason – Moncousu wasn't going to turn his back on a valuable prize offered on a silver plate. He agreed.'

'But what of all the regular hands and the marines?' Bungs said. 'How did the Irish rebels win the support of so many of the crew?'

'With the promise that everyman who supported them would receive a large reward when the ship arrived off the Irish coast – a purse full of silver coins. What poor sailor can afford to ignore that?'

'Did they say where the money was coming from?'

Eku shrugged his shoulder? 'The Frenchman didn't know, but with a fortune dangled before them they were easily bought over. Plus, the rebels were quick to remind their mates of the atrocities the British had done in Ireland in the past. Many of the men had memories of those times and many had lost loved ones so it was not hard to gain their support.'

Bungs said nothing. His eyes were wide. His mouth hanging half-open.

Eku continued. 'After the armoury was broken into, that's when Captain Liversedge was taken prisoner along with his officers. If they hadn't surrendered and done what he said, Captain Moncousu was going to string the captain and his officers up from the yardarm. That was what I was told.'

'It sounds like Captain Liversedge gave up his ship without a fight?'

'The French sailor said there was some fighting. Those that hadn't sworn allegiance were threatened with being tossed overboard or having their throats cut. The threats were real.'

'That's a lot of men to take on,' Bungs said. 'Near on two hundred, I would say. Why didn't we hear a ruckus?'

'I don't know. The French steward said some bodies tossed overboard so there must have been some fighting when the mutineers forced the rest of the 74's crew below decks. They were herded into the hold and the hatch covers were battened and locked.'

'Perhaps it was when we was practising the guns.' Bungs looked away, as if disinterested, and peered up and down the length of the deck. Mr Tully, having just descended from the hatch, was inspecting the mess to check all was well.

'Hey, Tully,' Bungs yelled. 'Lend us your ear for a tick?' He chuckled as he added, 'It best be your good ear.'

The lieutenant frowned. 'Mr Tully to you, if you don't mind. What's the matter, Bungs?' Striding down the mess between the swinging tables, the lieutenant replied, 'I haven't got time for your tittle-tattle.'

'It's not my title-tattle this time,' the cooper said adamantly. 'Eku, here, has a bit of tasty gossip which I'm certain the captain will want to chew on.'

The lieutenant regarded the Negro. 'Is that right, Eku?'

The Negro shrugged. 'If Bungs says so, I guess it must be.'

Mr Tully knew the cooper well enough to trust his judgement.

'On your feet, sailor. Let's do it now while the captain's not too busy.'

In the great cabin, Oliver Quintrell listened intently while the seaman repeated the details be had shared with the cooper. Though the eventual outcome of what had happened came as no surprise, the captain was grateful to be supplied with the full picture of how command of the 74 had been taken from its captain.

'This situation is diabolical,' Oliver said. 'A disaster.' He sat for a moment digesting the information.

'Is there anything else you have not told me?'

Eku swore he had related all he could remember.

'But it makes no sense, from what you say. The Irishman has the most supporters yet Captain Moncousu appears to have sole command. Why is he not sharing it with Murphy?'

'That's easy,' the West Indian replied. 'Murphy is a landsman and doesn't know how to sail a ship. The Irishman needed the French captain to take command and navigate.'

'Thank you, Eku. That information is indeed most helpful. Now I know the size of the enemy force, the distribution of men and where their loyalties lie. That knowledge will be imperative when I confront the 74 next time. In the meantime, return to your watch.'

Bending his head and shoulders to the doorframe, Eku departed leaving the captain in a quandary. Although he was able to mull over the makeup of the ship's complement aboard the third rate, there was nothing he could do for the present. Because of the time spent discharging the prisoners to La Désirade and subsequently allowing two days for the carpenters to complete the rudder and other necessary repairs to *Flambeau*, the 74 now had several sailing days' advantage over him. That, however, was not a major concern. In prime condition both frigates were capable of making good speed. They were fast, sleek, well-coppered and relatively weed-free. The 74, on the other hand was an older ship with a bulbous hull and although her bottom was copper-sheathed she wore a green petticoat beneath her waterline. The weeks spent idling in Guanabara Bay had contributed to that. Aside from that, her masts and spars were thick and heavy and, even though she could boast an enormous press of sail, Oliver was confident the man-of-war could not outrun the frigates in a chase.

The challenge now was to locate the 74 in the North Atlantic and that was the sort of challenge Oliver Quintrell enjoyed.

A few hours later, the captain sat down at the dining table in his cabin and rolled out a chart of the North Atlantic Ocean. With the help of his sailing master, he intended to chart the course they would expect the 74 to take if it was heading for Brest.

'It's a big stretch of ocean out there,' the sailing master said.

'Indeed, but it narrows as we near the Scillies and we'll catch them long before that, you mark my words.'

'Aye, but that 74 will make good speed now he doesn't have the Frog in tow,' Mr Mundy remonstrated.

'But think on this *Perpetual* and *Flambeau* can make better time than that cumbersome man-o'-war and with an unruly mob of disgruntled Irishmen on deck and an ungrateful French captain in command, anything might happen between now and then.'

'What if they changed tack and headed for Jamaica after all?'

'Mr Mundy, I know their general heading and am confident we will find them,' Oliver replied. In his opinion, Captain Moncousu would not head for Ireland even though he had agreed to do so. And Murphy, being no sailor, would be totally unaware from the navigational charts what their true position or charted course was.

For once, the sailing master did not dispute that likelihood. 'Wait till they get close to Europe. Let's see what happens then.'

Having split the *Perpetuals* between two ships, Oliver's immediate concern was the shortage of men. It was of little consolation to him that the third rate was also limited in its crew numbers. But the fact remained that most of the seamen serving on the 74 were Irishmen and the others Frenchmen who did not speak or understand English. Oliver wondered what sort of atmosphere existed on the gun decks where the two distinct groups were thrown together.

An interesting situation, he thought.

Armed with the information he had received from Ekundayo, Captain Quintrell considered the sailors belonging to his own command who had Irish blood. He wanted to know the mentality of seamen who could possibly be disloyal at heart. He needed to know how rational they were, how their minds worked and what drove them. He had been at sea in various capacities since his youth and had served alongside Irish, Scots and Welsh men, as well as Dutchmen, Norwegians and even some Frenchmen as equals, but had never been confronted with a situation such as this.

He decided to speak with the ship's surgeon again and, despite Mr Parry's warning to tread carefully, there were questions he needed answering and Jonathon Whipple was the only one he could ask.

When Oliver confronted the doctor again in the cockpit, there was a palpable air of tension when the subject of Ireland was broached. 'I seek your help, Jonathon. I need to know how you rate the Irishmen currently aboard *Perpetual*. Are they any different to the rest of the crew?'

The doctor considered his answer before speaking. 'In my opinion, the Irishmen aboard *Perpetual* are no different to their countrymen serving on other ships in His

Majesty's Navy. And, I believe, Irishmen make up the biggest proportion of sailors in most ships' crews.'

'That is possibly correct,' Oliver admitted. 'The Irish are well represented in all ranks. But of all the common sailors you have encountered, how do you find them?' Oliver asked.

'Most are lively, good humoured, prone to cheekiness and to taking the Word of the Lord in vain. Otherwise they are not dissimilar to the rest of the crew. But, let me remind you, when sailors are called into action and stand side-by-side against the enemy, it matters not how they speak or where they come from. Their blood is the same colour when spilled on the deck.'

'But you observe them through a physician's eye, not that of a fighting captain.'

Jonathon searched for his answer. 'Serving on any navy ship – and I have served on three – I see men with disfiguring scars, others with patches over empty eye sockets. I see men who tap about the deck on turned wooden legs, annoying those trying to sleep on the deck below, and I see those who cannot count to ten due to the loss of fingers on each hand. Yet they climb aloft, or haul on a line, or man the capstan or windlass and no one stops to enquire if they are Irish or English, or whalers or Deal longshoremen.'

The captain gave a slight nod of the head as he rubbed his finger and thumb together – the only full digits remaining on his damaged right hand.

Dr Whipple continued. 'I have treated more seamen for boils, rashes and the flux than from injuries resulting from sea battles. And more men die aboard ship from common illnesses than from wounds received fighting the enemy.' He sighed. 'In time, those wounds heal and scars fade and the fighting is forgotten but for the men of Irish heritage it is different. The wounds and the scars they suffered defending their cause run deep and never heal.'

Oliver was puzzled. 'Please explain.'

Jonathon's face screwed, as if with pain. 'Seven years ago, in Ireland, many suffered from hardship and were subjected to torture and inhuman treatment. It was the time they learned to dodge bullets from the redcoats' muskets, and side-step pikes thrust by the militiamen. They were made to witness their homes and villages being put to the torch. Many saw their families locked behind barred doors and heard the heart-rending screams of women and children as thatched roofs were set alight and the buildings engulfed in flames. Besides watching their families burned alive, many were obliged to draw a bloodied pike from the body of a son or brother in order to defend themselves. They did not hear the rush of air escaping from the victim's lungs but the gurgling dying cry for liberty.

'The sounds and sights of such events are embedded in the soul of every Irishman who ever fought or witnessed the atrocities of the '98 rebellion. It is those indelible images that have forged such a strong bond between them. It is the reason many have reasserted their sworn oaths as brothers over the years. Those men will never submit or surrender to British rule. Despite the passing of years and the semblance of peace between Britain and Ireland, the spirit and zeal of the United Irishmen will smoulder like a slowmatch and they will strive for independence no matter how long it takes.'

A moan from one of the cots swinging lazily to the Atlantic's swell reminded both men of their present situation. The doctor quickly checked on his patient before returning to the conversation.

Though uneasy, and treading carefully, the captain addressed the captain's next question. 'Would Irishmen aboard a naval vessel regard you differently because they know you are Irish born? Would they hold you in high esteem? Would they question your allegiance?'

'As you are doing now?' the doctor asked directly.

Oliver did not respond.

Jonathon continued. 'You asked earlier about the five men who left the ship in Rio. They never once visited the cockpit. But working in my capacity as surgeon on a British ship, it would not surprise me if they presumed my loyalty was to the Crown.'

'As a warranted naval physician on one of His Majesty's ships, surely that must be the case,' Oliver said.

Mr Whipple's face gave no indication as to a commitment one way or the other.

Aware of the intrusive nature of his questions and the doctor's reticence to furnish a direct reply, Oliver refrained from pursuing that line of inquiry. The little he knew of the doctor's early life, he had learned when he first joined *Perpetual* in Portsmouth. At the time, however, there was something in the doctor's appearance which had struck him as rather strange. His hair was cropped close to his head in the fashion worn by revolutionary Frenchmen. But the short cropped coiffure was also that of Irish rebel farmers – the Croppies. Oliver wondered if the doctor's family had been actively involved in the 1798 uprising or in the years of upheaval preceding it.

Was the doctor a revolutionary? Oliver asked himself. He doubted it. *Was the doctor sympathetic to the Irish rebels?* He did not know.

'Might I be so bold as to ask what faith you worship? Is it possible you follow the Church of Rome?'

The doctor laughed but his eyes did not smile. 'Why do the English believe all Irish are Catholics and tar them with the same brush? Do you not know that the United Irish Party was formed by Presbyterians and a wealthy Protestant group who opened their hearts to the other faiths and the disadvantaged, including the rural labouring class? Did you know the plight of the peasant farmers who were mostly Catholics? Most worked small parcels of land of less than a handful of acres – a small patch of earth barely big enough to support one cow or a few sheep and hardly enough dirt to feed a family for a year. Yet, from the pittance that land provided in a good year, those farmers had to pay their tithes to the church as well as rent to wealthy landlords. In bad years, when the crops failed, nothing could save them from starvation.

'Whatever the status and faith of these *rebels*, they were united in their aim to free Ireland from the British oppressor. Whichever religion they chose to follow was of little consequence.'

Despite feeling slightly uncomfortable, Oliver listened carefully. He appreciated the doctor's candour but there was still more he wanted to know about the men standing against him. He continued his interrogation. 'Do you speak from personal experience?'

'No,' Jonathon Whipple replied sharply, 'I was not living in Ireland at the time, but the stories carried across the Irish Sea were repeated to me many times by close friends. Often their words were recounted so vividly I felt I was present.'

Oliver reflected on where he was at that time – with the Mediterranean fleet, he believed. 'When serving at sea, news of events happening in Britain is slow to filter through.'

'It was the twenty-first of June, 1798 to be precise,' Jonathon Whipple reminded.

'I recollect reading a brief notice when we returned to harbour. It spoke of a glorious victory over rebel forces.'

'No doubt it failed to mention the atrocities committed by the loyalists and the human suffering that followed as a result?'

'As I said, the report was brief, a matter of only a line or two.'

The doctor took a deep breath. 'Vinegar Hill,' he said, 'is in County Wexford, not far from where I was born and raised. It was the last stand of the United Party rebels. Twenty thousand men, women and children – mainly poor Catholic peasants – armed with pitchforks and handmade pikes stood against the British loyalist forces made up of ten thousand men.'

'Only half the number.'

'Indeed, but the British had the advantage of trained soldiers armed with muskets with fixed bayonets, and cannon. The Irish did not stand a chance. Even as they retreated, they were bombarded by the infantry's heavy artillery fire and, when they ran for cover, they were mowed down by the swords and sabres of the British cavalrymen. After the fight, the bodies were left on the ground to rot, while the women who were captured were raped – often by several men. The rebel hospital was torched and the wounded who were unable to escape were burned alive.'

'Many fights are ugly,' Oliver admitted and waited a moment. 'Was that the last of the battles?'

The doctor shook his head. 'No. Skirmishes continued with cruel atrocities reported from both sides. Throughout the fighting, the United Irishmen were buoyed by the promise of a mighty French force that would arrive by sea and land on the west coast. They were convinced the French troops would defeat the redcoats and the militiamen and help Ireland gain its independence. But it was a vain hope.'

'I read that a French force landed. Is that not correct?'

'True. However, the large force that had been promised to help liberate the people never materialised. Only a small number of troops were landed from a handful of French ships and, shortly after the soldiers disembarked, they were captured by Cornwallis's men.'

'What followed?'

'They were shipped back to France.'

Oliver was surprised. 'And the Irish rebels?'

'Without the support that had been promised from France and from some of their own regions, they were overcome. Their leader, Wolfe Tone, was captured and sentenced to death but chose to cut his own throat while awaiting execution. Many of the insurrectionists were put to death while eighty of the United Irish Party's leaders were tried and exiled to America or France. Hundreds of others were sentenced to transportation to New South Wales, the prison colony at the other side of the world.'

Oliver's thoughts flashed to the political prisoner held aboard the 74. *What was his role in this mutiny?*

The doctor continued. 'Though thirty thousand men, women and children died, the conflict merited only a paragraph in the London papers. The articles commended the British soldiers on their success. I doubt anything ever appeared in the *Naval Chronicle* as there was no British naval action.'

'Thank you, Jonathon.'

'The five men who left the ship in Rio,' the doctor continued. 'Though I spoke with them very briefly when they first came aboard and I examined them physically, I know little more of them than the names as they appear in the muster book. Mr Parry described them as being like any other lubbers, although better than pressed men in that they were eager to learn shipboard skills. However, they appeared rather secretive and preferred to keep to their own company.'

'I need to know which side they were aligned to.'

'You mean were they rebels?' the doctor asked. 'Were they members of the United Irishmen's Alliance? Or were they loyalists or militia of the British forces?'

Oliver nodded.

'From my brief conversations, I learned they hailed from Wexford, as I do. The sixth man, Michael O'Connor is from Kilkenny. But their demeanour raised some uneasy feelings that have not left me since the men disembarked.'

Chapter 17

O'Connor

Returning to the great cabin, Oliver Quintrell was wary of the ramifications of what he had heard. Divided loyalties, lack of discipline and constant murmurings were the harbingers of mutiny. Yet, men of many nationalities served Britain's most important service and jibes and jokes about the Scots, Welsh and Irish were accepted as normal chitchat in the mess. Yorkshiremen mocked cider-swilling yokels from the south while sailors from Cornwall were forever accused of raising false lights and seducing ships onto the rocks for the purpose of plunder. Deal longshoremen were seen as smugglers while those from the area of London Docks were not to be trusted. It was said they would cut your throat for a pinch of snuff. Aboard any ship, deep-seated hatred and long-standing jealousies, if left to simmer long enough, could eventually boil up into a full-blown mutiny. Similarly, it only took a handful of fiery voices to rekindle old grievances and feed a fire.

Mulling over the words the doctor had spoken, Oliver considered the names of a string of Irish captains who had risen to the rank of Admiral and wondered if their backgrounds had ever been brought into question. If such a man was not pilloried for his heritage, was it his heritage that had elevated him to his position of authority?

A knock on the cabin door interrupted his thoughts.

'Begging your pardon, Captain,' Casson said. 'O'Connor's here for the work you have for him.'

Oliver glanced at the pile of assorted papers and correspondence on his desk needing attention. 'Thank you, Casson. Allow him in.'

'Sorry to disturb you, Captain. I came to collect the inventories for copying.'

Oliver Quintrell looked up. The freckle-faced red-headed Irishman hovered in the doorway. Though he was of similar age to himself, at only a little over five feet tall, he looked more like a boy than a man. Despite only having been aboard for a short time, O'Connor was already a regular visitor to the great cabin where at times he worked under supervision but, more often, undertook his work unattended.

The captain studied his features. If there was any subterfuge or evil intent in this man's mind, it did not show in his face. 'Come in,' he said. 'I wish to speak with you.'

The Irishman nodded and entered, taking the chair that was indicated to him at the end of the table.

'For several weeks now, you have been performing whatever assignment I have given you and I have been satisfied with your work. Your hand is neat, you demand little instruction, and I cannot fault your accuracy. However, there have been rumours spread about you that I am obliged to investigate.'

O'Connor did not appear surprised.

The captain offered him the opportunity to respond.

'I know what you are referring to, Captain. Accusations have been levelled at me in the mess and on deck, especially since the third rate was taken.'

Oliver tilted his head to one side and listened.

'I have been mocked, jeered and called names, and threatened, not only because of the way I speak and look, but because my name was entered in the muster book at the same time as the five Irishmen who left the ship and have since caused havoc aboard the 74.'

'I must ask you to reply to those accusations so I can consider how to deal with them and with the rumour mongers?'

'I will answer your questions honestly. It is the only way I know.'

Oliver expected nothing less. 'You assured me you did not know the other Irishmen before you left England.'

'I did not lie when I told you I met them in an ale house only days before the six of us stepped aboard the ship bound for America. You know what happened to that vessel.'

The captain nodded. 'Continue.'

'From the first night on board, they were buoyed by eager anticipation and talked about New York and a new life. They told stories about fellow countrymen who had settled there with their families and made a good life. That kind of talk was not new to me. It was the escape many poor Irish folk dreamed of.'

'And were you of the same mind?'

'I thought America would offer an opportunity for me to advance myself as there was nothing for me in Liverpool at the time.'

'You had a job.'

'But that was all,' O'Connor said.

Oliver studied the man sitting bolt upright. 'Tell me about the five men. You must have learned something about them before the ship foundered – their characters, their ambitions, their backgrounds.'

'It was impossible not to,' the scribe said, tossing his head back, 'confined, as we were, in a cramped cabin on the orlop deck. For hours each day, we were pressed shoulder to shoulder and, at night, we slept three to a bench unable to roll over or change position. I could not help but listen to their chatter and overhear their whisperings.'

'Were they Irish rebels?'

He nodded. 'Too right, they were. They had fought for an independent Ireland and were proud of that fact.'

'Fought against British rule?'

'What else?' the Irishman said. 'They killed, maimed and murdered without question or conscience. Each conflict they fought was bloodier than the last and the reprisals were even more horrific. They fought alongside an army of peasants armed with pikes and pitchforks, and when they had no weapons they used their fists, fingers and teeth. You can do a lot of damage to a man's face with those weapons alone.'

'Did you fight?' the captain asked.

'No, but it was hard not to get caught up in the uprisings.'

The captain asked him to continue.

'Eight years ago, I worked in Dublin Castle as a clerk for a shipping agent of the Honourable East India Company.'

'For the East India Company itself?' Oliver queried.

'No. The HEIC did not have an office in Dublin. All its business was conducted through a shipping company. It was interesting work as the agent dealt with all manner of people regarding maritime, military and revenue matters. It was also a recruiting office for the Bengal Army. My job, as a writer, was mainly copying correspondence and the postage of letters.

'One evening, when I left the Castle to go home, I was gathered up by an angry mob thronging the street and, though I tried to escape from the crowd, I was forcibly carried along. We had gone no more than one hundred yards when I was grabbed by a pair of soldiers and dragged from the street and thrown into the back of a cart with several others. In a way, I was lucky. I heard later that the mob was halted at a barricade where a company of armed militiamen was lying in wait for them with loaded muskets. Many died that day.'

'But you got away?'

'No. There was no escape. It was already dark and, like the others in the cart, we didn't know what was to become of us or where we were being taken. I had never felt so much fear. Eventually we arrived at Kilmainham Gaol where we were dragged from the cart and herded into its dungeons. It was dark, dank and cold. The guards issued us with a single candle to serve for light and warmth and said it had to last us for two weeks. The other four men in my cell were dressed in clothes typical of poor country folk, whereas I was wearing the tailored coat and trousers I wore to my desk. The sounds and smells of that place were repugnant and the cries unimaginable. Some of the cells had women and children in them but they received no special treatment.

'Three weeks passed before I was brought before a judge. Fortunately, having had a few coins in my pocket, I had managed to get word to several reputable friends who visited me. They spoke on my behalf and convinced the judge I was not a rebel. To my relief, the Court pronounced me not guilty and I was allowed to walk free. My fellow prisoners were not so lucky.'

'Did you return to the Castle?'

'Only for a short time. One day there was uproar in the courtyard close to where I was working. The bodies of a group of insurgents were brought into the Castle's yard on a large wagon and dropped in full view of the secretaries' windows. It was the intention of the authorities to display them as trophies. The poor souls, including some women, were cut and sliced every which way. Their bodies were filthy and blackened with blood and mud. After several hours in the hot sun, one of the mutilated carcases moved. The man was not dead. The soldiers found it amusing. One stood over the man, removed the bayonet from his musket and drove it through the man's throat. When the other soldiers cheered, he twisted it in an act of bravado. It was a sickening sight. I had to leave. I could not stay any longer.'

Oliver paused before addressing his next question. 'Are you a British loyalist?'

Michael O'Connor shifted in his seat and looked uncomfortable. 'I was asked that question almost as many times as I was asked if I was a rebel. My answer was always the same: I am an Irishman and I love Ireland but I hated what was happening to my country. The uprisings divided my people. I saw friends and neighbours torn apart. Loyalties were sworn and broken. Murder, treachery and retribution were commonplace and it was impossible to know who to trust.' He sighed deeply. 'I did not take sides, though it was hard not to do so and, in the end, I found it easier to take a ship from Dublin and sail to Bristol. My plan was to sail to America but I had little money, so I travelled north to Liverpool and went to the offices of another agent of the Honourable East India

Company and offered them my services. I was lucky. I was given a job as a writer and commenced work the following day.'

'Was your employer satisfied with your work?

'Always. I was a good worker.'

'Then what made you leave?'

'It was the memory of those ear-piercing screams falling within earshot of the Ministers of Government, knowing full well that the torture was allowed to continue. I could not stay. I was desperate to make a new life for myself in a new country. I am not young and I would like to take a wife and have children who will grow up in a place without fear.'

'And now' Oliver said, glancing about him. 'What of your present situation aboard *Perpetual*?'

The Irishman shrugged. 'I find myself in a similar bind to that which I endured in Dublin. I know I am not trusted. On deck, sailors point and talk about me. They call me foul names because they saw me come aboard in Ponta Delgada with the five troublemakers and assume that I am of the same mind as them. Even now, I sense undercurrents of hatred and feelings of animosity against men of Irish birth. But I swear I am not like them and I thank you for allowing me to stay on board and for providing me with a purposeful occupation.'

'And of the sea itself?' Oliver enquired. 'How do you regard a life being confined within a ship once again?'

'I have no complaints. I have my own hammock and I like the sea,' he said. 'It provides a feeling of seclusion, and every mile we sail carries me further from the land I escaped from. The sea itself is wild and unpredictable and can claim a man's soul as quick as a militiaman's bullet, but that is its nature and I accept it.'

'But the sea is not devoid of mortal conflict,' Oliver said. 'You witnessed that off the Fernando de Noronha Islands where men fought each other tooth and nail like savages, and would have torn each other to shreds given the opportunity.'

O'Connor acknowledged the captain's comments. 'Despite that, I see the ship as a place of sanctuary. It's like a church. Its walls surround me, comfort me and protect me. And, while *Perpetual* is my home, I will fight with my life to defend it.'

Though the Irishman's words had satisfied the captain as to his integrity, it had also given him concerns regarding the underlying feeling of discontent aboard his ship. 'Thank you, Michael. For the present, return to your other duties on deck and ignore the ugly talk. I will put a stop to that.'

Throughout the conversation, Oliver had been engaged, not only with the man's words but with the lilting tones and accent in which he delivered them. It was only after the door had closed that he recollected hearing the same resonance from Captain Gore of HMS *Medusa*, the officer from whom he had accepted the cases of Spanish treasure in Gibraltar Bay – the very treasure his present mission was connected with.

He remembered how Captain Gore had shared a meal aboard *Perpetual* with him and his officers and had impressed everyone with his cordiality –particularly the young midshipmen. For over an hour he had delighted them with stories of his exploits, of successful missions and others of misadventure. Every element of that evening was fixed in Oliver's head and he remembered how the captain had told him that he had been born in Kilkenny in Ireland. The ring in his voice was the same as O'Connor's.

Oliver shook his head. It appeared that this whole episode in his life was revolving around Irishmen.

Chapter 18

Flotsam

'Deck there!'

'What do you see?' the midshipman called.

'Something in the water two points off the starboard bow.'

'A sail?'

'No. Something floating on the water,' the lookout called. 'It could be a body.'

'How far?'

Before an answer came back from aloft, Mr Tully grabbed a telescope, leapt into the shrouds and climbed the rigging to the foretopgallant yard.

'Less than half a mile ahead,' was the reply.

Having studied the object with and without the glass, Ben Tully wasted no time before returning to the quarterdeck and ordering one of the midshipmen to go below and beg the captain attend him on deck. After calling for the maintop-sail yard to be backed to slow the frigate, he waited for the captain to appear on deck.

Within minutes of the changes to *Perpetual*'s canvas, *Flambeau*'s main top-sail yard was similarly braced and both ships slowed allowing the lookouts to investigate the flotsam.

Having pointed his telescope to the object that the lookout had reported, the captain joined Ben Tully leaning over the starboard rail. 'It's a body alright,' the lieutenant announced. It was floating face down in the water.

'Do we ignore it or haul it aboard?' the lieutenant asked.

'If it has not been weighted down in the appropriate manner, then I doubt it was afforded any burial rights. I think, therefore,' Oliver said, 'it should be hoisted aboard and, if nothing else, we can provide it with a decent burial. That is the least it deserves. Bosun, a boat in the water and rig up a whip with a sling, if you please.'

With sails backed, *Perpetual* rolled and pitched on the Atlantic swell as the body drifted slowly towards it. With nothing but the monotony of the vast expanse of ocean having been borne by the crew for the past three weeks, the arrival of a corpse provided a welcome break from continuous boredom. Sailors streamed up from below to witness the body being retrieved and carefully dragged to the side of the boat without the limbs being torn from the torso. The *Perpetuals* who had sailed with Captain Quintrell in the icy regions of the Southern Ocean remembered the effects submersion could have. Those were memories they would rather forget. Mindful of this, the coxswain threw a tarpaulin over the corpse before it was hoisted to the deck and placed flat on a canvas hammock.

'Let me see it,' Oliver said.

When the midshipman drew back the cover, there was an instant intake of breath from those standing close by.

'Not a pleasant sight,' Oliver said, turning to his first lieutenant. 'Kindly ask Dr Whipple to join me. And clear this rabble away.'

With several hands having seen the damage to the corpse, word quickly spread around the deck and was relayed to the sailors in the forecastle. A fleeting glance had revealed eyes gouged out and, from the open mouth, the tongue had gone too. There were puncture marks dotted over the bare torso and the fingers and toes had apparently been cut off.

Apart from the signs of inflicted wounds, the body was bloated as was to be expected. But, being thousands of miles from land, it raised the question, what ship had the man fallen off or been thrown from? Was he alive when he'd gone overboard or was he already dead when he hit the water? How many of his injuries had occurred before he died? Had he died as a result of being tortured? Apart from those questions there remained the mystery of who he was. The captain was not the only one wanting to know the answers.

Aside from those questions, could it be assumed the dead man had come from the 74 and, if so, by calculating the prevailing winds and flow of the Atlantic current, was it possible to calculate the probable location of the third rate?

It took Dr Whipple only a matter of minutes to make a brief appraisal of the corpse. He then requested the body be delivered to the cockpit so he could make a more thorough examination.

Having spoken only briefly with the surgeon on deck, Oliver allowed an hour for him to examine the corpse before stepping down to the cockpit.

'May I enter?' Oliver asked, from the doorway.

'Of course,' the doctor replied from the far side of an operating table that had been constructed in the centre of the cockpit. Standing over his subject, he still held a knife in his stained hand.

Oliver approached slowly. The sight that confronted him was more appalling than that which he had witnessed on the deck.

Lying on his back, on a stained white sheet, the man's torso had been opened from neck to navel and horizontally across the chest from one armpit to the other. The entrails and other organs, that had been removed, had been placed in several buckets near the doctor's feet. The empty shell on the table resembled a butcher's carcase rather than a human body.

Choosing not to look into the wooden pails, Oliver cleared his throat. 'This is the sort of work you did at the Borough Hospitals, I believe?'

The surgeon nodded, placing the knife in a water butt on the floor. 'That is correct, and I thank you for giving me the opportunity to conduct a thorough post mortem examination.'

'I am hoping you can supply some information about this man. If not his identity, then perhaps how and when he died?'

'I believe I can confidently answer those questions and more. First,' he said, pointing to the man's trousers, which had been removed and were neatly folded on the floor. 'If I am not mistaken, these are regular duck issue as supplied by the purser on all naval vessels. Therefore, I contend this man was a Royal Navy seaman.'

Without touching them, Oliver viewed the item of clothing. 'I agree.'

'Furthermore, the anchor tattooed on his arms would confirm his occupation and, from the tar staining his palms yellow and his broken fingernails, I would assess he spent most of his days aloft in a ship's rigging furling canvas to the yards.'

Oliver was impressed.

'Added to that,' he said, 'the man's feet have a distinct calloused ridge across them. That is the skin's response to years of friction sliding along a footrope.'

'A topman?' Oliver queried, surprised at the conclusion arrived at so quickly.

'Indeed,' he said. 'But now, for the obvious and somewhat appalling injuries the body displays.' The ship's surgeon continued, pointing to the man's side, arms and the loose skin incised from his chest. 'These puncture marks have been caused by the teeth of small fish trying to make a meal of him. It appears a larger fish has nipped off several fingers and toes quite cleanly. I am surprised a shark did not make a more complete meal of him.' Leaning forward over the face, he placed his index finger in one of the open orifices. 'As to the eyes and tongue, which are also missing, I put that damage down to the voracious appetites of wandering seabirds. They are attracted to shiny morsels and unlikely to refuse any delicacy offered to them.'

Oliver was amazed. 'So, it would appear, when he entered the water this man was uninjured.'

'That is so and the question you will ask next is – did he fall or was he thrown into the sea?'

Oliver nodded expectantly.

'I can confidently say he did not fall from the rigging either to the deck or directly into the sea. If he had, there would be obvious damage to his skull, neck or limbs. He would have suffered breaks or dislocations and shown evidence of bleeding about the head. I could find no such injuries.'

'Perhaps he jumped overboard of his own free will.'

'Are you suggesting suicide?'

Oliver nodded his head. 'It happens.'

'And it is a possibility I considered,' the doctor said.

The captain was surprised. 'What makes you say that?'

He glanced to one of the wooden pails on the floor near his feet. 'From my examination of the man's stomach contents and his overall body appearance – discounting the bloating effect caused by submersion, I would say this man was less than thirty years of age, had been strong, fit and healthy but had recently been starved. Perhaps the sea was a means of escape.'

Oliver took a step back from the table. 'Thank you, Doctor, I appreciate your assessment, but I will not enter suicide as the cause of death. If that were the case, I could not provide this sailor with a Christian burial. However, I can accept that he died of natural causes, albeit malnutrition, and was buried at sea. It is possible he was sewn into a hammock and subsequently slipped from it.'

'So be it,' Jonathon said. 'I have no problem with that.'

'Just one more question. How long has the body been in the water?'

'In my estimation, three to four days.'

'Thank you, Doctor. Your advice has been enormously helpful. I will arrange for the body to be buried in the morning. Kindly prepare the remains accordingly.'

With the Admiralty's chart of the Atlantic Ocean once again spread across the table in the great cabin, the captain and Mr Mundy studied it, reflecting on the strength and direction of the winds in the past five days. They referred to the ship's log and considered the speed *Perpetual* and *Flambeau* had been making, and their bearings. They also spoke of the state of the sea, the surface waves, the swell and the underlying currents. Armed with this information they independently calculated where the body was likely to have entered the water and, if it had come from the 74, which seemed the most logical explanation, what the present position of HMS *Stalwart* might be.

After considerable debate, the captain and sailing master finally agreed and an adjustment to the ship's present course was called for. With word passed to the helm and news related by speaking trumpet to Mr Parry aboard *Flambeau*, the two frigates took up their pursuit of the man-of-war.

Though he did not discuss the matter with his sailing master, Oliver was troubled by certain aspects of the information the doctor had given him. He had learned from Ekundayo that around two hundred British sailors had likely been locked in the 74's hold. If this sailor, whose body had been recovered from the ocean, was one of that group and he had died from starvation, was it possible many other sailors similarly confined were dying at that very instant?

It was imperative to catch the 74 as quickly as possible and wrest it from the fiends who had taken it.

Two days later, a signal from *Flambeau* announced that another body had been spotted off its beam. *Perpetual* immediately hove to, while the French frigate wore around in a near complete circle to swim up alongside the corpse and pluck it from the water. There was no need to transfer the body to *Perpetual*, as Mr Parry's report was sufficient to convince Captain Quintrell that not all was well aboard the 74. Unlike the previous body, however, this seaman had died as a result of several violent wounds inflicted by cutlass blade or knife. The fact this body was not bloated indicated it had not been in the water very long.

'It would appear we are following a trail of corpses,' Oliver commented rather flippantly to the ship's surgeon. 'I wonder how many are out there that have not been spotted.'

Jonathon Whipple's expression was grave. 'I fear what is up ahead will be no laughing matter.'

Chapter 19

Mayhem

With the dawn of a new day, members of both watches were on deck at sunrise scanning the sea for more floating bodies or a ship. Word had filtered from the quarterdeck that the 74 was not far ahead and the two frigates were in pursuit. Surprisingly, the macabre discoveries had perked the spirits of the crew and there was an air of anticipation in the mess and on the forecastle.

The discovery of yet another corpse confirmed the captain's suspicions but also elevated his concerns. Like the body sighted by *Flambeau* earlier, the injuries were deep and deadly. Blood, which had dried as hard as mortar, was still caked in the wounds.

The tension on board was high. The officers paced the deck, screwing their eyes or squinting at the ocean through the lens of a telescope.

'Do you see anything?' Mr Tully shouted to the foremast lookout.

'There's a grey smudge on the horizon but it could be a cloud.'

As usual Mr Tully climbed aloft where the lookout pointed to what he had described.

The lieutenant rubbed his eyes, cleaned the lens on the cuff of his shirt and looked again. 'I agree,' he said. 'A grey smudge. It could be the tip of a rising cloud but it could also be a pyramid of canvas with its hull buried in the ocean.'

Together the pair watched and waited for any change but the blot on the horizon neither rose nor dissolved.

'If it was heading this way, it would be hull-up by now.'

Mr Tully agreed. 'If it's a ship, it's heading away from us.' Looking at the firm bosoms of canvas all around him, it was obvious *Perpetual* was sailing well. She was carrying all her sails including studding sails alow and aloft. The French frigate mirrored her canvas. 'Keep an eye on it,' Mr Tully advised the lookout, 'I'll inform the captain.'

With the news relayed to the quarterdeck and then to *Flambeau*, both the helms were adjusted by a couple of spokes bringing both frigates in line with the object on the horizon.

'Would a warning shot be worthwhile?' the sailing master asked.

'Not yet,' the captain replied. If it is *Stalwart*, the lookouts will identify it soon enough. For the present, I prefer to be sure it is the ship we are chasing rather than alarming some other vessel.'

It was more than half an hour before the lookout confirmed a three-masted ship on the horizon with its hull almost visible. In his opinion, it was a line-of-battle ship and probably the third rate they were looking for, but it was flying no colours.

Sailing with a fresh following wind, the two frigates were making nine knots, but any evidence of the pair gaining on the 74 was hard to see. The sailing master announced it would take several hours to bring the ship into range of their guns, but three hours later, Captain

Quintrell was satisfied that they had *Stalwart* in their sights and gave the order, 'Mr Tully, call all hands. Prepare for action, and pass the word to Mr Parry on *Flambeau*.'

'Aye aye, sir.'

Unable to anticipate who or what they would find aboard the third rate, the captain ordered a shot to be fired from one of the bow chasers. The response was almost immediate and surprised everyone. A white flag was run up on the 74's signal halliard. However, that reply failed to answer the captain's question as to who was in command, and it raised another other question: *Was it a ruse?*

The captain received his answer when the ship backed its sails and the ensign was hoisted. Cheers rang out simultaneously from the decks of both frigates which immediately came alive with activity. As if suddenly endowed with renewed vigour, the sailors streamed aloft to shorten sail, pull in the stuns'l booms, put another reef in the topsails and furl the courses. This allowed the frigates to slow as they closed on the warship.

When the name on the third rate's transom was clearly visible to the naked eye, *Perpetual* bore away to its larboard side while Mr Parry ordered *Flambeau* down the starboard beam. Not knowing what reception they would receive, both frigates' gun ports were open and the gun crews were standing ready for action.

After a brief conversation between *Perpetual* and the third rate, spoken through a brass trumpet, Oliver called for two boats to be put away. With the wind whipping up three foot waves on top of a strong swell, the waiting craft pitched and bounced, thudding heavily against the frigate's hull.

With the coxswains already aboard, the crews quickly took their seats. Captain Quintrell, two of his senior officers and six marines occupied the first boat, while more marines jumped down into the second. With spray from the wave tips making for a wet ride, it was fortunate it was only a short pull to the 74.

Stepping aboard, everyone was struck with the same sense of shock and abhorrence. Those feelings were immediately etched on the men's faces. While Captain Liversedge, in unbuttoned undress uniform, was waiting on deck to greet his fellow captain and the side boys lined the gangway sounding their pipes, it was the startling consequences of a recent fight that grabbed Oliver Quintrell's attention.

The deck was stained with blood – not scattered crimson spots as if dripped from a paint brush, but great swathes and streaks in plum and yellow-brown tones. With an attempt to wash the evidence from the deck, the swabbers had created the backcloth palette for an angry watercolour painting. The scuppers were stained rusty-red along their full length while the gunnels, rails and timber lockers bore cuts and gouges from blades hacking into them with lethal force. But most shocking of all was a large angular pile, heaped to chest high, covered in an expanse of torn sailcloth. Protruding legs and arms announced what was hidden beneath the canvas.'

'In Heaven's name,' Oliver exclaimed. 'What happened here?'

'Let us go below,' the captain said, drawing him away and indicating towards his cabin. 'We need to talk.' A feeling of great heaviness was evident in William Liversedge's voice.

Hardly able to avert his eyes from the scene, Oliver handed his pistol to Mr Tully and followed his friend to the great cabin. On entering, William made no excuse or apology for the state of the room and appeared oblivious to the wanton damage which spoke of a fierce fight that had taken place in that part of the ship. Oliver blinked. The scene bore little resemblance to the fine drawing room-like accommodation he had visited, only a few weeks ago, in Guanabara Bay.

While a pile of broken chairs, tossed into one corner, was the only measure taken to clear the debris, that effort failed to hide proof of the violent confrontation that had occurred. The elegant drapes, ripped from the casements lay in tatters while goose down, spilled from a slashed cushion, decorated the floor like flakes of snow. The carpet was still sticky with blood.

Trying hard not to be distracted, Oliver expressed a warm greeting. He was genuinely pleased to be reunited with his friend. With refreshments already prepared and waiting on the table, Oliver was grateful to accept a drink and invited his friend to relate his story in his own time.

Stalwart's captain said it had been hard to control his emotions at the relief he felt when he heard *Perpetual* together with *Flambeau* had been sighted. 'How did you manage to come up on us in this vast ocean?'

'Floating bodies,' Oliver relied bluntly. 'You left a trail.'

'I did not know,' Captain Liversedge said. 'I am sorry.'

'It seems much has happened aboard the 74 since we spoke several weeks ago.'

William Liversedge shook his head several times as if trying to deny the things that had happened or attempting to dispel the raffle of distasteful images cluttering his brain. 'So many dead,' he said, speaking to himself. 'As you can see, there are many still awaiting burial.'

Oliver knew those matters should be attended to without delay but first he had to uncover the problem. 'I learned that your ship had been taken and am relieved to find that you have now regained control.'

The third rate's captain nodded but showed no sign of elation.

'You must have taken prisoners? Where are they?' Oliver asked.

'In the hold.'

Oliver thought of the French sailors who had been held in *Flambeau*'s hold. 'I trust they are secure and under guard,' he said.

'I believe so.' But the voice lacked conviction.

Oliver poured another glass of wine for himself and one for his friend. 'Can you tell me what led to this assault? I wish to be of assistance.'

After a long sigh, Captain Liversedge began. 'Two days ago, my crew, who had been confined below decks by a group of evil mutineers, rioted. I was told later that my men were not being fed and were desperate to escape. On discovering an axe and handspike buried in the ballast, they broke open barrels of water, biscuits, beef and potatoes and, being half-starved, ate ravenously till many were sick. Then they helped themselves to wine, beer and spirits and gorged themselves until they were raving drunk. In this state of inebriation, a group of them smashed the hatch cover, despite being fired on by the French soldiers guarding them. Several died from musket shots and others were injured, but before the soldiers could reload and reinforcements arrived, the mob burst through to the orlop deck. From there they spilled along the companionways, climbed to the gun decks and headed for the forecastle and quarterdeck. It was not only their freedom they wanted, but they were desperate for fresh air after having been deprived of it for several weeks.'

Sitting across the table, Oliver remained silent.

'Moving *en masse* from one deck to the next, the crew set upon anyone in their path irrespective of whether they were English, Irish or French. Only Moncousu's sailors, in their quaint nautical garb, were easy to identify.

'Though unarmed, I understand my men fought as if they were deranged – punching, kicking, gouging and biting anyone who obstructed their path. As they progressed through the ship, they collected whatever items they could to use as weapons – handspikes, boathooks, screws, rammers, pawls and belaying pins. And when they reached the armoury, they added pistols, muskets, hangers and cutlasses to their arsenal.'

'Where were you at this time?' Oliver asked.

'I was locked in a cabin in the midshipmen's quarters, separated from my officers. I had lost track of how long I was there. With no light, save for a faint glimmer spilling through the cracks around the door, I never knew if it was night or day and with my feet and arms pinioned, I was incapable of doing anything.'

'Did you hear the ruckus taking place?' Oliver enquired.

'I heard a commotion,' Liversedge said, 'but I did not know where it was coming from or what it meant. At first, I feared my ship was under attack. I am ashamed I did not free myself before this terrible incident took place. Only when my men released me and I came out on deck did I witness the full extent of the mutiny.' He paused and sighed heavily. 'It was the most ungodly conflict imaginable.

'The fighting was hand to hand and brutal. Amongst those fighting, one of the first people I recognised was

Captain Moncousu. He was being restrained by some of my men. I was told he had surrendered his sword but his own men either didn't see or didn't care. They neither lowered their weapons nor ceased fighting. There was no shortage of those wanting to fight. Heads continued to pop up from the waist and hatches and, as each sailor stepped onto the deck, he was hit, kicked or stuck with whatever implement was on hand without any enquiry being made as to his identity or allegiance. The men crawled over each other like animals with cutlass blades flashing in the sun above their heads. When arteries were severed, blood spurted as freely as water from a drinking fountain. The deck was a charnel house with bodies covering every square inch. So many bodies.' He sighed. 'As the ship pitched and heeled, they rolled on the deck like seals in the shallows on a South American beach. It was hard to walk in any direction without stepping on some limb or head, be it attached to a body or not. The scuppers flowed red with blood and the sea beneath bloomed crimson. It was terrible.'

'You and your men must have fought bravely,' Oliver offered.

'I cannot remember who I fought or how many. Having exhausted the pistol I'd been given, I brought it down on a Frenchman's skull before flinging it over the side. I recollect gripping a dirk in my left hand and hearing the constant clang of metal on metal. I still hear it ringing in my ears. I was without my sword, but without rules or mutual respect, it was no place for swordplay. Yet, I vividly recollect swinging a cutlass blindly about me not knowing if it was friend or foe I was making contact with. At one point, I raised my right arm to protect my face and at the same time thrust the point of the knife into the belly of a man leaning over me. For a second, his expression changed as I pushed him from me. He looked puzzled, but he didn't fall and kept on fighting with the hilt protruding from him.'

'But your men succeeded in extinguishing the riot.'

'Eventually,' Captain Liversedge said. 'With my officers beside me, we forced the mob to the rails where some scrambled over frantically and jumped into the sea. Others were pushed overboard with blood spurting from their wounds. Several fell backwards over the rail into the waist. I remember the sound of dull thuds when their bodies hit the gun deck. They never returned.' He took a sip of wine. 'When we gained the upper hand, we started driving them back. Then, all of a sudden, the remaining Frenchmen and the irate Irish insurgents turned about and dived for the hatches. We followed them down from one deck to another, lunging at them all the time, clambering over dead and dying victims in the companionways, pushing them deeper into the ship until there was nowhere for them to go apart from the hold.'

'Where your men had previously been held?'

'Indeed. They had no alternative. Soon after, the stragglers were rounded up and pushed in with them also. Gratings were laid over the hatches to replace the covers that had been broken and a strong guard was placed on the hold.'

'You turned the tables completely. Well done.'

'But at what cost?' William sighed. 'How pleased I am to see you. Once again I am in your debt. You can be assured the Admiralty will hear of this.'

Oliver brushed off the comment. 'Now is the time to address the present situation. You have bodies that are long overdue for burial. The sun is taking a dire toll. They must be disposed of urgently.'

'I know that,' William said. 'But how can those sailors be identified? How can I give them all a Christian burial?'

'Permit me to advise you. In times of war, when fighting is most intense, bodies are cast overboard without a second thought. What occurred here on *Stalwart* was a battle.' He paused for a moment. 'I suggest you assemble your men forthwith. Read the burial rights over the dead and then dispose of the bodies into the sea? You cannot afford time to bury each man with the regular ritual.'

'I suppose it must be done that way.'

'It must,' Oliver said. 'We are three or four days' sailing from Ushant and the entrance to the Channel. You cannot leave the dead on deck any longer. Those carcases are already leaking and I guarantee the stench from them will precede you, and your ship will not be welcome in any port. If you delay casting the corpses adrift, the beaches of England and France will be littered with rotting corpses for weeks. My advice is to dispose of them now and let the sea do what it does best.'

Captain Liversedge admitted he had been remiss in not attending to the dead earlier. 'I will give the order right away. Will you stay for the service?'

Oliver agreed, though he had no desire to witness another burial service especially with so many corpses. But, with the anguish and exhaustion of the incident resting heavily on the shoulders of his fellow captain, he was conscious his support was needed.

'When that matter has been attended to,' Oliver said, 'I will return to *Perpetual* and will escort you to Spithead.'

William Liversedge thanked him and, after splashing water across his face and drying his hands, the pair repaired to the quarterdeck.

'There is one thing I can relieve you of,' Oliver said. 'The two women you accommodated for me. I trust all the women aboard survived.'

'They did, but there was also the boy. I have been told he has not been seen for some time. What has become of him is uncertain. It is possible he fell overboard and drowned.'

Oliver smiled. 'The boy is safe and well. But what of the Irishman who led this insurrection. His name was Joseph Murphy. Where is he now?'

William Liversedge pointed up into the rigging. 'I was not familiar with any names, but if you look to the starboard main yardarm you will see three ropes' ends dangling. I was told the French captain had no intention of sailing to Ireland though he had given his word to the rebels. A week ago Moncousu, claimed sole control of the 74 and had three of the ringleaders strung up. It was a cruel half-hanging with the noose not tight enough to strangle the men immediately. I did not witness this but was told the trio hung and kicked and moaned till late into the night when they eventually succumbed. Ironically, that is an Irish practice, I believe. Apparently, Captain Moncousu found the whole exercise amusing.'

'Only three men?' Oliver queried. 'Originally there were five.'

Captain Liversedge nodded. 'Perhaps the other two are amongst the bodies on the deck.'

'And where did Moncousu intend to take this ship?'

'Brest, I believe.'

'Hoping to run the gauntlet of the British blockade.'

'Perhaps he intended to fly the British jack until he was in the harbour.'

'He was an ambitious man,' Captain Liversedge said.

'A misguided fool, in my eyes. And what of his bold plans now?' Oliver asked. 'Where is he?'

William Liversedge cast his eyes down to the planks. 'The captain's blood is decorating the deck. He got what he deserved. At the height of the riot, Moncousu escaped yet again and was yelling and screaming at his men to attack and retake the ship. He threatened to string up anyone who opposed him. By this time, however, everyone had had enough of the fighting, deceit, anger and uncertainty and, though I did not witness it, he was rushed by an incensed group of men – of what nationality I do not know. He was murdered where we stand and his body hacked to shreds. His remains were not a pretty sight and were thrown overboard even before the fighting ended.'

'You have suffered much, William. I feel responsible for bringing this trouble to you.'

'You are not responsible, Oliver,' Captain Liversedge said and forthwith excused himself to make the necessary preparations to conduct the burial service.

With the canvas covering removed from the pile of carcases, and a few additional bodies dragged up from below, the corpses, trailing blood, body fluids and, in some cases, entrails were dragged to the entry port and lined up alongside each other.

At the bosun's prompting, the assembled company removed their hats and stood in silence on the heaving deck. The burial service was duly read committing all the bodies to the sea. Without further ado, each victim was placed onto a wooden hatch cover and the flag was briefly draped over it. Each one remained there only for the time it took for the timber to be inclined and the body to plunge over the side. Lacking canvas shrouds and cannon balls, the manner in which they were consigned to the deep was one of convenience, speed and necessity. Despite some of the victims being French, others Irish, others British, and many being Catholic and others Protestant, no distinctions were made.

With heads bowed, the ship's company maintained that attitude throughout the service. While the now-familiar fetid stench was tolerated by the 74's crew, the sailors serving under Oliver Quintrell's command were physically sickened by it. Like whalers whose hands stank constantly of blubber, those men given the unenviable task of dragging the bodies to the side would find the vile smell impregnated their skin and would stay with them for days.

From start to finish, the service took over an hour and as soon as the bodies and body parts had been cleared away, buckets of sea water were hauled up and washed across the deck. A concoction of lye and ash from the galley-fire was then sprinkled along the planks to help remove the worst of the stains. After that, a division of sailors attacked the deck with bristle brushes and swabs.

It was with much relief when the formalities were concluded and Oliver Quintrell and his officers were able to climb down the ship's side to the boats and return to the frigate. The hour was late, but having moved into the higher northern latitudes, it was not dark when the boats bumped up alongside *Perpetual*. Apart from the captain and some of his officers, the boat carried Mrs Pilkington and Mrs Crosby. A canvas chair was quickly rigged to whip the women onto the deck.

Their arrival prompted a spontaneously warm welcome, Connie Pilkington being almost bowled off her feet when Charles Goodridge ran up and threw his arms around her waist. Her eyes immediately clouded with tears. Having been told he was feared drowned, she was overjoyed to see him.

Dr Whipple, standing nearby, waited politely to offer his good wishes. Taking the young woman's hand and holding it between his own, there was much he wanted to say. But he barely had sufficient time to express his joy and relief at finding her well and restored once more to *Perpetual*. After a brief exchange, he was obliged to follow his medicine chest, bag and some personal dunnage down the steps to the waiting boat to be transferred to the third rate. His presence had been requested to assist the ship's surgeon in administering to the many injured and dying sailors who were overflowing the 74's cockpit.

Chapter 20

The 74's Hold

Having slept a full watch of four hours and eaten a cooked breakfast, Oliver came on deck feeling refreshed. Despite the many questions he still had for Captain Liversedge, he decided those matters could wait until they dropped anchor in Spithead.

'Mr Tully, double the lookout, if you please. I expect we will encounter some merchantmen when we enter the chops, not to mention ships of the Channel Fleet and Frenchies from Boulogne or Le Havre.'

'Aye aye, Capt'n.'

A fair wind filled the sails of all three vessels and the plaintive cry of seagulls wheeling above the mastheads heralded the fact they were closing on the coast.

On deck, Mrs Pilkington stood alongside Charles Goodridge, her hand resting on his shoulder. Beside her was Mrs Crosby and her husband – the ship's carpenter who had been returned from *Flambeau* after several weeks of absence. Oliver was pleased to see the family and friends reunited. He regretted that Mr Parry was not able to join him on the quarterdeck. His lieutenant's command of the French frigate would not end until it was handed over to the prize agent in Spithead.

While contemplating the set of the sails and noting the occasional luff of the royal, the captain's attention was suddenly alerted by the muffled sound of musket fire. He glanced to Mr Tully, standing by the binnacle. He had also heard the noise. It was not of one shot but several and they came from the direction of the 74. Although the ship was sailing slightly ahead of the two frigates, heads could be seen scuttling along *Stalwart*'s deck and disappearing into the waist or down through the hatches.

'What in Heaven's name is happening now?' Oliver cried.

As he spoke, the 74's mainsail was clewed up, the topsail yard braced around and the ship slowed to a stop.

'All hands on deck!' Oliver ordered. 'Luff up!' A similar order was relayed by Lieutenant Parry on *Flambeau*.

Within minutes, the two frigates closed on the 74. When *Perpetual* drifted to within pistol shot, Captain Quintrell hailed the deck.

A seaman replied with the aid of a speaking trumpet. 'The prisoners in the hold have gone crazy,' he announced. 'Captain Liversedge needs help.'

The thought again flashed through Oliver's mind that this could be a ploy to lure him and his men aboard in order for *Perpetual* to be taken. But on seeing Lieutenant Hazzlewood, the man who had served with him as a middie, hovering by the gangway, he was reassured. Cupping his hands, he shouted across the water: 'Inform Captain Liversedge I intend to come aboard. I will bring men and marines and provide whatever assistance is required.'

The 74's lieutenant acknowledged and immediately disappeared from view.

In the time it took to lower two of *Perpetual*'s boats, Captain Quintrell and a dozen of his men armed themselves with pistols and cutlasses. A dozen marines were been assembled along the deck their muskets already primed and bayonets fixed. The boats had hardly touched the water before the contingent clambered down and filled the thwarts. With spray splashing over the bows and the boats being tossed by the waves, it was not an easy pull for the rowers or a comfortable transfer for those aboard.

Despite the support of well-armed men and marines following closely behind, Captain Quintrell climbed to the deck of the 74 with trepidation. In one hand he held a cocked pistol, while his sword hand remained free. Stepping onto the deck, he was wary of what sight would greet him this time.

His fears were allayed when Lieutenant Hazzlewood stepped up and greeted the captain. The deck was clear and apart from the occasional raised voices coming from below, all appeared quiet. There were no sounds of shooting, no crashing of steel, no cries of pain and no canvas-covered pile of bodies. However, the lieutenant was obviously agitated.

'Good to see you, sir' he said quickly. 'The captain is in dire need of your help.'

'What has happened?'

'The prisoners rioted. They are behaving like wild beasts. Captain Liversedge told me the French and Irish sailors in the hold have formed themselves into two separate mobs and are intent on slaughtering each other.'

'Where is the captain now?'

'He's in the hold. He went below to try to talk some sense into them.'

'You accompanied him?'

'Not inside. He said for me to lower the cover after he and his men had entered and not to allow anyone in or out until he gave the instruction.'

'You did that?'

'Yes, Captain. And I placed an armed guard at the hatch.'

'Who is with Captain Liversedge?'

'The second lieutenant and some of the crew. They are armed but they are badly outnumbered. I don't know how long they can hold out before the mob takes over.'

'Come with me,' Oliver said. 'I am going below'.

'Take care, captain.'

Oliver nodded and followed Mr Hazzlewood down through the ship. When they reached the grating over the hatch, the lieutenant released the bar securing it and slid the cover back a few inches. Oliver peered through the gap but could see nothing.

'I shall need more light,' he demanded. 'Much more light.'

'Captain Quintrell is that you?'

Though reassured to hear the voice of the 74's captain, it sounded distant and his words lacked their usual verve.

'I am coming below. I have men with me,' he shouted back then turned to the lieutenant. 'Remove the grating and stand back, but be ready.'

Standing by the hatch cover, Oliver sniffed the air. The stench that invaded his nostrils was strange. The hold reeked of brine, but not the salty brine swept from the ocean but the pickling brine of the galley when cauldrons of beef, pork and preserved vegetables were boiled. The smell almost took his breath away. But the shouts and curses and threats held his attention.

After waiting until two more lanterns were handed to his men, Oliver ordered the hatch cover to be removed completely and he stepped down.

With Mr Tully on his right shoulder, Ekundayo to his left and several seamen and marines following closely behind, the captain descended carefully, unsure of the reception awaiting them. He stopped when he reached the bottom of the ladder. 'Secure the grating,' he called.

Beneath his feet, the ship's ballast, usually firm with blocks of pig iron embedded in gravel, was soft and slimy. The shiny black surface appeared to slither slowly from side to side like a giant black serpent.

Ignoring the wetness penetrating his shoes, Oliver dug his feet firmly on the bottom and peered into the gloom. Closest to the steps was a small group of men, including some in uniform. The cocked pistols in their hands were levelled at two larger groups whose faces and identities were obscured in the darkness. Some shadowy figures hung back skulking within the hold's dark recesses. Others stepped forward defiantly brandishing weapons, their blades catching the light of the flickering glims. Between the groups, several bodies were sprawled on the ballast. It was evident an ugly confrontation had already taken place.

'Where are you?' Oliver called.

'I am here,' William Liversedge cried from the group nearby.

With his eyes slowly adjusting to the murky gloom, the tenseness of the situation was revealed. But the sight of William Liversedge standing at the head of his men concerned him. The captain's hair was dishevelled and beads of sweat glistened on his forehead. Though he was armed with a pistol in one hand and a cutlass in the other, both hands were trembling.

The Frenchmen were huddled closely together at the far end of the hold – their shirts, hats and striped trousers marking their identity. They numbered about thirty but were making no effort to move.

At the opposite end was a much larger, noisier and more aggressive group. From their dress they appeared British. From their accents, they were obviously Irish.

Oliver moved forward with his small armed forced and edged towards Captain Liversedge.

'They will stop at nothing,' the 74's captain said. 'They are armed and seem intent on slaughtering each other. And us too. They must be kept apart.'

As he was speaking, two of the marine's muskets exploded and two more bodies crumpled to the deck.

'Stay back!' Oliver yelled.

The man who had been hit moaned and squirmed like a cut worm on the slime but no one attempted to assist him.

With cutlasses brandished above their heads, the mob of Irishmen cursed, seethed and struggled with each other, throwing blows and curses at their own countrymen. Standing out at the front of the mob was one red-headed Wexford lad and another man, standing taller than the others in the group. It was Joseph Murphy.

'*Saoirse nó bás*!' the red-head yelled. The others joined in the cry for freedom or death.

'They are intent on killing each other,' Captain Liversedge repeated.

'Perhaps we should afford them that privilege,' Oliver replied.

'*Saoirse nó bás*,' Murphy cried, before breaking from the group. With a cutlass raised above his head he launched himself towards Captain Quintrell.

Oliver pulled the trigger and two muskets shots rang out simultaneously. Two Irish men dropped while Murphy fell forward impaling himself on a broken barrel stave. He did not get up.

Undeterred, another man took up the rebellious cry and the process was repeated.

'How many of you want to die,' Oliver yelled. 'You serve your country nothing by ending your lives in a stinking ship's hold. You have already forfeited your liberty and freedom. Death is waiting for you. Is that what you want? Is that what you are fighting for?'

The cries were silenced. No one moved.

'Surrender your weapons,' Oliver cried, 'or make this hold your grave.'

After the first cutlass was dropped to the ballast, grips were reluctantly released and others followed. The order was repeated and slowly an array of weapons fell from the Irishmen's hands. Cutlasses, knives and other implements were collected by two of the 74's marines and passed up through the hatch to the deck above.

Oliver turned and faced the other group. 'You Frogs will do the same. Captain Moncousu is dead. Your life rests in the hands of the ship's captain. If you are lucky, you will be delivered to an English port and treated as prisoners of war. You are enemies of the Crown and if you do not surrender now you will be shot. The choice is yours.'

Ekundayo repeated the order in French and immediately the sailors lifted their arms above their heads.

'If you do not want to die here with these Irish dogs, move from there. Follow my men to the deck. I will decide what to do with you later.'

The Frenchmen wasted no time in making their decision. Stepping carefully, they slid towards the steps.

'Clear away the hatch cover,' Oliver called to the guards. 'Marines, escort these Frogs to the waist. Restrain them with irons and keep them quiet until Captain Liversedge and I are done here.'

Ekundayo again relayed the instructions and the French sailors started pushing forward.

As Oliver watched the last few Frenchmen climbing the steps, another two shots rang out. Smoke rose from the muskets of the 74's marines.

'Back where you were!' Captain Liversedge yelled. With little choice, the Irishmen cursed but complied. Oliver nodded to his friend. Some degree of order had been restored.

Treading carefully in order not to slip, *Stalwart*'s sailors followed their captain up the steps to fresher air. Following his own men, Oliver Quintrell was the last to climb out. Before leaving, he turned and addressed the Irishmen.

'You men are a disgrace to the British Navy, a disgrace to yourselves and a disgrace to your country. For the riotous behaviour you have demonstrated on this ship you will be tried for mutiny and many of you will hang.'

With all the weapons removed and all but one lanterns remaining, Oliver Quintrell backed out of the hold. The grating immediately thudded down on the coaming leaving the irate Irish to argue and fight among themselves.

Captain Liversedge was waiting on the orlop deck. 'I thank God you came to my aid,' William cried. 'I was holding an empty pistol. I had exhausted all possibilities of overcoming those fiends and had no way of removing myself from the situation I got myself into. I don't know how much longer I could have held them off.'

Oliver reassured his friend that all would be well.

'More bodies,' William said. 'What do we do with them?'

'My men will assist. They must be tossed overboard.'

'So many young lives wasted,' William said, shaking his head. 'Such a waste.'

But Oliver knew there was much to attend to and no time for sentimentality. 'With your permission, I will speak with your officer on deck. The sooner we reach Portsmouth, the better.'

William Liversedge agreed. It was obvious there was little fight left in him.

An hour later, with the two captains sitting together in the main cabin, Oliver questioned his friend.

'What sparked this latest riot? I thought the matter had been resolved.'

'I thought so too,' William said. 'At least long enough to see us safe home. But, before setting upon each other, the two mobs turned their attention to the remaining barrels in the hold.'

'But you were not starving them, were you?'

Captain Liversedge laughed derisively. 'Certainly not.'

'Then what?' Oliver asked.

'Word had reached them that four chests of Spanish treasure were hidden in the barrels. As you know, many of my men had witnessed the transfer in Rio and when the men were forced into the hold and saw the barrels had been smashed by the British sailors, they presumed they had been searching for the silver.'

Oliver Quintrell rolled his eyes in disbelief.

'When we forced them below, they were still carrying the weapons they had been fighting with – axes, knives, cutlasses and pikes. They found those implements handy to prise the bands from the barrels or to stove in the staves. Once a few had been opened every sailor joined in. It was like the inmates of Bedlam had been let loose. Starting from the topmost level, they smashed every barrel they could reach then started grappling with each other. That was when my men had no alternative but to fire into the mob to try to bring some order. Several were shot and others wounded, but at least they stopped their riotous behaviour and I was able to separate them. That is when you arrived'

'Did they find what they were searching for?' Oliver enquired.

'No, I think not, but they had not reached the lower levels. They did, however, stove in barrels containing pork and beef, sauerkraut, lemons and beer empting them all into the hull. As you would have noticed, it's a gluey, stinking sewer that boasts an armada of ship's biscuits swimming on its surface. It will be impossible to pump out. Like night water it will have to be shovelled up and removed a bucketful at a time. I fear it will take days and the Navy Board will not be impressed.'

'This is truly unfortunate,' Oliver said, 'I am sorry that you were the one to suffer because of a promise I made long ago.'

William Liversedge was exhausted. 'What should I do, Oliver?'

It was a cry for help rather than a question.

'Trust me – now the two groups are apart you will have no problems. Bury the dead and set all sail. Leave the Irish prisoners where they are. Two days from now we will raise The Needles and, the following morning, anchor in Spithead. With the permission of the Port Admiral, it is possible you will be able to enter Portsmouth Harbour and convey your prisoners directly to one of the prison hulks where a court can be convened to hear the mutineers' case.'

'What of recovering and delivering the Spanish treasure?'

'Leave that to me,' Oliver said.

Chapter 21

Portsmouth

The early morning arrival in Spithead of a 74-gun ship of the line in convoy with a British frigate and a French prize was met in the port town with excitement. Along the ancient battlements and on both sides of the harbour's entrance, crowds gathered and watched in silence. Small children clung to their mothers' skirts after being told the father they had not seen in years was coming home. With that came the promise of food on the table and perhaps a pair of much needed shoes. On the wharfs, old salts, who had been refused berths on other ships, waited to see where the ships would dock. If the navy was desperate for men, there was a chance they could sign and return to sea. The possibility had been kindled by harbour talk that French squadrons were being recalled from across the Atlantic and that the Spanish were supplying their ships in readiness for a combined attack on the British fleet.

While the arrival and departure of line-of-battle ships was commonplace and a fleet could sit in Spithead for several days without drawing any attention, mention of His Majesty's frigate *Perpetual*, which had spent time in Gibraltar, jogged a few memories and set a few tongues wagging.

The previous year, the *Gazette* and *Naval Chronicle* had published details of Captain Graham Moore's success in taking several Spanish treasure ships in a deadly battle off

Cape St Mary. On his return to England, the majority of the treasure taken from the Spanish fleet had been discharged and conveyed to London. Though little was written of it at the time, word that the cargo consisted of gold ingots, gems and minted silver had spread like wildfire. But the frigate, *Medusa*, Captain John Gore, which had taken part in the action, had been severely damaged in the encounter and unable to return with the other ships. Having limped into Gibraltar Bay after the battle, it had undergone a refit there and arrived in England some weeks after the rest of the fleet. It was rumoured that during his stay in the colony, Captain Gore had entrust several chest of silver coins to a British frigate. Word quickly passed that the newly arrived 32-gun frigate, *Perpetual* was that ship.

As for the 74, talk of trouble aboard the third rate had not yet made landfall but news of the mutiny would quickly be relayed by the crew of the pilot boat once it touched the quay. It would be some time, however, before the facts would appear in the local papers and, even then, not all the information would be made known.

For the wives and children, mothers and sweethearts of those who had served aboard HMS *Stalwart* it would be a long wait until the third rate was able to enter the harbour and take up a berth along the quay. Despite this, many wives would head to the gates at the entrance of the naval dockyard where they would wait patiently under the great arch until the hundreds of sailors had been paid off and passed by heading to the nearest tavern. Sadly several women would wait days until the final sailor had departed and the gatekeeper turned them away. Only then would they realise their fate – they were now widows.

The Port Admiral's cutter was the first of many small boats to sail from the harbour's entrance to meet the newly arrived vessels in Spithead. While a flotilla of lighters and barges headed for the 74, the cutter's sights were set on the British frigate.

After the customary formalities were attended on *Perpetual*'s deck, the Port Admiral was invited below, while the local pilot familiarised himself with the ship itself. The meeting with the high ranking officer in the captain's cabin was brief but cordial and Oliver Quintrell and his senior officers were afforded a genuinely warm welcome home.

'Tell me, Captain Quintrell,' the Port Admiral enquired. 'I understand the Admiralty's orders delivered to you in Rio de Janeiro indicated you were to transfer the Spanish silver you were carrying to Captain Liversedge aboard HMS *Stalwart*?'

'You understand correctly,' Oliver replied.

'But by doing that, you were aware the consignment would be in jeopardy if the 74 fell into French hands.'

'That was a concern.'

'So, tell me, Captain. Have you returned with the cases intact? Can I take it that the consignment of silver is stowed safely aboard?'

'It is indeed – securely hidden within four barrels. Might I suggest that when these barrels are off-loaded and conveyed to their ultimate destination, they are escorted by a company of marine guards?'

The Port Admiral was delighted to oblige. 'I will make the necessary arrangement as soon as I go ashore. The country owes you a debt of gratitude, Captain Quintrell. You must be pleased.'

'No sir, I am not.' Oliver's blunt reply shocked the elderly gentleman charged with command of the most important naval port in Britain. 'I am, however, thankful to see this consignment arrive safely in Portsmouth. I made a commitment to Captain Gore in Gibraltar. Now I am free of that obligation and the Navy Board or the Lords of the Admiralty can decide to do what they will with the cache of silver. As for myself, speaking to you confidentially, I believe the treasure was stolen by a convoy of British ships at a time when Spain was still our ally. As such, I wish no thanks for my actions or any public mention of my name regarding this matter.'

'So be it,' the Admiral said. 'I will pass on your instruction and will arrange transport for the consignment and a guard to accompany it as soon as possible.'

From the quarterdeck, Oliver bade the Port Admiral farewell and waited by the rail until his boat had pulled away. It was heading across Spithead towards the 74, no doubt to extend the same cordial greeting to Captain Liversedge and his crew.

At midday, the French frigate was made ready to sail. Under the prize agent's directions and with Simon Parry on the quarterdeck, *Flambeau* proceeded through Portsmouth Harbour's narrow entrance and headed for the Gosport foreshore situated across from the naval dockyard. Once the ship was moored, the sailors who had manned her would be ferried back to *Perpetual* to collect their pay before being discharged. After a thorough examination by the agent, a decision as to the ship's future would be made. Whether it would be refitted and renamed to serve as a British frigate or converted to a coal or prison hulk or sent to the breakers' yard was yet to be decided.

With the tide almost full, *Perpetual* entered Portsmouth harbour and was warped to the wharfside adjacent to the dry-dock having been assured that as soon as the dock was empty it would be given priority to enter. Oliver was amenable to the idea. The excessive time dallied in the tropics had profited him little but had encouraged the fine growth of green weed from keel to waterline, even though the hull was coppered.

As it was, Oliver Quintrell's mission and his commission had come to an end but he hoped their Lordships in Whitehall would soon have new orders for him. He had already expressed to his fellow officers his firm hope that he would be returned to *Perpetual*, but that decision would rest with the Sea Lords. In the meantime, he intended to spend time with his wife and relax in his home on the Isle of Wight. He had missed his walks and morning swims on the Bembridge beach and looked forward to standing on solid ground which did not sway beneath his feet.

During that time, he would hope to hear news of the prize he had brought in and the sum it would return to be distributed accordingly between the officers and crew.

On a more discordant note, it was very likely Captain Liversedge would face a formal inquiry regarding the events that had taken place aboard *Stalwart*. He had lost his ship, though subsequently regained it, and he had also lost many men. If the matter was brought to a trial or hearing, Oliver had committed himself to attending, either on board ship in Portsmouth or at the Admiralty in Whitehall. It was not only his duty to tender an account of the events that had taken place but, as a friend, he was anxious to support William Liversedge who had fought bravely against, not one, but two enemies and was now weighed down with the whole wretched affair.

By four o'clock, the same afternoon, *Perpetual* was moored alongside the dockyard's stone quay ahead of the 74 which was buzzing with activity. Piled high on the dockside were numerous sacks filled with putrid waste, the juices from them leaking in rivulets back into the harbour. Nearby were cartloads of barrel hoops and dozens of bundles of wooden staves sufficient to keep the coopers in work for quite some time. Several dray wagons and various carriages were lined up along the wharf adjacent to both ships.

From *Perpetual*'s larboard rail, the captain along with Lieutenants Parry, Tully and Nightingale, watched as a man was escorted from the 74 and marched across the yard guarded by four marines. He was the Irish political prisoner who had been exiled from Britain. Having spoken with him briefly, Oliver had found him to be both polite and an excellent conversationalist. Though he was not an extremist, he had known both Robert Emmet – the leader of the '98 rebellion, and Michael Dwyer – a soldier who had fought for the rebels against the British at Vinegar Hill, and still held their ideals and conviction in high regard. To be exiled was a lenient punishment when compared to that of Robert Emmet who, only two years previously had been sentenced to be hung, drawn and quartered.

Captain Liversedge had reported that the prisoner's behaviour on board the 74 had been exemplary and, while the Irish rebels had released him for a time during the riot and put pressure on him to join their struggle, he had refused to be drawn into the conflict, argued against their course of action and attempted to mollify the men. Oliver wondered if this political exile would ever reach America or the Antipodes. He would probably never know.

Doubtless, he would spend the next few nights locked up at the dockyard's cells. Then, for convenience, he would be transferred to one of the prison hulks in the harbour, perhaps one which accommodated French prisoners. Oliver feared it could take months or years before a decision was made as to his future. Had he been a Frenchman, an end to the war would guarantee his release. But there was nothing anyone could say or do that would alter this man's situation and, as time passed, he would be forgotten.

Glancing along the quay, Oliver's attention was taken by a group of seamen in whom he had placed his trust. Laughing and joking, they were in good spirits, as they tossed bags and sea chests onto a hand barrow. These were the men who had safeguarded the ship's secret throughout its eventful and, at times, harrowing recent voyages.

Amongst them was William Ethridge the young shipwright who had originally come from Lord Montagu's private shipyard on the Beaulieu River. Oliver wondered if he would return to Buckler's Hard or would seek employment in the Royal Navy dockyard at Portsmouth. Or perhaps he would remain in the port and sign up on another cruise.

Also standing with the group was Ekundayo, the broad-shouldered West Indian, whose shiny black head towered above the rest. And Bungs, the old cooper, whose voice could be heard above the others – the feisty old seadog whose mind was as sharp as a length of hoop-iron honed to a knifepoint on the grindstone. Sensing he was being observed, Bungs looked across to the ship and tossed a cheeky wink in the captain's direction.

Hintuition, Oliver thought and lifted his hat acknowledging the members of his crew. 'Enjoy your time ashore, gentlemen. Be wary of the press gangs and keep a keen eye out for the broadsheets. As soon as *Perpetual* is refitted and ready to sail, notices will be posted.' The group joined in three huzzas for the captain and all promised they would be back.

Stepping gingerly from the ship, Mrs Crosby was helped onto the dockside by her husband. Mrs Pilkington followed with the doctor close behind her. Having already said their farewells on the ship, Mr Crosby shook hands with the doctor and embraced Connie Pilkington in the manner a man would embrace his sister-in-law or cousin, promising they would meet up again very shortly. Oliver thought it unlikely the carpenter would sign with him again but rather that he would gain employment in the dockyard so he could remain in Portsmouth with his wife. With the tools of his trade and bags already loaded on the back of a waiting gig, the couple were the first to be driven away.

An ageing wagon pulled by an equally ageing draft horse, creaked under the weight of bags and boxes, jars and wooden chests – the property of Dr Whipple. Other cases, bottles and pieces of equipment were still being added. Mrs P and the boy, Charles Goodridge, who had accepted an offer to travel into town with him, had very few possessions.

Stepping from the frigate, Oliver strolled across the yard to where the group was standing. After greeting them politely and wishing them well, he drew the doctor aside.

'I am sorry to farewell you, Jonathon. Please remember: there will always be a place for you as ship's surgeon should you wish to join me on my next command.'

'Thank you, Oliver. For the moment, I am undecided as to my future. I have things to attend to in London but, aside from that, I intend to take rooms in Portsmouth. I believe a naval town, in times of war, will appreciate the services of a well-practised surgeon.'

'Indeed it will,' Oliver said, glancing across to Consuela Pilkington and Charles Goodridge. 'And what of the widow and the boy?' he added.

The doctor smiled as he spoke. 'Mrs Pilkington is also undecided as to her future. Her wish is to return to Gibraltar but I have advised her against that. It would be best to wait until the colony is fully recovered. There is always a chance the malignant fever could return, as it has done in the past. In the interim, I have asked if she would consider accepting a position as housekeeper in the rooms I propose to rent. I have offered to pay her a wage which will provide her with a degree of independence. If she so wishes it.'

'And the boy?'

'She asked if I could offer accommodation to Charles also. She assured me he would make himself useful and work for his keep.'

'And your answer?'

'I agreed, of course.'

'I am delighted to hear that,' Oliver said. 'And you must continue to hone your skill in stick fighting. It strikes me as a rather antiquated and sometimes barbaric form of fighting but I have witnessed how very effective it is.'

'Less barbaric than wielding a sabre, I think. But, yes, I will continue and I intend to teach the boy. That will give me a deal of satisfaction. Also, it is my intention to hire a tutor or enrol him in school. I have not yet broached this with Connie, but I think she will support the idea. As you know, he is a rather precocious lad and very bright.'

Oliver smiled. 'Might I suggest the naval college and, if the lad's taste for the sea remains constant, I insist it should be encouraged.' Oliver lowered his voice. 'Dr Whipple, kindly do me the honour of permitting me to support this young man. I would like to sponsor his education – school fees and other incidentals.'

'That is very generous, Oliver,' the doctor said. 'But I have heard you speak vehemently on the evils of privilege and patronage.'

'That is true. However, I will make an exception in this case. I trust my contribution can be made in a confidential manner.'

The doctor nodded.

'As you know, I have no son to follow me to sea and I would take pleasure in following Charles's development.'

'But why this lad? Surely you have nephews or young cousins?'

'There is no question in my mind as to why I should choose this boy. Without Charles Goodridge, we would not have arrived in Portsmouth with a fine French prize for which every man aboard will be entitled to a share, including your good self. Without Charles, it is unlikely Captain Liversedge would have command of the 74 and without Charles's bravery our freedom and indeed our very lives may well have been forfeited.

'Young Charles proved he has courage and ingenuity beyond his years. If he continues to study and learns well, I will further sponsor him aboard a post ship as a midshipman. Say nothing of this to the lad but keep me advised of his progress.'

As they were speaking, the pair's attention was drawn to an angry outcry. Perched atop the wagon Charles Goodridge was busily rearranging the position of the doctor's more precious items, much to the aggravation of the driver who had placed them there. Turning his head to the two gentlemen now watching him, Charles Goodridge waved in the happy-go-lucky manner of any ten-year-old.

Standing nearby, Consuela Pilkington smiled at the boy's antics, her dark Iberian eyes flashing in the spring sunshine. For a fleeting moment she reminded Captain Quintrell of Susannah but he did not allow the memory to linger.

Extending his hand to the doctor, Oliver bade him farewell. 'I wish you and your party good health and good fortune. I am sure we will meet again before very long.'

'We will indeed, Captain. Thank you for everything. God speed.'

With the doctor and his party departed and most of the crew paid off, Oliver returned to the ship but had no intention of remaining aboard longer than necessary.

With no pressing engagements, Mr Parry had agreed to remain in Portsmouth where he would be able to follow *Perpetual*'s progress in the dockyard. Oliver hoped a new commission would follow very quickly and that he could return to the frigate that had been his home for almost a year.

Returning to the quarterdeck, he was alerted by the rumble of wheels of two large wagons, each drawn by a pair of black Shire horses as they moved slowly away from the dockside. Securely lashed to each wagon were two large barrels bearing no specific markings and apparently of no significance apart from the fact they were accompanied by a guard of marines walking on either side. Having watched them being removed from the ship's hold, Oliver Quintrell was familiar with the consignment.

'What will become of the contents?' the sailing master enquired.

'I doubt they will remain in Portsmouth. I reckon they will be sent to London when a suitable mode of transport becomes available.'

'I understand the Irish rebels found nothing of value in the barrels they smashed aboard *Stalwart*? So what was packed in those barrels you sent to the 74 when we were in Guanabara Bay?'

'Cases of copper, iron and wrought nails – courtesy of Mr Crosby, and packed into the barrels by Bungs himself. I believe the weight was about equal to that of the cases of silver coins.' He grinned. 'Image the frustration of the Irishmen when they frantically smashed the barrels in the 74's hold. They were searching for something that was not there.'

'And the silver was aboard *Perpetual* throughout the voyage?'

'Indeed – it never moved an inch from its original location.'

* * *

Printed by Amazon Italia Logistica S.r.l.
Torrazza Piemonte (TO), Italy